SEARCHING
FOR MY
DAUGHTER

BOOKS BY LIZ TRENOW

The Lost Soldiers (published in the UK as *In Love and War*)
All the Things We Lost (published in the UK as *The Poppy Factory*)
Our Last Letter (published in the UK as *Under a Wartime Sky*)
Searching for My Daughter

The Last Telegram
The Forgotten Seamstress
The Hidden Thread (published in the UK as *The Silk Weaver*)
The Dressmaker of Draper's Lane
The Secrets of the Lake

LIZ TRENOW

SEARCHING
FOR MY
DAUGHTER

bookouture

Published by Bookouture in 2022

An imprint of Storyfire Ltd.
Carmelite House
50 Victoria Embankment
London EC4Y 0DZ

www.bookouture.com

ISBN: 978-1-80314-363-7
eBook ISBN: 978-1-80314-362-0

This book is dedicated to the memory of my uncle, John Walters,
1913–2013

PART 1

1

RUSSIAN / BRITISH BORDER, GERMANY, JULY 1945

She expects to feel elated, even triumphant, after all those gruelling days of trudging towards the border post, of fighting hunger, dodging danger, battling exhaustion. But when she finally reaches it, all she feels is a drab, grey sense of anticlimax.

The queue is long, but that barely matters. She is perfectly used to waiting. For the midnight knock at the door, for her number to be called, for the next meal of watery soup, the sound of a gunshot, for the last gasping breath of the woman sharing her bunk so that she can steal the concealed crust, for the end of another ten-hour shift in the factory, for the unknown destination of another interminable march. For the morning to arrive, for night to fall. For another day of life.

Sustaining her through every moment of waiting, at the end of every queue, every roll call, every railway line, every dreary junction and every span of time, has been the tiniest flicker of hope: Rosa's face, her eyes bright and expectant, arms outstretched in readiness. What does it matter if she has to wait a few more hours if it means she might one day walk into those arms?

There must be fifty people ahead of her, snaking into the

distance towards a gateway with armed guards at either side. No one is moving. Many have given up any expectation of doing so and are resting on the ground, their backs against the tall chain-link fence topped with coils of barbed wire that marks the official boundary between the Russian and British sectors. At least in this queue they are allowed to sit. There are no soldiers shouting or threatening them. And no dogs, thank goodness. The dogs in the camp were even more terrifying than the guards.

She glances along the line of nondescript figures, stripped of any identity by exhaustion and poverty, their faces prematurely aged from fear and starvation, their threadbare clothing concealing all clues to nationality, origin or occupation. But they have a common purpose, seeking to escape from something, to discover a new life or return to a semblance of one they once enjoyed. No one speaks, of course. Strangers don't much, these days. They are wary of everyone and weary of news, with its exaggerations, its false hopes, its lies.

She sits down on the dusty ground, takes off her mismatched boots, massages her blisters and slips from her pocket the last crust of bread she's been saving, concealing it in the palm of her hand out of habit, stealing small, surreptitious mouthfuls. No one takes any notice, or seems inclined to snatch it from her. There is a chill wind blowing through the fence, but yesterday's clouds have cleared and a weak shaft of sunlight slices between the buildings onto the silent, patient queue. She's been walking all night and feels suddenly, overwhelmingly weary.

Her eyes are just beginning to close when a kerfuffle at the head of the queue shakes her awake, her heart pounding with fear. A man is being frogmarched out of the gate by the guards.

'Off you go. And don't come back.'

The ejected man curses loudly, waving his arms and tearing at his clothes. 'What am I to do?' he wails in Polish-accented

German, his eyes wide with desperation. 'If I go home, they will kill me.'

No one responds. The queue seems to turn in on itself. People lower their heads, wrapping coats, scarves or scraps of blanket tightly around them, eyes to the ground. There is no solidarity among these refugees. Under the watchful eye of the British guards, no one is prepared to risk showing sympathy for an angry stranger.

After a further hour or so, she has stiffened up so much she fears she will never walk again. Then, quite suddenly, the queue moves. She counts as exactly thirty people are admitted through the gate and marched across the compound before being ushered into a low wooden building on the other side. As the rest of the queue shuffles forward, her heart lifts. If this is the pattern, she might even reach the gate before the end of the day.

She wonders what happens once you arrive inside that building. Will you be expected to queue again, waiting to be called for interview? And where are the people who failed to be given a visa? As far as she can tell, no one apart from the Polish man has been sent away. She hardly dares to hope that this means most people get through.

As though answering her thoughts, a group of around eighteen men, women and children emerge from another hut and are marched briskly towards the gate by the guards. Their shoulders are slumped in resignation and their faces lowered. No one makes a fuss. What is it they've done, or not done, she wonders, what papers or other proof are missing? They are ushered back onto the street, the men taciturn, some of the women silently weeping, the children's faces aged beyond their years as they cling to their parents' hands.

What lies ahead for these poor people? More trudging, more starvation, more terror? 'Please, please let that not be me,' she mutters under her breath. She has no papers at all, no proof, of course. Who does these days, except those who can afford to buy false ones?

A tinny bell on the town hall begins to chime: it is three o'clock. The queue is stationary again, and has grown so long behind her that she can no longer see where it ends. The afternoon draws on, the wind changes direction, becomes fiercer. A storm is coming. She prays that the rain will hold off, at least until she can find shelter. Her stomach is rumbling painfully, and the old beer bottle in which she carries water is empty.

At last, as dusk approaches and she is starting to despair, there is more movement. The gate opens, people shuffle through. She leaps to her feet and gathers her belongings. As the queue inches forward, she finds herself holding her breath. The guards are counting, in English: nineteen, twenty, twenty-one. She couldn't bear it if they close the gate before she gets to it. Nearly there. Moving forward again. Twenty-six, twenty-seven, twenty-eight ...

Just as she reaches him, the guard raises his hand. 'Wait there, madam.' She pauses obediently, watching enviously as the admitted group cross the courtyard and enter the wooden hut thirty metres away. It feels so near, but so far out of reach. There are fractious shouts behind her, and people break rank, pushing forward and buffeting her, almost knocking her to the ground. The guard frowns and starts to close the gate.

It is her last chance. 'Please, sir. I have been waiting since first light and have no food or water.'

He looks down at her, surprised. 'Your English is good, madam.'

'I am a teacher of your language, sir.' It is true, but she finds it surprising to believe now. That was long ago, in another life.

'Come on then, quick.' With a sudden decisive movement, he grasps her shoulder, guiding her roughly through. The gate clangs behind her, and a furious roar rises from the crowd behind. Ahead, another guard is beckoning her forward. Her feet move automatically, as though in a dream.

I'm coming, Rosa.

It is a long, low building with only a single window, and as her eyes adjust to the gloom, she can see rows of people, men, women and a scattering of children, already filling wooden benches along each side and down the middle of the room. It is warm and dry, but the smell is powerful: of unwashed bodies, filthy clothes and feet that have been laced in boots for far too long. She finds a corner and sinks to the floor, clutching the piece of paper a guard has thrust into her hand. With a sickening jolt of recognition she registers the number 341 written on it, and hopes the coincidence is not a bad omen. Roughly tattooed into the tender flesh of her inside arm is 341089.

It is almost silent in the room apart from an occasional wheezy cough, or the whisper of a mother comforting a child. Someone lights a cigarette and the aroma of tobacco smoke is welcome, helping to mask the smell of desperate souls.

A soldier arrives carrying two buckets. 'Clean drinking water. Help yourselves,' he says, clanking them down either side of the hut.

People shuffle forward, queuing patiently to drink from cupped palms or to fill containers: bottles, jam jars, old teacups, chipped enamel mugs. The water revives her, lifts her spirits. I am warm and dry and inside the English sector at least for now, she says to herself. Just a few more steps and I will once again hold my daughter in my arms. She returns to her small square of floor, sits down and closes her eyes.

Someone is shaking her shoulder. 'Wake up, madam. You can't sleep here, I'm afraid.'

She drags herself into a sitting position, slowly starting to remember where she is. Around her, the benches are empty.

'What? Where is everyone?' she says, before remembering to speak in English.

'The office is closed for the weekend,' he replies. 'You'll have to come back on Monday.'

Surely this soldier isn't telling her she will have to wait three more days and then queue outside all over again? She pulls herself to her feet, her bones creaking like an old woman's, so much older than her forty-five years.

'Sir, I beg you. I have been travelling for two weeks now and have walked many miles. I have no food, nowhere to stay. Please don't turn me out onto the streets again.'

He shakes his head. 'Sorry, madam. That's the rules. All the officers have left for the evening, and you can't stay here.'

In her head she hears her daughter's voice. *Be strong, stand up to them. Don't let anyone bully you, Mama.* It wasn't always the best advice, as she'd learned to her cost. In the camps it could earn you a blow from a rifle butt or worse. But this man is being polite; he isn't waving a gun. Besides, he's English. She's got little to lose.

She draws herself up as tall as she can and looks him directly in the eye. He's only a boy really. But for the shock of bright ginger hair and the splatter of freckles on his cheeks he could be her Wilhelm.

'Young man,' she says, in as firm a voice as she can muster. 'Have you heard what happened in the German camps? Have you seen the photographs? The piles of bodies, the thousands dead?'

He nods slowly, thoughtfully, his eyes lowered. 'I have, madam. Terrible business.'

She takes a breath. 'I was there, sir. Somehow I survived, by the grace of God. But the rest of my family were killed and the only thing I have to live for is the hope of finding my beloved daughter, who is in England. And you tell me I must go back outside and sleep on the streets for the weekend, trying to fight off drunken Russian soldiers, because all your officers have gone home to their comfortable beds?'

He shuffles his boots and clears his throat. 'Wait here, madam. I'll see what I can do.'

2

'Come,' Jack shouts when he hears the knock at the door.

Since when has he become so imperious? he wonders. He hates all this army hierarchy stuff. The air force was so much less formal. But it is an army commander who runs the Control Commission, and landing this job as an intelligence officer has allowed Jack to defer his discharge and stay in Europe. He has no intention of going home to the UK to work in his father's factory just yet, thank you very much. After five long years at a prisoner-of-war camp, he is only just rediscovering the will to live, and now he's ruddy well going to enjoy himself.

As a bonus, he's been promoted to officer class, which brings unexpected privileges. The food in the officers' mess is considerably better, the drinks measures dangerously generous and the chevrons on his shoulders make a serious impression with the girls, especially classier ones like the commander's secretary, Lisa, who he is meeting this evening.

It will be their first proper date. Until now it's just been flirtation, teasing, all very proper. With her boss liable to emerge from the next-door office at any moment, there's been little chance of much else. But last week she slipped Jack a flyer about a dance being held at the US army base just ten miles away. 'Fancy this? There'll be lots of booze, and the size of their steaks is fabled.'

'Might do,' he said, playing it cool. 'How about you?'

She lowered long eyelashes, coyly. 'I was hoping you might offer me a lift.'

'I don't have a car, Lisa.'

'You have a motorbike, don't you?'

'You'd be happy to ride pillion?'

She nodded. 'I'll wear slacks.'

Much as he dislikes large gatherings of drunken army types, especially Yanks, the prospect of Lisa clasping him tightly round the waist ten miles there and ten miles home again was too good to resist.

'Of course.' He glanced at the flyer, checking the start time. 'Seven o'clock on Friday, then?'

But now it is almost 6.15 on that very Friday evening and he needs to return to his room, smarten up and get across town to the HQ building, where Lisa will be waiting for him. Instead of which, Private Squires is standing in the doorway, cap in hand, looking apologetic.

'What is it, Ginger?'

The private clears his throat nervously, Adam's apple bobbing in his narrow neck.

'Spit it out, man, I'm in a hurry.'

'There's a woman in the waiting area. She won't leave.' A pause. 'Sir.'

'What kind of a mouse are you? Tell her to come back on Monday.'

'It's just ...' Ginger tails off, cheeks flushing.

'Just what?'

'She's been in a camp, she says. One of *those* camps. She's suffered terribly, sir. You can see it in her face. She pleaded with me. About drunken Russian soldiers. I didn't have the heart.'

'Oh, for heaven's sake, Squires.' Jack gives an exasperated sigh, dropping the duffel bag containing the extra jacket he put in at the last minute for Lisa. 'I'll sort her out. You go on home.'

'Thank you, sir.' Ginger salutes, clicking his heels.

'Enough of that formal nonsense,' Jack says. 'Just give me the keys. I'll lock up.'

She is huddled on the floor, and his first impressions are of an old woman, her face carved by starvation into sharp angles and framed with a grey halo of short wiry hair, a shabby coat of indeterminate dusty brown, mismatched boots tied with string and a pitifully small bundle of belongings. She scrambles to stand, drawing herself up to a proud height, and fixes him with a fierce, defiant expression, her dark eyes blazing. Now that he looks more closely, he realises that she is younger than he first assumed – perhaps in her fifties. His mother's age.

'Madam,' he begins. 'As my private has already explained ...'

Her gaze slips sideways, taking in the gold bands on his sleeves. 'So he lied to me, your private. He said the officers had all gone home.'

It takes him aback for a second, this sharpness of observation, her command of grammar. 'Your English is very good, madam.'

Her expression softens. 'I used to teach the language, once upon a time. In the *Gymnasium*.' The elite schools for clever kids.

'But I am afraid it makes no difference. I cannot interview you tonight.'

'I don't see why not. You are here, and so am I. I have no money, no food and no place to stay. I've been walking for two weeks to get here. Now you tell me I must go back and take my chances with the Russians until you deign to reopen your border post on Monday?'

Her vocabulary and English idioms are impressive, too. 'May I ask why you wish to cross the border, madam?'

She sighs. 'My family were all killed in the camps, sir. I survived only through good fortune. My only relative in the world, a daughter, is in Britain.'

He's heard such heartbreaking stories so many times before that he's become almost hardened to them. His resolve stiffens. They can't help everyone. There is a quota for visas and they are nearing this month's limit already.

'Look, my private was correct, madam. My colleagues have gone home, and without them I cannot complete the paperwork this evening, even if I wanted to. You will have to wait, I'm afraid.'

'Then I shall wait here.' She sits down firmly on a bench and gathers her belongings around her. 'I shall be perfectly happy here until Monday.'

'You cannot wait here,' he says, taking a step towards her.

'Then you will have to carry me out, young man,' she says, folding her arms defiantly.

Jack glances at his watch. It tells him he is already late for Lisa. His fingers feel for his holster, the gun nestling warmly beneath his jacket. He is about to grasp it when something gives him pause. Is he really going to threaten this woman? And what if she resists? He wouldn't put it past her; she's already survived who knows how many threats to her life. His hand falls to his side.

'Madam, I shall ask you politely once again. Will you please leave, and return on Monday morning?'

She looks up at him with those fierce eyes. 'Tell me, young man. Are you aware of what the Russian soldiers will do to a woman?'

He gapes, struggling for a response.

'Let me put it another way,' she says. 'Have you ever been raped?'

'Erm, no, madam, I have not,' he finally manages.

'I do not recommend it,' she says, tersely. 'But since you

have never experienced it, you will not understand what it is like to be a woman alone and homeless in the Russian sector. Or to what fate you are sending me back there.'

He's heard the rumours, of course. Surely they don't rape women of her age? But the fire in her eyes leaves him in no doubt.

He glances at his watch again, thinks of Lisa waiting, and makes up his mind. 'Okay. I have a plan. It's against the rules, but if you are prepared for me to lock you in here tonight, I will return in the morning and we can have a conversation then. Is that acceptable to you?'

She doesn't smile or show any sign of gratitude. 'That will suit me well, sir. It is warm and dry and there is water left in the bucket. Off you go for your rendezvous, or whatever it is you are so late for.'

Is he crazy? If anyone discovers what he's done, he could get sacked or even, if she causes trouble, court-martialled. But it's worth the risk: he suffered enough inhumanity from his captors, and he's not about to turn into one of those brutes, not now, in peacetime.

'You must remain perfectly quiet, you understand, and I will return at eight o'clock tomorrow morning, before anyone else finds you.'

She nods gratefully.

He locks the door firmly behind him.

In the office, he rifles through all the desk drawers, but all he can find is a half-eaten bar of chocolate, a dried-up slice of cheese and a slightly wrinkled apple. Better than nothing, he says to himself, retracing his steps.

The woman has already made herself at home. She is stretched out on the bench, head resting on her folded coat, sparse belongings on the floor beside her.

'Is it morning so soon?' she says, sitting up.

'I brought you these. Sorry I can't lay my hands on anything more exciting.'

She examines them. 'This is a feast, sir. Thank you,' she whispers.

Does he hear her voice breaking? He doesn't wait to find out. 'Sleep well, madam. I will see you in the morning.'

Lisa is still waiting in the anteroom to the commander's office, a portrait of contained fury: cheeks pale, teeth clenched, hands balled into fists, the sweet smile a thing of his imagination. It is 7.30. 'So you decided to grace me with your presence at last, Captain Preston?'

'I'm so, so sorry,' he says, panting a little. He's just run across the courtyard. 'Some woman refused to leave the waiting area and everyone else had already scarpered so I had to deal with her.'

She raises a sceptical eyebrow. 'And what did you do, to deal with her?'

'Long story,' he says. 'So, are you still up for the Yankee party? I could eat a horse.'

'That's probably what we will be eating, by the time we get there.'

'What, horse?' He's confused.

'When the Yanks run out of cows.' Her eyes soften a fraction.

He laughs now. She's forgiven him enough to tease. 'Well I don't care. It'll be delicious, whatever it is. Come on.'

With her arms clasped tightly around his waist and the brisk air whipping past them, Jack feels the lifting of his heart that signals once more that he is, after all, glad to be alive. Yes, he will always feel a terrible burning guilt about all those who didn't make it: the crew-mates who died when their planes came down, fellow prisoners who tried to escape and got shot for it, others who defied guards and were so badly beaten they never recovered, the ones who simply succumbed to sickness. But in his better moments he knows he has a duty to repay that debt by living his life in the best way he can.

How he loves the German countryside. No proper mountains near here, sadly. For that he would have to travel a hundred miles east to the Harz range or, for real peaks, further south to Switzerland. But on his rare days off, these wooded hills make for good summer hiking, the wide rivers and lakes perfect for swimming, if a bit chilly. And it is great biking country, with twisty lanes and long open stretches of road where it's possible to do a ton on a good day, without a pillion rider, of course. He's not going to risk terrifying Lisa.

Jack considers himself fortunate to be here. His parents continue to write, begging him to come home as soon as he can. In his replies he emphasises the importance of the work he is doing as an intelligence officer, encouraging them to believe he is helping to keep the Western world safe from Nazis and other riff-raff of the Third Reich trying to flee punishment for their vile, vicious crimes. The reality is that until recently, most people trying to cross between the sectors are genuine refugees, poor, innocent souls simply trying to return to the places from which they've been uprooted by six years of war, or to find the rest of their scattered families.

But news of the impending Nuremberg trials has shaken remaining former Nazis out of complacency. Having believed that by keeping their heads down they would get away without retribution, it is becoming clear that after starting at the top, the Allies are determined to root out the middle and lower ranks too. At least once or twice a week, these days, Jack will meet someone who rings alarm bells. It is likely to be a lone individual, usually a man but occasionally a woman. Over time he has developed a sixth sense for the story that doesn't ring true, or something about the set of the chin, a restless knee or a failure to meet his eyes under questioning.

It has been drummed into all the intelligence officers that in these circumstances it is important to stay calm to avoid giving any hint of suspicion. The suspect is invited into a separate room, unaware that they are being observed, while waiting, through a one-way mirror set into the wall.

Their behaviour when left alone is often revealing. Some, habituated to hierarchy, use the time to preen themselves in the mirror, combing hair or straightening ties in readiness for meeting a person of superior rank. Others pace the room anxiously, unable to conceal the military precision of their stride. Some open briefcases and shuffle papers that are almost invariably false.

Watching from the other side of the glass, Jack and his colleagues will be simultaneously sifting through files of photographs of 'most wanted' men and women to see whether they recognise any similarities. Height, shape of hands, fingernails, moles and scars are their usual focus, since escaping Nazis use all manner of techniques to disguise themselves.

Of course, the records are woefully incomplete, and more often than not it is instinct that leads the team to stage two: intensive questioning over a period of hours, even days. They never use force, of course, or the less savoury techniques the Russians are said to employ: sleep deprivation, persistent loud sounds, sudden bursts of recorded screams, binding the captive into uncomfortable poses for hours on end. Even mock executions, he's heard.

The more subtle British way – verbal tricks and dogged persistence – takes longer but, they believe, leads to more genuine confessions. Jack finds the process distasteful but strangely satisfying: how an individual who at first presents as strong and self-righteous will slowly crumble and finally admit that, yes, they were connected to the Nazi Party but of course their role was entirely passive. They were a junior underling and were forced to take part for fear of their own lives.

Only once did they find someone dying, his face furiously flushed and limbs writhing in agony, the faint smell of burnt almonds leading to the discovery of a cyanide capsule still clenched between his teeth. Any suicide is considered a failure.

When Jack and Lisa arrive, the party is in full swing. The steaks are delicious, the best he's had in years, and he doesn't care whether it is horse or cow. Lisa was a responsive pillion rider and is proving to be a delightful companion, laughing at even the weakest of his jokes and earning him envious glances from nearby Americans, all tall, clean-cut and absurdly handsome. The pale cold Yankee beer is a perfect thirst-quencher after the frantic jitterbugging he has done his best to approximate.

Again he reminds himself that he is an exceptionally lucky man. The evening flies by, and suddenly seems to be drawing to an end. The leader of the band announces the last number and Lisa is grasping his hand, pulling him back onto the dance floor. This is the moment for cheek-to-cheek intimacy, perhaps even the chance of stealing a kiss.

But even now, as they smooch to 'In the Mood', he finds his mind wandering back to the woman at the border post. The memory of the encounter has left him uneasy. What on earth possessed him to allow her to stay in the waiting room? What a dereliction of duty, a lapse of his usual strict discipline. Not for a moment did he question whether she was lying, and he didn't even think to check her bag for weapons or explosives.

He prays she is not making any disturbance that might lead to her discovery. 'I felt sorry for her, sir' was hardly likely to wash with the commander, and Jack's position in the Control Commission would surely come to an abrupt end, also cutting short this promising liaison with Lisa. He tightens his arms around her, feeling her warmth, trying to lose himself in the music and the moment.

It is six long years since his heart was broken, and this is the first time he's experienced anything even remotely approaching the desire he felt in those distant days. When he nuzzles Lisa's neck, she responds by turning her face upwards. Their lips meet, and all thoughts of the other woman evaporate.

3

Miriam stirs, shifting stiffly on the wooden floor. As she opens her eyes and blinks warily in the pale light, her stomach contracts in that familiar grip of dread. Sleep offers escape, but each morning heartless reality floods in once more. Her mind whirls. Where is she? What is this place? What horrors await her? What threats, beatings, physical trials? Will there be any food today?

And then she remembers. This is the border-post waiting room inside English lines, and she will be interviewed this very morning by that sweet-faced young officer. Or so he promised.

Last night the cheese and apple helped to ease the hunger pains in her shrunken stomach, and she waited an hour before starting on the half-bar of chocolate, savouring it tiny nibble by tiny nibble, inhaling the glorious taste of each morsel as it melted on her tongue. The surge of sugar was as powerful as any shot of schnapps, and she actually chuckled out loud from the pure pleasure of it.

Afterwards she settled down to sleep, her head resting on the kitbag in which she had carried her few belongings across Germany, walking, hitching rides, begging food and water, hiding at night in undergrowth or abandoned ruined buildings, anywhere out of sight of Russian troops. Now, for the first time in years, she felt safe.

As she closed her eyes, an image of her daughter appeared, more clearly than she'd experienced it for many months. It was the last time she had seen her: February 1939. Gossip was rife about mass arrests and everyone was desperate to leave. The station concourse was so crowded with families that she feared they would never get to the train in time.

'Say goodbye here, Mama,' Rosa had said. 'We'll have to push our way through to the platform.' She'd hugged each one of them in turn, her brother Willi, father Hans and then finally Miriam, who had given up fighting the tears that now streamed unchecked down her cheeks. She cupped Rosa's face with both hands and kissed her, then held her as tightly as she possibly could, as though trying to transmit the protective force of her love into her daughter by some kind of magic.

Daniel, Rosa's husband of just a couple of weeks, had shifted uneasily beside them, and then grabbed his wife's hand and torn her away, almost forcefully. 'We have to go. Now.' His normally placid face was tight with tension, his eyes wild. 'Or we'll miss the train.' As they were dragged apart, Rosa turned to look back, deep eyes brimming with tears, strands of thick auburn hair falling across her face, mouthing the words 'I love you'.

'I love you too, my darling.' Miriam heard her own voice ringing round the empty hut. 'Not long now, God willing.' And then, beneath the faded Union Jack pinned to one wall and the kindly eyes of King George VI beaming down from his photograph opposite, she slept more soundly than she could remember.

Now it is morning. She pushes herself to a sitting position, then stands and walks to the sole window, set into the door through which she entered from the courtyard the previous evening. The small square of frosted glass is reinforced with a grid of fine wire and she can see nothing through it, but from the level of light she imagines that it must be well past dawn, possibly even approaching eight o'clock. Her stomach rumbles. That is the problem with eating. Your body always wants more.

She goes to the other door, the one through which the officer appeared, pressing her ear to it, straining for sounds, footsteps, voices. All is silent. She will have to wait. There is a little water left in the bucket and she lifts it to drink, swilling it around her teeth, before allowing the last few drops to fall over her face. She wipes herself dry with the hem of her blouse. Morning ablutions, she thinks, smiling to herself. Such luxury.

At last she hears the faint sound of a tinny church bell and holds her breath, counting. Eight o'clock. At the same moment, footsteps approach and a key rattles in the lock. She stands to attention, smoothing her hair and brushing down her skirt out of habit, although of course it makes no difference. The young officer enters, bleary-eyed, his uniform jacket creased as though it has spent the night in a heap on the floor, which makes her feel less embarrassed about her own dishevelled state.

'Good morning, sir. Thank you for keeping your promise.'

'You slept well, I hope? No disturbances?'

'I was perfectly warm and comfortable and entirely undisturbed, thank you. The chocolate was delicious.'

'Good. Now, come with me.' He seems to be studying her face. 'I will try to get you a cup of coffee. It's only the bottled concentrate stuff, but it tastes okay.'

Coffee? Real coffee? Not the ersatz variety, made of chicory and acorns? In the camps you could have killed, or been killed, for less. 'That would be most welcome, sir,' she says, remembering the power of British understatement.

He leads her along a corridor and into a small, stuffy room that smells of new paint and cigarette smoke, the only decoration the ubiquitous photograph of the British king. On the opposite wall is a mirror, from which she averts her eyes: the very last thing she wants to be reminded of is how aged she has become, frown lines carved into the skin around her eyes, her hair already grey and still growing out from the lice shave they all received after liberation.

'Take a seat, make yourself comfortable. I may be a little while,' he says.

He returns about ten minutes later bearing a tray with two cups of delicious-smelling coffee and a brown paper bag, which he pushes towards her. 'I missed breakfast myself, so I grabbed a couple of these from the bakery.' He tears open the bag to reveal a little miracle: two crispy bread rolls – *white!* – filled with what looks like sausage. 'Help yourself.'

At first she resists the temptation to stuff her mouth like a ravenous animal, trying instead to take small, ladylike bites, chewing them carefully. But the smell of fresh bread and the tang of the meat sandwiched between layers of creamy salted butter gets the better of her. They munch together in silence until all that is left are a few crumbs on the table. She is about to gather them with a licked fingertip as usual, but holds herself back. She needs to impress this young man.

The coffee, sweet and aromatic, is like nectar. A small sigh of appreciation escapes her lips, which makes him smile. He is a kind man, she thinks to herself. Surely he will take pity on her?

He opens a paper form, picking up a pen. 'So, first things first. Your name?'

'Mrs Miriam Kauffman. Two effs.' She notices his pen hesitating, and spells it for him.

'Maiden name?'

She tells him.

'Place of birth?'

'Hamburg, Germany.'

'Address?'

'Neuer Steinweg 38, Hamburg. It no longer exists, sir. The whole street has been obliterated.'

She'd been planning to head home just as soon as she was strong enough, until she met a fellow survivor at the rehabilitation hospital who, it turned out, had once lived in the next-door road. 'Don't bother,' she was told. 'The whole place was blown to smithereens in '43.' She tried to find out more, asking anyone who might know. She eventually managed to piece together the grim story: the Allied bombing, along with high winds and dry weather, had caused a firestorm, an inferno reaching high into the sky that sucked all the air out of cellars and shelters so that the occupants suffocated before they could be burned. The updraught was so powerful that it swept bodies into the air like so many dried leaves. Asphalt on the streets burst into flame, and spilled fuel oil ignited and turned canals and the harbour into rivers of fire.

No, it would be a waste of time returning to Hamburg. There was nothing left for her there and her heart was calling for her in England. She headed instead for the nearest border post.

'Nationality?' the officer asks.

Once she would have been proud to say the word, but now it fills her with shame. 'German, sir.'

'Your religion?'

'Jewish.' Those two syllables are so bound up with deep, sickening terror.

But he writes it down, his face impassive. 'Passport?'

She shakes her head. 'I have no papers. All gone. The only thing I have is this.' She pulls up her sleeve. He winces as he acknowledges the numbers roughly tattooed on her skin. She dreads the next question, the one she will never fully answer: how on earth did you survive? The shame seems to burn deep inside, like a dark red stain. She will never reveal it, so long as she lives. But he barely hesitates.

'Profession?'

'English teacher.'

'We have noted your excellent command of the language, madam. Where did you learn to speak it so well?'

'As a young woman I spent four months living with an English couple in Hamburg, looking after their children. The father was in shipping. Everyone spoke English to me and expected me to speak it in return. I learned fast, and it has stood me in good stead. Later, I studied your great literature at university.'

'Impressive.'

'Who are your favourite authors, sir?' she dares to ask. From reading Charles Dickens and Jane Austen she feels that she already knows much about British society, even though she has never visited the country.

The question seems to stump him; his cheeks flush. Perhaps, like so many men, he does not read books. But she is already warming to him: a gentleman, formal but respectful, with not an ounce of aggression despite the telltale bulge of the holster visible beneath his uniform jacket. Good-looking, too, with his light curly hair and hazel eyes, the ready smile, the gentle way of talking. Not your typical army type, not at all.

His pen is poised over a new section of the form, ready to write. 'What is your reason for seeking a visa to England?'

She clears her throat. 'I wish to find my daughter, sir. She is my only living relative. As far as I know, no others have survived.'

He acknowledges the words with a single nod. It is a familiar story.

'Do you have anywhere to stay in England?'

'I hope to stay with my daughter in London. At least at first.'

'Her address?'

She was concerned when Rosa wrote to say they had moved to London. At first, when they were lodging with a family in a small English town, Daniel commuting by train each day to work at his office in the city, she felt reassured that they would not be in any danger should war break out. But then a hastily scribbled note arrived: *D wants to be closer to the office so we're in temporary lodgings in London for a few weeks until we find our own place.*

That was so like Daniel, she thought angrily, putting himself first, with no consideration for his young wife. An arrogant, selfish man. Rosa had never loved him, she felt sure, but marrying him was a means to an end, her route to freedom and safety, and possibly for her family too. Not that it had worked out that way.

The officer is looking at her, waiting.

'I'm sorry. What did you say?'

'Your daughter's name, please?'

'Rosa.'

He holds her gaze for an unsettling second. 'Rosa. That's a lovely name.'

'After her grandmother. Some people say it means beautiful flower, and she certainly is that.' She watches, reading upside down, as he writes: *Rosa Kauffman*.

'Oh, er, no. Sorry. She is not Kauffman, sir. She is married.'

'Dammit,' he swears, strangely ruffled, as he crosses the name out. 'What is her name now?'

'Levy,' Miriam says. 'Mrs Rosa Levy.'

His pen seems to freeze in space and he looks up at her with penetrating eyes. 'Let me get this right. Your daughter's name is Rosa Levy?' He emphasises each syllable as though he doesn't believe her. Her heart pounds, and beneath the table her legs start to tremble. 'Rosa Levy? You are sure?' he repeats.

She forces herself to answer. 'I am perfectly sure. That is my daughter's name.'

'Her husband's name, please?'

'Daniel Levy.'

The officer looks at her wide-eyed, disbelieving, as though she's said something perfectly outrageous. He stands suddenly, pushing his chair away with a sharp scraping sound that makes her jump. 'Excuse me, madam. There is something I ...'

Then he rushes from the room.

Miriam feels paralysed by panic. She does not move a muscle, not even turning her head.

Whatever has just happened? The interview seemed to be going perfectly well. He'd brought her coffee and a roll. What changed? He even smiled at the mention of Rosa's name, and complimented it. But his reaction when she mentioned Daniel was nothing short of astonishing. She struggles to think what she has said wrong. Has Daniel committed some crime? Perhaps he is on a list of suspects the British are searching for. Surely he is not a spy?

The officer is gone for what feels like half an hour but is probably only a few minutes. She imagines the worst: he will return with a strong-man colleague and clamp her in handcuffs, march her to a prison cell and interrogate her about Daniel and Rosa.

She racks her brains: what could an engineer and his young wife, a girl barely out of college, have possibly done to offend the British authorities? It is six long years since she's seen either of them, five since she's received any communication. It distresses her to imagine they might have broken the law in a country that has provided a safe haven.

There was always something odd about Daniel, though. She and Hans knew his parents through the community, and although they seemed friendly enough, their elder son always appeared rather formal, stand-offish. Hans was more tolerant. He told her not to be critical – 'he's probably just shy' – but she suspected that the boy considered himself superior to the other young people in the community. He was very bright, of course, and everyone seemed to hope that he would bring new zest to the faltering family business.

She was surprised when Rosa began courting him. Her beautiful, lively, popular daughter, going out with this serious, studious older boy? He was tall, she'd admit that, but not especially handsome, with his dark complexion and thick hair that grew so low on his forehead that he appeared – she berated herself for thinking it – almost Neanderthal.

'He's at least three or four years older than she is,' she muttered to Hans. 'If not more. Whatever does she see in him?'

It was a relief when Rosa finished the relationship. 'He's so dull, Mum, so intense. He even asked me to marry him! Imagine. I'm nowhere near ready to settle down just yet – it's time to have fun.

But the Nazis put paid to any fun, Miriam thought miserably, and Rosa ended up with Daniel anyway.

When is that wretched British officer going to return, to end the gut-wrenching anxiety of waiting? Only then does Miriam notice that the door to the little room is not closed properly. It sits ajar.

She waits, and time passes. Eventually curiosity gets the better of her. She stands and walks silently to the door, slowly pushes it open as quietly as she can, and peeks out.

4

Hearing Rosa's name for the first time in seven years leaves Jack winded, as though someone has punched him in the solar plexus.

His thoughts scramble to rationalise what he has heard. Surely it is a simple coincidence? Levy is a fairly common German name, after all. He's met several women called Rosa in this very interview room, and Daniels are two-a-penny. And anyway, what are the odds? Thousands of people, tens of thousands even, are trying to move between the sectors every day, at dozens of border posts, French, American, Russian and British, strung across Germany. Not in a million years would he expect to encounter anyone he knows.

But then, as he stands outside in the corridor, clinging onto the door jamb and trying to gather his breath, he is overtaken by the conviction, a feeling so deep and so intense it seems to hurt his bones, that it really *must* be her. *His* Rosa. This woman is Rosa's mother.

His reaction on meeting Miriam Kauffman in the waiting room the previous evening troubled him. He was unable to put a finger on it, and dismissed the notion as fanciful. There was

something in that starved and exhausted face – the strength and
determination, the proud bearing, perhaps – that caused him to
be kinder and more trusting than he would normally allow.

And now he knows why. He must have felt some subcon-
scious affinity. He can see no obvious family resemblance,
although that is hardly surprising given what she's been
through. But where is Rosa? The last he heard, she and Daniel
were thinking of heading to America, although he didn't rate
their chances once war had been declared. He lights a cigarette
with a shaky hand, and the first drag leaves him dizzy as the
memories surge back, almost overwhelming.

The first time he heard Rosa's name was six years ago. It
feels as though it was yesterday and yet at the same time like
ancient history, as though he has known her for all of his life.

'Jack. *Jack!*' His mother's imperious calls echoed across the
twilight to the garden bench where he liked to retreat for a quiet
smoke. He was eighteen and had recently returned from six
months of blissful independence, staying with family friends in
Austria for work experience and polishing his languages before
returning to London to study French, German and Latin in
readiness for his final exams. Now he was in limbo, suspended
somewhere between being a student and becoming a working
man, whatever that meant.

He hated being back at home, resenting his mother's
pernickety house rules and irritated by the childish energy of
his younger brothers. Some days he felt like packing a small
rucksack and walking away, going wherever his feet took him.
He wanted to return to Austria, but the news from Europe was
alarming. At home there was talk of war and conscription.

His father's expectations weighed heavily. As the oldest of
four, Jack had always been only too aware where his duty

would lie. He was expected to join the family's small engineering business and eventually take over from his father as managing director. But how could he spend his whole life – his *whole* life, for goodness' sake! – stuck in a small market town, going to work in the same place day after day, dealing with inanimate machines, difficult customers and a workforce totally reliant on him to generate business and pay their wages? He wanted so much to be free of those expectations, free to travel, to live in many different countries and learn the ways of the world.

His mother's insistent call had disturbed these gloomy thoughts. 'Jack? Jack! Where are you? Come at once and welcome our guests, you rude boy.'

Irritated, he stood, stubbed out his cigarette and straightened his trousers. They were his best summer cotton, pale blue, matched with a pale blue checked shirt. His mother had insisted. 'They'll be here around seven,' she'd said. 'Go and put on something decent, would you? Can't have them thinking they've come all this way to stay with a family of tramps.'

He rounded the corner of the house to find his three other brothers standing in a reception line, introducing themselves to the visitors, shaking hands one by one in a ridiculously formal way. What a curiously mismatched couple, he thought. The man was tall and dark-complexioned, with thick brown-black hair, and held himself in that terribly stiff way some Germans had. He was wearing a heavy woollen coat more suited to winter than a warm spring day. The woman was at least a foot shorter than her husband and looked much younger, girlish even. A single thick plait of auburn hair fell down her back, glinting in the sunshine.

'Herr Levy,' his father said. 'Please meet my eldest son, Jack.'

The man reached out his hand, but just at that moment the woman turned her face to Jack, and he was so distracted he found himself unable to tear his gaze away. It was the kind of face that seemed to have a source of internal illumination. The eyes, deep brown and framed beneath the delicate arch of perfect brows, glittered with an expression of ... was it amusement, pleasure or just politeness? Her teeth showed small and white between sensationally red lips. He found himself imagining what it would be like to kiss her, to press his tongue between those sweet, inviting ...

'Jack! Shake hands with Mr Levy!' His father's command brought him back into the moment.

'Very pleased to meet you, Jack,' Levy was saying. His grip was firm and businesslike, that of a man who knew what he wanted and would stop at nothing to get it. 'Please call me Daniel. And this is my wife, Rosa. We are really most grateful for your kind hospitality.'

The woman's hand was soft and smooth, gentle and yet firm. The touch of it was intoxicating, like a shot of the very best malt whisky.

'Come in, come in. Bring their cases, boys,' his mother commanded, and Jack stood back from the melee as his brothers jostled to prove their manliness. 'You must be exhausted after your long journey. You are just in time for supper. Come with me and I will show you to your room. It has a splendid view.'

As the woman passed him, she gave him the sweetest of smiles. A heady breath of perfume, reminiscent of his mother's stand of sweet peas, wafted on the evening air. Jack inhaled it like a precious gasp of oxygen, and it made him giddy and unsteady on his feet as he followed the couple inside.

Now, six years later, he is standing in the corridor, lost in his memories. And the woman who might be Rosa's mother is peering at him from the doorway of the interview room, with a terrified look on her face.

5

Miriam is startled to discover that the officer is right there in the corridor just a few feet away, smoking a cigarette. He turns and stares at her intensely, as though seeing her for the first time.

'Is something wrong?' she asks.

'No, nothing's wrong,' he replies, although the look on his face tells her otherwise. 'Go back inside and I will join you just as soon as ...' He waves his cigarette in the air.

After a few moments he returns to the room and takes his chair opposite her once more. He leans forward across the table. 'Mrs Kauffman, can you tell me a bit more about your daughter and her husband?' His voice is gentle, but she is instantly on high alert. She is familiar with this tactic: he's going to take a softly-softly approach to the interrogation, lulling her into a sense of false security. Well, she has nothing to hide. She will tell him everything she knows.

'Rosa is my elder child,' she begins. 'She has – had – a younger brother called Wilhelm. We call, er, called ...' Her voice falters.

The officer is listening intently, his eyes fixed on her like rifle sights.

'We were desperate to get our children out of Germany, you understand.' She swallows before continuing. 'My son Wilhelm, we call him ... called him Willi, anyway, he was fifteen, young enough to go on the Kindertransport, and we managed to raise the cash, but at the last minute there was a problem with his papers and they wouldn't allow it. Rosa was nineteen, just too old. And then a family we knew, the Levys, they have a son called Daniel who had been offered a sponsorship by a British business contact of theirs. They ran – used to run – a small engineering business, and he was about to apply for the travel visa to Britain. Daniel and Rosa had courted a few years before, but now he was asking her to marry him. In this way she would be eligible for a visa, too. He was offering to save her life.'

The officer nods. His eyes are softening, his expression becoming almost dreamy. She begins to see the boy he once was, before war hardened him.

'Please go on,' he says, quietly.

'Things were getting so bad for us Jews, you understand. Rosa married Daniel just two weeks later, and the visa took a month to come through. And then they were gone. I have not seen her since.'

That scene at the train station swims into her brain: the noise, the crowd, the smell of soot and steam, and through it all the brave, beautiful face of her daughter, fighting back tears while trying to put on a smile for her parents.

'Did you hear from her once she reached England?'

'Yes, she wrote each week. Until the war, when everything stopped, of course. But she was very happy, living in a beautiful part of the countryside with a generous family, and Daniel was working at their London office. I never knew the details, but it might have been the sales end of the company. They made fans for ship and aeroplane engines, I believe, so trade must have been quite brisk with the threat of war.'

At this moment, something extraordinary happens. The officer rocks back on his chair and gives a great bellow of laughter, and then another, slapping his thigh and then holding his hands up in the air, as though in supplication. Miriam freezes, astounded and horrified by this outburst; she has no idea what to think. Has she accidentally incriminated herself in a way that he finds amusing? Some of the camp guards would jeer when prisoners begged for mercy, but this laugh has a different sound to it.

'I'm so sorry,' he gasps. 'But I must stop you there. Something extraordinary has happened, the strangest coincidence. I hardly expect you to believe it.'

'Please go on, sir.'

'It is like this, Mrs Kauffman.' He beams across the table at her. 'It seems barely credible, but I knew your daughter and her husband, very well. My name is Jack Preston, and I am one of the sons of the family that Daniel and your daughter stayed with.'

Miriam gapes at him. Surely this is some kind of trick. Is he drawing her into his confidence so that she will divulge further information? But now she comes to think of it, the name Preston does ring a bell, somehow, somewhere. Perhaps she heard Daniel speak of it, or Rosa wrote it in a letter. Her head is spinning, and he is watching her, waiting for a response.

'I ... I don't know what to think, sir,' she begins, cautiously. 'Am I really to believe this? That your father is the fan manufacturer who sponsored Daniel?'

The officer nods.

'And that you really do know my daughter?'

'Indeed I do, madam. She and her husband lodged with my family for eight months.' His smile is so genuine that a chink of hope lodges in her brain. Is he telling her the truth, however extraordinary that might seem? All her natural mistrust, learned through years of experiencing lies and abuse, seems to slip away and the words tumble eagerly from her mouth. 'How is she? Is she well? Do you know where she is living?'

The officer holds up a hand. 'I'm sorry, but I have not seen your daughter since August 1939. She and Daniel went to live in London, I believe, and I joined the air force. Unfortunately I do not have an address for her.'

'What about your father? Would he have an address? Did Daniel continue working for him?'

His expression becomes serious again. 'It was a bit difficult. Daniel left the company, you see. I believe he wanted to get to America, but visas were very hard to come by at that late stage.'

Her hopes slump, but Captain Preston is still talking: 'Listen, Mrs Kauffman, once you are in the UK, you will be able to find her yourself, I'm sure.'

She gapes at him. 'You will give me the visa?'

'Oh yes. Of course.' He smiles again. 'If you will bear with me for a few minutes, I will collect the paperwork, and after that is completed, you will be free to continue your journey and the search for your daughter.'

Once again she finds herself alone in the stuffy little room listening to the pounding of her own heart, although this time it is with astonishment rather than terror. Has this really just happened, or is it some kind of dream? She has the overwhelming sensation of floating above the table, looking down on it and on herself, this ragged old woman who has been clinging to a single strand of hope, a flimsy thread that has been her lifeline for so many years and through so much hardship. And now someone has thrown her a ladder with sturdy rungs, leading to her daughter. All she has to do is summon the energy to climb it.

Jack Preston is back in the room and she looks at him with new eyes, this man who is turning out to be her saviour. 'First we have to complete the application form.' He pushes the paper across the table, along with a classy fountain pen still warm from his breast pocket. 'Print your full name and the date, then sign here.'

He passes her another sheet with a carbon paper duplicate. *Proof of Identity*, it reads. *I, the undersigned, do declare that I am the person identified in this document.* She fills in her name, maiden name, date and place of birth, last known address, nationality and religion.

'Normally we would need more proof of identity,' he says as she writes, 'but how can I mistrust you when you are Rosa's mother?'

'It is my lucky day, sir.'

'And mine, Mrs Kauffman,' he says, grinning like a boy once more. He really has a very charming way with him, she thinks. 'All you have to do is sign both copies and date them, here. Then the top copy is yours to keep, until you can go to the embassy in London to apply for a new passport.'

She signs and dates, passes it back to him. He scribbles his initials beside her signature, removes the carbon copy, then takes out a rubber stamp and ink pad. Two sharp thuds later, and it is complete.

'And finally, this.'

It is a small piece of paper with a British coat of arms printed in red at the top, the ferocious-looking lion and the equally alarming unicorn facing each other across a shield. This is the moment she has been waiting for, dreaming of, for months, even years.

The United Kingdom visa. Her ticket to Rosa.

Miriam emerges from the border post blinking in the bright sunlight. She feels giddy with astonishment, still trying to comprehend what has just happened, and her feet are so light she feels like skipping. Carefully stowed in the inner pocket of her coat – she dares not risk leaving them in her rucksack – are the two precious documents. In her hand is an envelope the officer handed her just as she was leaving. 'Open this when you are away from the border post,' he instructed.

The chain-link fence and the line of miserable refugees in the border queue are just a few hundred yards behind her. She is still breathing the same air as them, yet she has entered a different world and feels a sudden glorious sense of freedom. The burden of fear has lifted, or so she thinks.

A car screeches past, and at the sound of a sudden loud report Miriam throws herself instinctively to the ground, cradling her head in her arms and trembling with terror. As she sits up, dusting herself off, she realises that it must have simply been an exhaust backfiring. How long will it be before she can hear loud noises and not assume it is gunfire?

She continues walking until she reaches the town square. Ahead is what looks like ordinary civilian life, people going about their normal Saturday business: businessmen in suits, girls giggling arm in arm, mothers with babies in prams, old ladies with their shopping baskets. This is the British sector. There are no Russian soldiers. No one will fire at her. The rule of law applies here – or at least this is what everyone has told her.

A small market is being set up, and the place is bustling with activity. She stops, astonished to see pyramids of vegetables: carrots, sticks of white celery, ruby beetroot, brilliant green cabbages. A nearby stall has stocks of meat, sausages and brawn; such riches she has not witnessed since the start of the war. Queues are already starting to form.

The sight brings tears to her eyes. It is years since she has seen anything like it. The clock on the town hall chimes ten o'clock. Just two hours ago she was waiting in that small, stuffy wooden hut, still fearful of what faced her. How could she have predicted the extraordinary stroke of good fortune that seems to have beamed down on her like a powerful ray of sunshine? What has she done to deserve such a blessed coincidence?

Her sense of exhilaration is only slightly tempered by the knowledge that although the precious identity card and visa might be in her pocket, there are still many problems to overcome. She has no money, no food and no place to stay. She is still many miles from Holland and the coast, where she will have to take a ferry to cross the Channel.

Suddenly drained of energy, she sits on the step of an empty shop, surveying the bustling square. People here are recovering their lives. Will that luxury ever be granted to her? Then she remembers the unopened envelope the officer pressed on her. She takes it out and rips it open.

Inside is a ten-mark note and a scrap of paper on which he has written, in a hasty scribble: *Buy yourself some food. Please meet me at the café on the square, five o'clock this evening. Jack Preston*

For the first time in many months, Miriam laughs out loud.

6

It is such a curious feeling, sitting at a table in this café as though it is something she does every day. She is a proper citizen, a legitimate customer, not someone trying to conceal their Jewish identity, not a beggar desperate for a crust of stale bread or a glass of clean water. For once, she has money in her pocket and is able to pay.

She has done her best to tidy herself up. At one corner of the market, tucked away from the main stalls, she discovered a stall selling second-hand clothing and bought a pair of navy blue slacks and a woollen jersey in a delicate pale green, the hopeful colours of springtime, all for three marks.

On the corner of a little street just off the square, she found a mossy fountain trickling pure spring water. Making sure there was no one watching, she dipped her hands into the pool and washed herself as thoroughly as possible, combing the water through her hair with her fingers. Then she found a park with some scraggy bushes behind which she was able to change.

Even these small adjustments make her feel more confident. It is more than three years since the day they arrived at the camp after that interminable train journey, herded into a windowless concrete bunker and told to undress. Then, of course, it was striped camp uniform pyjamas for everyone until they were rescued.

In hospital, after liberation, after the bathing, the shaving and de-lousing, they were given gowns, and then, when finally discharged, they were told to choose from a pile of second-hand garments in a damp, musty storeroom. Everyone complained that the clothes were probably stolen from dead Jews, but by then Miriam hardly cared. Working in the camp warehouses had long hardened her to such qualms.

All the women were advised to wear trousers, jacket and cap, to dress like men. It didn't take long to find out why. Russian soldiers were rapacious. They would make filthy gestures, laughing and shouting out words she was glad not to understand. They would corner you at any time you found yourself alone, day or night, and force themselves on you without inhibition. But if you pulled up your collar, stuck your hair into a cap and stayed in the shadows, you might, just might, avoid their attentions.

Miriam sat under the bushes to eat the *Apfelstrudel* she'd bought from the bakery in the square. Lifting the lid of the small white cardboard box, she pressed her nose close and inhaled deeply: the smell of icing sugar, cinnamon, apples and raisins was intoxicating. She did not stop until the inside of the box was cleared, with a dampened fingertip, of every single crumb of pastry and dusting of sugar.

Someone else was watching her as she ate: a skinny tabby cat. When she finished, she held out her sticky fingers for it to lick.

'Hello, little puss,' she crooned as the cat purred, raking her skin with its rough tongue and then stroking itself along her outstretched hand. She petted it, delighting in its soft warmth, its languid affection. How long was it since she'd caressed a cat?

Few domestic pets had survived during those war years; their meat was too precious.

And now the long day has passed, and dusk is deepening and there is a chill in the air once more. At ten minutes to five she went to the café, and the warmth inside was welcome. Despite the pretty new jumper, she is aware that she probably still looks like a tramp, and is grateful for the respectful manner in which the waiter brings a glass of water and asks for her order.

'I am waiting for a friend,' she explains. A friend? Is that what he is, this officer she met less than twenty-four hours ago, this man who claims to know her daughter? She still cannot quite believe what he has told her. She will know whether or not it is true, she supposes, when he fails to turn up, which she half expects. But then why would he lie to her? Why would he give her ten marks – apparently from his own pocket – if he didn't genuinely intend to meet her?

She waits as the clock on the town hall strikes five, the hand creeps round to ten past and the waiter looks at her across the café with questioning eyebrows.

'Still waiting for my friend,' she says, embarrassed. Now increasingly convinced that Jack Preston has spun her a line, she orders a coffee anyway. That leaves her with only four marks, which may be just enough to pay for a night at a hostel, she hopes. After that, it will be back to begging and sleeping under hedges.

At twenty minutes past, she sees his face smiling through the window of the café. He is here, as he promised.

'May I?' She gestures yes, of course, and he sits down, tugging off his cap and folding it into a neat roll on the table.

'I am so sorry to be late,' he says. 'My commander is a tyrant.'

The waiter arrives with her coffee and Jack Preston orders a beer. She carefully stirs in a few chips of sugar – free sugar, imagine! – and takes a sip, looking at him over the rim of the cup.

'Good?' he asks.

'Delicious,' she says. 'Two real coffees in one day. I hardly know myself.'

He watches her as she drinks it, slowly, savouring every mouthful. 'You look ... different,' he says at last.

She hears herself giggling, almost girlishly. 'Your generosity meant I could buy clean clothes and a delicious pastry for my lunch. I cannot thank you enough – for the money, for everything. I am really most grateful.'

'And I, for my part, am so pleased to have met you, Mrs Kauffman,' he says, graciously. 'I have spent most of today pinching myself. Rosa's mother turns up at my border post! I still cannot quite believe it. We have so much to catch up on.'

The beer arrives and he swigs it greedily before putting down the glass with a small sigh, wiping the foam from his upper lip with the back of his hand.

'Aah. I needed that. Shall we order food? I'm starving,' he suggests, and it is clear that he immediately regrets using the word.

She pretends not to notice. 'You have been so kind. I'm afraid there is not much left of the ten marks you gave me.'

'I'll pay, don't you worry.' He gestures to the waiter and asks what's on the menu.

'Meatloaf and dumplings. Delicious.' The waiter kisses the tips of his fingers with a theatrical flourish. 'Our chef has contacts at the US base.'

As he leaves, they fall into silence again. There is too much to say, and neither seems able to start. Then they both speak at once: 'Tell me ...' They laugh and he says, 'You go first,' and she says, 'I've done all the talking so far. Tell me how you met my daughter.'

7

Rosa. The name is like a sigh on his lips.

Earlier, Jack watched the woman walking away, with her mismatched boots and ragged overcoat, the old khaki knapsack over her shoulder, shaking his head in disbelief. Had that meeting really just happened? That stooped, starved figure – she'd stopped and waved just then, and he'd waved back – had turned his world inside out and upside down.

Just last night he took Lisa in his arms and enjoyed his first truly passionate kiss of many years, believing that perhaps, just perhaps, she might be the one to replace Rosa in his heart. But that kiss has already faded into a distant memory.

All these years he has tried to banish Rosa from his mind, and yet even in the worst moments of his life, the memories insist on reappearing. She was there during the terrifying twenty-four hours floating in that little rubber life raft after they'd been forced to ditch into the North Sea on a freezing night, as he held in his arms the only other survivor, his navigator, Scotty, who was mortally wounded and slowly slipping into unconsciousness.

She was there when he found himself alone on the ocean,

hallucinating from pain, hunger and thirst; when he was picked up by a German gunboat and treated with such kindness he found it difficult to believe that their two countries could actually be at war, their armies trying to kill each other. And as he slipped in and out of consciousness in a pristine hospital bed, where the nurses were charmed by his fluent German, and expert military surgeons patched him up with impressive skill before shipping him off to the prisoner-of-war camp.

At all these times he felt Rosa by his side.

Camp was different; so brutal, so hard-edged, that at first his sole focus was day-to-day survival. There was food and fuel to be sought, negotiations with guards to be had, letters to be written, entertainments, classes and other distractions to be devised to keep up morale. They had all seen the might of the German army and were under no illusions: the war would not be won easily unless the Yanks climbed off the fence and decided to join in. They were likely to be stuck here for years. The goal was to survive without starving, falling ill or getting shot. There was little space in his head for dreaming.

Some people tried to escape and their methods were certainly ingenious: tunnelling, wire-cutting, work-detail breakouts. Most attempts ended in disaster, and some of the men died. They never heard news of those who made it and how they managed to travel through German-occupied territory, let alone get across the Channel, without being detected or betrayed.

As the months passed, even though the tension and fear never went away, the men became resigned and time began to weigh more heavily. It was then that the memories of Rosa returned, more vivid than ever.

Now, improbably, he is sitting in a café opposite her mother, and she is asking him to tell her all about how they met. It feels surreal, as though he is in a dream.

He wants to blurt it out: to confess how he fell hopelessly in love with Rosa from the very first moment he set eyes on her, and the ecstasy of discovering that she felt the same; how he believed to his core that such a powerful love could not be denied, his absolute certainty that she would divorce Daniel and they would live happily ever after. How, even now, the very mention of her name sends shivers down his spine. How she occupies his dreams.

But ultimately she turned him down, and that still cuts like a knife, alongside the embarrassment he caused his family. His mother's words ring in his ears: 'You should be ashamed of yourself, Jack, taking advantage of a young woman when she is so dependent on our help. A *married* woman. Whatever were you thinking of?' And now here he is, in danger of admitting everything to Rosa's mother. He checks himself, trying to compose his expression.

'She is a beautiful young woman,' he says now, quite simply. 'Daniel is, well, more formal, and harder to get to know, although my father said he was an excellent worker and very efficient. His help was very welcome at that time because so many of the men were going off to fight.

'But everyone adored Rosa. She was so willing and helpful and my mother frequently said she could never manage without her. We were eight in the house – me and my three brothers were all at home – and there was so much to do, what with Ma's good works as well.'

'Good works?'

'Raising money for various causes, old people's homes, the church restoration fund, you know? Rosa was happy to pitch in,' he says. 'And she got along with everyone.'

'She was always a good girl,' Miriam says, quietly. 'It makes me very proud to hear you speak of her like this. But ...' She hesitates.

'But?'

'Was she happy? With Daniel, I mean? It was all such a

rush, their marriage, and she really did not have any other choice. She never said anything bad about him, but I did wonder.'

What has she heard? Did Rosa write to her? How much should he say? The truth is that even by the time they reached England, the marriage was already showing signs of strain, although they did their best to conceal it. Raised voices could sometimes be overheard from their bedroom, causing Ma to raise her eyebrows and mutter: 'It's hardly surprising, given what they've been through and what they've had to leave behind, poor things.'

One evening, when the dinner gong sounded, Jack emerged from his own bedroom to see the couple walking ahead of him down the corridor. Daniel put his arm around his wife's waist, but she shrugged him off and he muttered: '*Um Himmels willen, Rosa!*' For goodness' sake.

In public, all was calm and polite. They presented themselves as the perfect couple, but the tension between them was obvious. Daniel was clearly not an easy man, and although Rosa did her best to attend to his every need, it was not always with a willing smile. He had fixed views on the world and loved to rehearse them after supper, over a glass of brandy or two. After a couple of hours of his pontification, everyone, including Rosa, could be seen trying to conceal their yawns.

'They were fine,' he says to Miriam now. 'A very handsome pair they made, too.'

She nods, apparently reassured. 'When did you last see them?'

'It was the end of August, I think,' he says, deliberately vague, although he knows perfectly well the date: 22 August 1939, the week before the outbreak of war. He has not seen Rosa, nor received any word from her, since.

He'd signed up with the RAF knowing that his chances of survival were slim. Everyone knew it, although no one said it out loud. But he didn't care. Without Rosa, he felt as though he had nothing to live for.

So it came as a surprise when, having escaped death after the crash into the North Sea, he discovered that he very much wanted to live. After a while, letters from his parents began to arrive: a reminder of the England into which Rosa and Daniel had arrived, and a way of life – work at the factory, news of his brothers, Red Cross fundraisers, concerts and village fetes – that read like a fairy tale, blithely unaffected by the cataclysm happening on the other side of the Channel.

His replies were constructed to avoid anything the camp censors might consider sensitive information – they had little compunction in blacking out anything they didn't like, or even just refusing to send letters. Otherwise, he was careful not to say anything that might cause his parents more worry. He refused even to hint at the hunger, the humiliation and the threats, the numbing cold, the constant fear of what might happen next, or the stultifying boredom of camp life. Sometimes, reading them through, he couldn't help laughing at what he'd written: what with the special meals they managed to put together from Red Cross parcels, the quiz evenings, concerts and other theatrical entertainments, it sounded for all the world as though he was describing a jolly holiday camp.

What would he have written to Rosa, had he been able? Would he have told her the truth, as they swore they always would? It was one of the miracles of their friendship. From a tongue-tied boy had emerged a young man who could not only examine and acknowledge his own feelings, but also felt no embarrassment at expressing them.

When this is all over, he would have written, *I want to spend the rest of my life with you.*

After being released from PoW camp and going home for debriefing and recuperation before returning to Germany, Jack had risked asking his father whether he'd had any news about the Levys. The terse reply was that they had heard nothing.

'We were sorry to see them go,' he says now, to a backdrop of clattering in the kitchens behind them as the chef prepares their meatloaf and dumplings.

'They never wrote to you?' Her eyes probe his face, anxious for an answer.

He shakes his head. Some things are impossible to explain. And some things are best left unsaid.

When the food arrives, it soon becomes clear that the waiter was not exaggerating: the meatloaf is delicious. Jack finishes long before Miriam. She eats slowly and deliberately, savouring every mouthful and exclaiming her delight. 'Oh, this is so good ... Even the dumplings taste wonderful ... What are those herbs? ... And the gravy ... It is just as my mother used to make it.'

'I'm pleased you are enjoying it,' he says, taking a sip of beer. 'Can I get you something else to drink?'

'No, thank you. Water will be fine. I want to savour the food.'

The strain in her face has lifted, and as she smiles back across the table, he sees, perhaps for the first time, an echo of Rosa's smile; the smile that made him feel like the king of the world.

She answers his questions politely but seems to drift into long moments of thoughtfulness. If what he endured was terrible, whatever can it have been like for her? Waiting, fearing, never knowing whether the next day would bring arrest and deportation to heaven knew where. The tattoo tells him that that day eventually arrived for her and she was taken to a concentration camp, and he's seen enough photos of the liberation of Belsen to know that those places were hell on earth, unimaginable for anyone who has not been there. She doesn't offer any more, and he dares not press her further, not tonight, not at this first meeting.

At last, he can see that she is exhausted. 'We'd better find you a place to stay,' he says.

Her brow furrows with concern. 'I have no more money, I'm afraid.'

'You think I'm going to let Rosa's mother sleep on the streets?'

The waiter arrives with the bill and Jack asks him whether he knows of a guest house or hostel that is comfortable and not too pricey. The man tells them that there are rooms above the café, if that would suit. The room is small and modestly furnished, but Miriam is delighted: it will be the first time she has slept in a real bed between cotton sheets since she left the hospital, she tells him.

They agree to meet at ten o'clock the following morning to arrange her onward journey. They will go to the station and buy her a ticket through to the Hook of Holland, from where she can catch a ferry to Harwich. Jack checks his wallet: yes, he has enough marks, he thinks, and some notes in sterling for when she reaches England.

He leaves the café and stands in the square for a while, having a smoke, considering whether to get an early night or return to HQ for a drink in the mess with the lads. Although he is physically weary, his head is buzzing and he needs time to reflect on the extraordinary events of the day. There is a *Bierkeller* on the other corner of the square – he walks over, takes a seat in a quiet corner and orders himself a large flagon.

For so long he has tried to forget about Rosa; the memories were just too painful. Never in a million years did he imagine that he would find himself hatching plans with her mother, helping her find her daughter again. Cheered on by the rowdy company around him – mostly English servicemen – he downs his second flagon in five heroic gulps.

8

Miriam tosses restlessly in the soft bed, with its white sheets and wondrously puffy quilt.

Her stomach is uncomfortably full and her mind turns over the events of the previous day in minute-by-minute detail: waking in the reception hut, the tense interview in that stuffy room with the curiously wide mirror on the wall that looked suspiciously like two-way glass, the officer's kindness, bringing rolls and coffee, his shock when she mentioned Daniel's name, and her utter astonishment when this man, a complete stranger until that moment, told her that he knew Rosa. It was his father's company that had sponsored Daniel. His family had effectively saved her daughter's life.

And now he is offering to help her get to England. A train journey and a ferry crossing will bring her onto the same soil as Rosa – she is almost there already. There are organisations in London that help people find their families. It is possible, just possible, that they might be reunited within a few days, or weeks at most.

She is exhausted but cannot sleep: she climbs down from the high bed and paces the floor for several minutes, then opens the shutters to peer down at the town square, where people are still out and about, chatting in groups, walking arm in arm, sitting at café tables. This is what normal life looks like. This is what she might be doing with Rosa, just a few days from now. Seeing the sights of London, spending time together, chatting, laughing, embracing ...

She grabs a bolster from the bed and wraps her arms tightly around it until her heart calms and she feels comforted enough to return to bed, and to sleep.

Next morning, Jack Preston is at the café, as arranged. He enquires after her in that polite English way, 'I trust you slept well?' and orders coffee and cheese rolls.

'Do you not have rationing here?' she asks as the food arrives, white bread with fat chunks of cheese. 'The rest of Germany is starving.'

He shrugs: 'Of course, but there's also a thriving black market. The Americans have shipped in all kinds of meat, dairy, wheat. Like the waiter said last night, it pays to have connections.'

When they finish eating, he reaches into an inside pocket and hands her an envelope. 'This should get you to London and pay for food and lodging for a couple of days, until you can get yourself sorted.' She peers into it, counting twenty marks and ten pounds sterling, before pushing it back across the table. 'No. I cannot accept this. It is too much. I will never be able to repay you.'

'You will be helping me as well,' he says, returning it. 'You want to find your daughter, and I want to see her again too. I'm sorry we don't have an address for her any more, but I think you said you had friends there who can help you search?'

'There are organisations,' she says. 'Jewish organisations.'

'I've put my English address inside. My parents will

forward anything to me if I'm still over here. You will let me know, won't you, when you find her?'

'Do you suppose your parents have heard anything from Daniel and Rosa recently?'

Jack Preston's handsome brow furrows, and he shakes his head. 'I doubt it.'

Something in his tone alerts her. 'May I enquire why? Was there something wrong?'

He pauses. 'Let's just say there was a small difference of opinion,' he says at last. 'Which is why Daniel could not continue to work for the company.'

Daniel was such an impatient character, she always thought. Little wonder they didn't get on with him.

'But you think they're probably still in England?'

She is relieved when he nods in agreement: 'Chances are Daniel found work in London and they're still there, although I suppose they might have tried again for the US after VE Day.'

'VE?'

'Sorry, Victory in Europe. The eighth of May.'

'What we called the Day of Liberation. We celebrated in the hospital,' she says. 'The Russians all got very drunk and forgot to feed us, but we forgave them because we were so grateful to them for liberating us.'

Her memories of those first few weeks are sketchy. They were rescued from the camp by Russian soldiers and driven to a former airbase converted into a hospital and convalescent home. She was so weak that she could barely walk unaided, struggling to breathe from the pneumonia and hallucinating from the typhoid fever. They didn't expect her to survive.

Although few of the Russian nurses spoke German, they managed to communicate somehow. They were endlessly kind and careful, administering medicines for the fever and slowly introducing food: liquids only at first, then mashed vegetables.

Considering the general scarcity of almost everything, it was a minor miracle how well she was cared for.

Jack gives her advice about the journey, and after breakfast he walks with her to the station and they find a train leaving in just an hour's time to Duisburg, from where she can connect with another train to The Hague in Holland. Ferries from The Hague arrive in a place called Harwich, from which there is a direct train to London. She remembers now Rosa describing their travel plans: she will be taking much the same route.

When it comes time to say goodbye, Jack holds out his hand.

'Safe journey, Miriam Kauffman,' he says. 'And good luck with your search. Don't forget to let me know as soon as you find Rosa.'

'I promise,' she says. 'And I bless the day I met you, Captain Preston.'

As they shake hands, slightly awkwardly, she feels the solid strength of the man and his genuine goodness, as though it is somehow radiating through his uniform.

The sea crossing is calm, and by late afternoon Miriam gains her first glimpse of England. It is disappointing. She imagined white cliffs towering above a slate-grey sea, but then remembers from long-ago geography lessons that the white cliffs are on the south coast, and this is the east.

Later, sitting on another train, she can just about make out through the gathering dusk that they are travelling through flat, featureless countryside past estuaries and muddy marshes, then hedges and brown fields, green pastures with cows. Looming clouds threaten rain once more. The landscape is punctuated by small villages of pink-painted cottages with thatched or tiled roofs dominated by outsize church towers.

As they draw into London, she sees ranks of tiny houses squashed together. They are drab and run-down, with narrow gardens and scarcely any green spaces between them. Closer to the city there is bomb damage: whole streets demolished and replaced with mountains of rubble. This is what Hamburg probably looks like, she thinks to herself.

Since learning that the Allies had bombed her home city to smithereens, she'd wondered whether it had really been necessary to punish ordinary people. That they needed to put airbases, factories, docks and railway depots out of action she could understand, but destroying people's homes too? Now she can see that the Germans bombed London in an equally undiscriminating way. What an absurdity war is, how meaningless. They should just have bombed Hitler himself instead of allowing so many millions to die pointlessly.

The confusingly named Liverpool Street station – 'But I want to go to London, not Liverpool,' she told the guard at Harwich, who kindly reassured her – is vast and cavernous, and hardly any light penetrates the steamy gloom. She finds her way through the maze of platforms and emerges into the street.

In the dim glow of the street lamps, she can see that the area around the station has been devastated. Rubble-filled gaps in the rows of houses remind her of broken teeth. Walls have fallen away, revealing the rooms once lived in, their wallpaper, furniture and personal belongings now open to the elements. She starts to worry about Rosa. Did she and Daniel stay here throughout the war, and if so, did they survive the bombs?

She is exhausted and hungry, and her shabby overcoat and mismatched boots provide little protection against the drizzle. Just a few streets away from the station she sees a sign: *Rooms for rent*. She knocks on the door, and after some minutes it opens, just a few inches. An elderly woman in a flowery overall peers suspiciously through the narrow crack.

'Can I help you, madam?'

Miriam puts on her best British accent. 'Good evening. I am looking for somewhere to stay, just for a few nights.'

'It's late.'

'Yes, my train has just arrived.'

'Where've you come from?'

She hesitates, reluctant to admit that she is German.

'From Essex.' It isn't a lie. She saw it on the signs: Harwich is in Essex.

The door opens wider. 'I have a vacancy as it happens. Five shillings a night. Do you want to see it?'

The room, on the second floor, is small and musty-smelling, but Miriam takes it anyway.

'Payment in advance,' the landlady says, holding out her palm. 'Don't want you doing a runner.'

Miriam takes out of her pocket the envelope Jack gave her, and unfolds the bundle of notes. 'I will stay for four days, please,' she says, peeling off a grubby blue pound note. But as she does so, others are dislodged and fall to the floor. She hastens to pick up the German marks, but the landlady has sharp eyes.

'What are those?' she says. 'Foreign money?'

Miriam's heart contracts.

'Show me it.' The woman looks at her sharply, eyes fierce. 'German money. You're a Kraut, then? Thought you could pull the wool over my eyes, did you? You aren't from Essex after all, are you?'

She pushes away Miriam's outstretched hand, and the proffered pound note.

'No. The room is not available.'

'But—'

'It's not me, it's the other guests. Some of them were serving men and they've seen what your people can do.' She shakes her head. 'It's just not worth the aggravation, dearie. Now off you go.'

By the time Miriam is ejected into the street, it is raining heavily. Her boots are leaking, the rain runs down inside her collar and her coat grows heavier as it absorbs the water. Her new trousers are also soaked. She sees a doorway to a closed office building and takes shelter. It's no good trying to find lodgings at this late hour looking as she does, like a drowned rat. She has survived worse than this, much, much worse, she tells herself, curling up in the driest corner. At least she is now, probably, in the same city as her daughter. It can only be a matter of time before they are reunited.

Not long, my darling, she says to herself. I'm coming. Nearly there.

PART 2

9

HAMBURG, 1938

It was wrong to have a favourite child, Miriam knew, but Rosa was her firstborn. She was always going to be special.

Hans had a good job in an upmarket furrier's shop, and Miriam was teaching at the *Gymnasium*, so they could afford to rent a fine apartment near the park in Hamburg. It was a good life, and they had many amusing, cultured friends, enjoying concerts and the opera or spending long evenings in cafés putting the world to rights. So when Rosa arrived, with those big brown eyes like her grandmother's, Miriam's life was complete.

When she discovered that she was expecting again, she worried that she wouldn't have enough love to spare for another child, but of course when Wilhelm was born she discovered that a mother's love is infinite. Rosa was lively and clever, always amusing them with her sharp wit. She did well at school, and Willi – as he soon became – was growing into a fine young man, excelling at sport. He seemed to have an endless stream of school friends, always at the front door asking if he could come out to play and join their team in the park.

The years flashed by in a blur of busy motherhood. Life was

almost perfect and at first it was easy to disregard the political shenanigans reported daily in the newspapers. That man will never get into power, everyone said. They tried to dismiss the ghastly gossip that spread like a plague, the outlandish stories that people related, more shocking with every telling. And yet, as time went by, came the slow acceptance that many of the stories were true and the fierce, crippling fear grew and grew like a cancer, a malignant cloud that hovered over and around them, denser and more suffocating with each day that passed.

First of all, Hans's employer, a man who had become a friend over the years, drew him into the back room and in a low, mournful voice told him that his services were no longer required. They could only use certain shops. Money grew tight, food grew scarce.

Then the terrifying night-time arrests began. People taken to prison, questioned and released, often with horrific injuries. It was all part of the regime's way of repressing the populace, everyone said. Ruling through fear. But never in a million years did Miriam and Hans imagine the midnight hammering might come to their own front door.

'Get back to bed, it's nothing to worry about.' Miriam shooed the children back into their rooms, her legs trembling beneath her flimsy nightgown. She felt so vulnerable as Hans opened the door and black-uniformed men filled the apartment. It was like something from a nightmare.

'Hans Kauffman?' the lead officer barked.

'Yes, that is me.'

'You are under arrest. You must come with us. Now.'

She rushed forward, screaming at them: 'This is outrageous. Arrest? What for? What has he done wrong?'

Hans took her hand, drawing her back, shushing her. 'I'll be back before you know it,' he said, calmly taking his coat from the hook. He kissed her and was gone.

Afterwards, as silence descended on the apartment once

again, the children crept out of their rooms and joined their sobbing mother on the sofa.

'Whatever are we to do?' she wailed.

'Don't worry, Mama,' Rosa said. 'There's obviously been a mistake. Papa will be home soon, you'll see. We will go to the police station tomorrow.'

But the days went by and their visits to the police station were met with scoffs, sneers and ultimately threats. 'If you continue to cause trouble, Mrs Kauffman, it will be all the worse for your husband,' they said.

Weeks passed and there was still no word. The police would not tell them why he was being held or whether he had been charged, and if so, what he had been charged with. They would give no date, no information on the possibility of bail. Miriam began to despair. Their savings were disappearing fast. The price of everything, especially food and coal, was rocketing. Life was becoming intolerable and many of their friends were trying to get out of Germany.

The rent was due, then overdue, and Miriam pleaded with the landlord, but in the end there was nothing for it: they had to give up the beautiful sunlit apartment next to the park that had been their home for years, since before the children were born. All they could afford was two rooms on the third floor of an ugly block in a run-down area of Hamburg, not far from the docks. Miriam tried to make the best of it, saying it was only temporary. They would leave Germany just as soon as Hans was released from prison.

Rosa had finished senior school with excellent grades and was all set for further study in English literature when she received the letter from the university. It made it perfectly clear that she would not be eligible for a place because she was Jewish – not said explicitly but plainly obvious. She told her mother later that she'd been sitting on the back step of the apartment block trying to figure out what to do next when she'd felt a hand on her shoulder.

'Are you okay?'

'Not really,' she had admitted, trying to smile.

'Mind if I join you?'

'Feel free.'

'My name is Marta Muller. We're on the same floor as you, I think. Cigarette?'

'I don't, thanks.'

'Try it.' Marta lit up, and passed the cigarette over. 'Don't inhale at first, or only a little bit, or it'll make you cough.'

Rosa coughed anyway, which made them both laugh, but she persevered and after a while began to enjoy it. Marta seemed nice, but she was blonde-haired and blue-eyed, the perfect Aryan, so Rosa was instantly suspicious.

The other girl seemed to read her thoughts. 'You don't have to worry. I know you're Jewish, and I've got nothing against Jews. In fact I think you are being treated abominably. My father is a communist. He's in jail, like your father – Frau Geller told us – so we're in the same boat really.'

'It's horrible, isn't it? Feeling so helpless. Have you had any word from him?'

'No, nothing. Mama is desperate. And there's only me to look after her.'

'Are you at university?' Rosa asked.

'I wish. I had a place but had to turn it down because we couldn't afford it. Without Papa's money we're poor as church mice. So I'm working as a waitress in a café.'

'And I've just been told I'm not eligible because I'm Jewish. It's so unfair, isn't it?'

The girls had become firm friends. Even when Marta confessed to Rosa with great embarrassment that her mother had warned her off fraternising with 'those Jews', they continued to meet secretly.

It was through Marta that the family were introduced to the neighbour on the other side. Seeing Miriam returning from the market with a basket empty save for a few poor-quality potatoes – all she could afford – Frau Geller invited her in for coffee and cake and Miriam broke down, admitting the plight in which the family found themselves.

Two days later, Frau Geller called round.

'May I come in?' she asked. 'I believe I may have some useful information for you.'

'Please, come and sit down.'

'My old school friend is poorly with tuberculosis and has been sent to a sanatorium for heaven knows how long, poor dear woman. What she's most worried about is how her husband is coping with their three children. His housekeeper has just left, and he's desperate. Do you suppose your daughter might be interested?'

Miriam tried to imagine what beautiful, headstrong Rosa might make of the idea, could imagine the toss of the auburn hair, the jutting of the chin, the incredulous look. Miriam and Hans had always impressed on Rosa that if she studied hard she could achieve great things. How would she respond to the idea of working as a lowly housekeeper?

'What kind of a man is he?' she asked. 'My daughter has only just left school.'

'Herr Steiner is a lawyer. Very respectable.'

'Would he mind if ... you know, our background?'

'He is a reasonable man. But for the moment I suggest you just don't mention it.'

For several days, Miriam couldn't bring herself to ask Rosa. But then, sitting down for another meal of turnip stew, Willi threw down his spoon and refused to eat. 'I hate vegetables,' he shouted. 'Why can't we have meat for a change?'

Miriam tasted the bitterness of shame: she couldn't even provide for her own family. Later, after Willi had gone to bed, she said to her daughter: 'I know a way we can get meat.'

Rosa was surprisingly receptive to the idea of becoming a housekeeper. 'It's only for a while, isn't it?' she said gaily, that first morning. 'At least it's not working in a factory.'

10

The Steiner home occupied the whole of the third floor of a building that must once have been a palace, overlooking the park in a smart residential area of Hamburg. Inside, it was not overly grand, but it was spacious and comfortable, with plenty of toys, games and musical instruments belonging to the three children Rosa was employed to look after. She was reminded, with a pang of nostalgia, of the apartment she'd been brought up in, the one they'd lived in until Papa was arrested and they'd had to move to those dark, cramped rooms near the docks.

'During the week, the children are at school and kindergarten. Your duties are to clean the apartment, shop for food, prepare the meals and do the laundry,' Steiner explained as he showed her around. 'You will pick up Anna from kindergarten at one o'clock, give her luncheon and take her to the park, then the other two finish school at three. I will usually be home by six o'clock. Before you leave, we will discuss what you should buy and cook for the following day's meals. Is that understood?'

'Yes,' she whispered, feeling overwhelmed.

'I didn't hear you,' he snapped, in his sharp, nasal voice.

'Yes, sir,' she said, more loudly. He was slim and pale-faced, and so tall she had to raise her chin to meet his eyes, and when she did, they were so piercingly blue that it sent shivers down her spine.

He regarded her silently for a long moment, up and down, as though she was some kind of farm animal at auction. A smile twisted his thin lips. 'Pretty little thing, aren't you? Have you any experience of childcare and housekeeping?'

'I've looked after my younger brother and my mother has taught me to cook.' It was an outrageous exaggeration. Yes, she had looked after Willi from when he was a baby. But cooking? She would have to get a crash course from Mama.

'Good, good. I suppose Frau Geller told you where my wife is?'

'Yes, sir. At a sanatorium in Switzerland. I hope she is feeling better.'

'Thank you, thank you. The doctors say it will take some time. So when can you start, Miss Kauffman?'

She took a breath. 'Tomorrow?'

'Half past seven, on the dot, please, so I may give you instructions. I must be at my office by eight.'

Right from those very first moments, there was something in the way he looked at her that made her uncomfortable. She didn't yet recognise it, but would come to know that look all too well in the coming months. All she could think of right now was the smile on Willi's face when she presented him with his favourite supper, a pot roast of beef brisket. Her mouth watered as she imagined it.

Being a housekeeper wasn't so bad, she told her mother after that first week. The children were pleasant enough and generally obedient, though the elder boy, thirteen-year-old Friedrich, was starting to copy his father's arrogant manners. The two younger ones were still keen to please.

Five-year-old Anna became her favourite; she was more biddable, and anyway they had more time together. She was blonde like her father, and usually demanded that her hair be braided each morning in complex ways that Rosa had to learn through practice. 'You have such beautiful hair, sweetheart,' she would say. 'Like the finest silk. It is best when it is natural.'

'No, I want the double French plait, like Mama used to make.'

The little girl was fiercely intelligent and talked all the time, asking questions to which Rosa sometimes had no answer. Why does the moon change shape? What happens to birds in the winter? How does cooked oatmeal get so gummy? When is Mama coming home?

The middle child, Wolfgang, was studious and reserved. You might have thought him slow but after a few weeks Rosa began to understand there was nothing wrong with his brain. He was just cautious. Still waters run deep, she thought, as she observed him avoiding conflict and deflecting his older brother's bullying ways. He would go far.

All seemed to be running smoothly until one day in September. As Rosa was returning from the morning walk to school and kindergarten via the market, it began to rain heavily. She ran to the apartment as fast as she could, only then noticing that Herr Steiner's coat was on the hook.

Hearing the door, he emerged from his study. 'Good morning, Rosa.'

'Good morning, sir. Are you working at home today?'

'I forgot this.' He held up a paper folder. 'It's for a case I am engaged on. But you are soaked to the skin, you poor girl. Haven't you got a coat?'

'I forgot it,' she said. It was a lie. She had grown out of her coat long ago and the sleeves came almost to her elbows, but there was no money for a new one.

'You will get a chill if you wear those damp things all day.'

Why was he so concerned for her welfare all of a sudden? He didn't usually notice her at all.

He disappeared into his bedroom and returned with a bundle of clothes. 'Here, why don't you put these on until your own have dried off?' As he thrust them into her arms, she smelled the perfume that must have been the one his wife wore, mingled with the stale musk of unworn garments.

'Oh, sir. I cannot. These are your wife's things.'

'Indeed. But she is not using them. And you can return them another day.'

'You are certain?'

'Perfectly certain. You are about the same size as Alicia. You can use our room to change in. Then you can bring me some coffee, please.'

It felt strange, changing into Alicia Steiner's clothing, a plaid skirt and a luxuriously soft cashmere cardigan in a deep shade of plum. It was not a colour Rosa usually wore, believing it would clash with her auburn hair, but as she looked at herself in the mirror, she realised that the tones actually worked. What she also saw was Erich Steiner, peeping around the partly open door.

'It suits you,' he said, smiling, unabashed at having been caught watching her. 'Better than it suits Alicia. You must keep it. She never wears it.'

'Oh, I couldn't,' Rosa said, whipping round to face him, her cheeks flushing the same shade as the jumper. How long had he been there? Had he seen her in her underwear?

'Now, how about that coffee?' he said.

'Right away sir.'

She brought the tray to the living room, where he was comfortably installed on the soft sofa, reading a newspaper. There was none of his usual impatience to get away.

'Come and join me,' he said. 'A hot drink will warm you up.'

She hesitated. This new informality was unsettling. 'Come on,' he urged. 'I don't bite.'

She went to get a cup, poured herself coffee and seated herself in an armchair opposite.

'So, Miss Kauffman, how are you getting on with my little monsters?'

She told him they were well behaved and how impressed she was with their table manners. 'You and your wife have brought them up very well, sir,' she said.

He asked her more questions, about their schooling, their hobbies, what they liked to eat. She found this level of interest in his children very strange, since he never usually paid them much attention. Then he said: 'I am visiting Alicia next week and she will want to know everything.' So that explained his sudden curiosity.

'She will also ask about you,' he went on. 'So you had better tell me. All I know is that you live next door to Frau Geller. She's an old friend of my wife's, as you know, but sadly fallen on hard times. So what about you? You seem a bright young woman, and well educated. Why are you working as a housekeeper?'

She had to tell him something, but would keep it to a minimum. She said she had just finished school and was waiting to hear whether she had a place at university.

'What will you study?'

'English, I think. Perhaps business, or law?' She had no real interest in the law, but thought that mentioning it might make him more favourable towards her. It worked.

'Law, eh? An excellent profession, although it is rare for women to reach the higher echelons. Are you a trailblazer, young Rosa?'

'I hope to be.'

'And what about your parents?'

'My father is a ...' she hesitated before deciding to lie, 'a businessman. My mother is a teacher of English.'

'What sort of business?' Rosa had never been in a court-room, but she imagined that being on the receiving end of this type of interrogation must feel quite uncomfortable.

'Retail. He was a furrier.' Her use of the past tense slipped out by mistake. 'I mean he is a furrier.'

Steiner's piercing attention missed nothing. 'Is, or was?'

'He had to give it up.'

'I'm so sorry. Ill health, was it?'

'No, not that.' She felt as though she was being forced into a corner. Steiner could find out easily enough from Frau Geller, after all. And if he discovered she was lying, she would probably get the sack. 'I am afraid he is in prison, sir. He is an honest man, has never been in trouble all of his life. We don't even know what he is supposed to have done wrong. They won't tell us anything at all.'

Steiner put his cup on the low table between them and leaned forward, elbows resting on his knees, his gaze piercing the air between them.

'I am sorry to hear this, Rosa. I may call you that, may I?' She nodded. 'Do you care to tell me more? I am a lawyer, as you know. I may be able to help.'

The atmosphere in the room felt thick. Rosa struggled to breathe normally. How had she allowed herself to be drawn into this admission? She was in for it now. If he went to the police, he would almost certainly learn that her father was Jewish, and then he would probably sack her. On the other hand, if there was a chance he might be able to get Papa released, wasn't it a risk worth taking?

'I know nothing more, sir, except that men came to our apartment and arrested him. We have been to the police station many times and they will not tell us where he is, nor what he has been charged with.'

He stood up now, a slight smile playing on his lips.

'Leave it with me, young Rosa. I will make enquiries and let you know. This has been a very pleasant little chat; it was nice to get to know you a bit more. But now I need to return to work, and you had better be getting on with yours.'

That evening, she felt like confessing everything to her mother, sharing her fears about this man, and her terror should he discover her Jewishness. But Mama returned home with a new set of worries: she had been back to the police station once more to ask about Papa and been told by an irritated desk sergeant that if she bothered them again, they would take her into custody too. Then the butcher she usually patronised had spat in her face and told her never to pollute his shop again.

'It is becoming intolerable here, my darling. Perhaps with the money you are earning we could get false papers for you and Willi.'

'No! I will not leave until Papa is released and we can all go together.' Rosa heard herself shouting, and then had to apologise. 'Sorry, Mama. It's been a long day.'

A week passed, and Herr Steiner said nothing more regarding enquiries about Papa. Rosa felt both impatient and relieved at the same time. Impatient because she desperately wanted to bring her mother a glimmer of hope. She had been so low recently, so lacking in her usual fortitude; it felt as though she was almost giving up. Relieved because she had convinced herself that as soon as he went to the police, he would learn why Papa was there, and that would be the end of her job.

What actually happened was the very opposite.

11

A fortnight later, Rosa returned from the market to discover the apartment door unlocked and Steiner in his study, reading papers.

'Good morning, Rosa,' he called. 'I hoped you would be back. I have news for you. Make coffee, two cups, then come to sit with me.'

Rosa had never been into his study before. On her first day, he'd told her firmly that it was out of bounds, and in any case, the door was always locked. The rest of the apartment, facing south over the park, with tall windows welcoming the sunshine for most of the day, had a cheerful atmosphere. But this room immediately gave her the creeps. It was dark and gloomy, over-powered by shelves of books and files from floor to ceiling on every wall except the one occupied by a window with a lowered blind. The only other source of illumination was a table lamp, creating a pool of light over the enormous mahogany desk behind which Steiner was standing, his face in the half-shadow. A pair of leather-upholstered easy chairs sat in front of a narrow coal fireplace, and the low table between them was covered with newspapers and periodicals. The room smelled of old books and stale cigarette smoke; she noticed an overflowing ashtray on the desk.

'Come in, come in. Please, take a seat. How do you like what Alicia calls my lair?' As he smiled, his teeth glinted in the light from the lamp, and Rosa shivered. It was easy enough to imagine him as a wolf.

'Now,' he said, after she had poured the coffee. 'About your father.'

Her heart was pounding so hard that her coffee cup rattled in its saucer. 'Yes, sir. You said you had news.'

'I have located Herr Kauffman,' he said. 'And discovered what he has been charged with.'

She held her breath.

'His crime is illegal trading,' he went on. 'You said he used to be a furrier?'

She nodded.

'He was caught selling furs, even though he is prohibited from doing so. And do you know why that is, young Rosa?'

Her heart ached for poor Papa, doing his very best and protecting his family by hiding it from them. And this was what he got for it.

'No, sir,' she said.

'It is because your father is a *Jew*.' He spat out the word as though it was poison. 'But of course that is not news to you, Rosa, is it? Because you're a Jew too. And in your great wisdom, you decided not to tell me, didn't you?'

What could she say?

'Answer me, girl.' The menace in his voice made her flinch. She gathered herself, took a breath and began the speech she had prepared for this moment.

'I did not tell you, sir, because I need the work and the money, because my family are starving. And that is why my father went on trading, I expect, although he did not tell us about it. We have had to move from our apartment into two tiny rooms and have barely enough to eat.'

She steeled herself to look up at him. He was lighting a cigarette. 'I am good at my job, am I not, Herr Steiner? I am a hard worker, always punctual. You often compliment my cooking, and the children like me. We are not religious Jews, we do not go to synagogue, we don't offend others with our habits. It is just the way we were born. Surely there is nothing wrong with that?'

To her surprise, she noticed a smile creeping across his face.

'Feisty little madam, aren't you? I like that in a girl.' He exhaled a cloud of smoke. 'Now, I don't personally have a problem with Jews, but you know the law of the land. Nevertheless, what you say is correct. You are a good worker and the children like you.'

He paused to take another draw on his cigarette, and blew a perfect smoke ring into the air above his head. 'So I may be able to offer you a deal. I know the police chief in this district personally – we are both in the party, of course – and he is a reasonable man. If you agree to my terms, we may be able to sort something out in regard to your father.'

He was smiling more broadly now. It was not going to be a good deal, or even a fair one, but he held all the cards, so what could she do but wait to see what he was planning to offer?

'What do you say, my dear?'

'I don't know what the deal is yet, sir.'

The burst of harsh, high-pitched laughter made her jump again. 'Oh, you are a little vixen. I find that quite delicious.'

She held her nerve. 'The deal, sir?'

He raised an eyebrow. 'Don't play the innocent, my girl. I think you know what I am suggesting. My wife has been away for three months now. Have you any idea what that does to a red-blooded man like myself? You would be saving your father and saving your job, too. Not to mention helping to save my marriage. Surely that is a good bargain all round?'

Her stomach contracted. 'Surely you don't mean ...'

'You know exactly what I mean, young Rosa.'

'But sir ...' She struggled to find the words. 'I am a good girl, an innocent girl. That is not what the job is supposed to involve.'

He shrugged, palms up. 'I am not forcing you to do anything you don't want to do. But if you refuse, you will be out of a job, and your father will probably stay in jail. It is your choice.'

Her guts were churning, her head spinning, her whole body beginning to tremble.

He stubbed out his cigarette, finished his coffee. After a few long moments, he stood, leaned over and took her hand. His voice modulated, he was almost purring. 'Come, Rosa. You know already what your choice is. Give me a chance to show you what you have been missing in your chaste little life. You might even learn to enjoy it.'

'Take off your clothes,' he demanded once they were in the bedroom with its thick carpet and luxurious linens, pervaded with the scents of Alicia's make-up and perfume.

She hesitated. 'Please, sir, not this.'

'Do it.'

There was no point in pleading. As she complied, her knees trembled so much she felt sure she would fall to the ground.

This cannot be happening to me, she said to herself as he stood back to appreciate her nakedness. Then she tried to steady herself with an internal voice: I can endure this. Whatever he does to me cannot be any worse than the treatment Papa is suffering in prison.

Steiner led her to the bed, laid her down and took off his trousers. Before she even knew what was happening, his whole weight was upon her, his mouth over hers, invading her, strong hands parting her legs, fingers pushing into her at first and then that thing. The pain was so intense she couldn't help crying out.

'Shut up, bitch,' he growled, clamping his hand over her mouth.

Her mind went blank and she seemed to be viewing this grotesque, bestial scene from above, at as though it were happening to someone else. He pounded into her for several minutes before grunting to a swift conclusion. As he slumped onto his back, she curled herself up into a tight ball and wept.

The clock in the hall struck twelve. It was just an hour before she should be at the nursery to collect Anna, and the shopping lay unpacked on the kitchen table, none of the housework done, the supper not prepared.

She hauled herself up from the bed and limped gingerly to the bathroom, gritting her teeth and trying not to cry out or retch as she washed away the blood. She dashed her face with cold water and looked at herself in the mirror. What she saw was an altered young woman, her hair in rat's tails, her cheeks pale, her eyes reddened. There were marks on her breasts that would surely turn to bruises. But after the tears, all she now felt was a deep numbness. This was not how she'd imagined her first time would be. Instead of giving herself to a man she loved, her body had become a bargaining chip, an instrument of a deal. Was this what her world had come to?

She crept back into the bedroom and, as she dressed, Steiner stirred and opened his eyes.

'Good girl,' he said sitting up and resting back against the luxurious pillows, regarding her with that terrifying predatory grin. 'You will get better with practice. Be ready for me every Tuesday and Thursday morning. I will talk to my friend the police chief to see what can be done about your father. But remember this, little Rosa,' he put one of his long, thin fingers to his lips, 'if you breathe so much as a word about this to anyone, your mother, your friends, anyone at all, I will make sure your whole family goes to jail.'

The rest of the day passed in a blur. As she returned with Anna to the now empty apartment, as she unpacked the food and prepared the meals, everything seemed so normal she could hardly believe what had happened. It was like a bad dream, but the soreness between her legs was a persistent reminder that the humiliation had been real, and there would be more to come.

When she got home that evening, she had to put on a brave face.

Surely the wrong outweighs the right? she asked herself silently. After all, it was what many married women had to do every night, whether they liked it or not. Perhaps she would, as Steiner had said, come to enjoy it. And surely anything was worth it to get Papa out of prison, so that the whole family could leave Germany and escape this horrible persecution, for however long it lasted. She had to grit her teeth and make the best of it. She fell asleep and dreamed of being on a ship, sailing across the ocean to freedom.

The following Thursday, she was ready for him. Perhaps he would have some news of Papa. Just as before, he asked for coffee before ushering her into the bedroom with its wide marital bed and all the reminders of his wife: the dressing table with her brushes and make-up, the smell of her perfume, the nightgown hanging on the back of the door. She tried her best to smile, to be sweet and submissive. But he was even rougher this time, more impatient, forcing himself on her too quickly, holding her down by the wrists. As he pummelled into her she felt the fury rising in her chest, imagined her hand plunging a kitchen knife into the soft skin of his belly.

But she must force down the anger and stay compliant,

until Steiner kept his side of the bargain. 'Have you any news of my father yet?' she asked afterwards.

'What do you want, miracles? Listen, little mouse,' he stroked her hair gently, almost affectionately, as she gritted her teeth and tried to smile, 'the law grinds slowly. It may take a while.'

The following week, he asked her to wear the negligee – Alicia's – that he had laid out on the bed. It was black and lacy; the knickers were split at the crotch. The idea of wearing such things was repugnant, but when she hesitated, he said: 'Do it for your father, little bitch.'

Another day he told her to bend over the bed and took her from behind like a rutting animal. Each time she tried to remove her mind to another place, but usually the pain and humiliation were all too real and she had no choice but to live through it, to survive it. Afterwards she ran to the bathroom to be sick.

Each time, she asked about Papa. Each time, he offered titbits of hope: the case was being reviewed; it was being considered by a judge; the hearing was scheduled for a month's time. Each time, she told herself to hold on just a few more weeks and it would all be worthwhile.

Steiner's demands grew ever more eccentric. 'You're too submissive. I want you to fight me off, like I am trying to rape you,' he told her, oblivious to the irony. She tried to act whatever part he wanted her to play, shy, innocent, terrified or fierce, but soon learned that his favourite was the mock fight, which grew increasingly violent. He pinched her, slapped her and held her down by the hair, calling her names.

'My dirty little Jewess,' he would grunt. 'You disgusting Jewish whore.'

Once or twice, he tied her up. She began to have nightmares: of him killing her, smothering her with those luxurious feather pillows and wrapping her body in the beautiful satin quilt.

Of course she said nothing at home, but Mama sensed something was wrong and questioned her endlessly. 'You don't have to carry on with this job if it makes you unhappy,' she would say, stroking Rosa's hair. 'We'll get by some other way, don't you worry.'

Rosa longed to tell her that Papa could be out of prison very soon, so that they could make plans for escaping, but didn't dare to raise her mother's hopes. And anyway, she would want to know why her daughter believed that his release was on the cards.

Each Tuesday and Thursday morning, she forced herself to get up, get dressed and travel to work as though everything was normal. It would be so easy to quit the job, to stop the twice-weekly torture, but she knew all too well what the consequence would be: Papa would suffer.

One Tuesday, she arrived at the apartment to find Steiner busy in the bedroom, setting up a cine camera.

'Perhaps you didn't know,' he said proudly. 'I only do law for the money. My real passion is making movies. You're going to be a film star, Rosa. Undress for the camera now. Slowly. Make it sexy.'

She loathed the idea of being filmed as he raped her. As time went by, she had managed with a reasonable level of success to submerge her anger at the twice-weekly humiliations, telling herself that this was just a mundane part of the job, a necessary evil, a means to an end. But now the record would be etched onto celluloid for ever.

The filming soon became a regular feature, and Steiner produced ever more bizarre costumes for her to wear: leather, lace, chains, hoods and eye masks that left her fumbling in the dark.

One afternoon, after returning from school, the older boy, Friedrich, invited her to his room. She went with a willing smile, expecting to be shown his latest balsa-wood model aeroplane. But she knew as soon as he closed the door and turned to her with a furious glare that something was terribly wrong. At thirteen, he was already taller than her, and his eyes, so blue and pale, were just like his father's.

'What are you doing with Papa in his bedroom?' he hissed. 'All that disgusting stuff without your clothes on. Are you a prostitute?'

Rosa gaped at the boy. How could he have known? 'Whatever are you saying, Friedrich?'

'Don't try to deny it. I've seen you. In Papa's films.'

'He's *shown* you his films?'

'He shows them to his friends on a Friday night,' he said. 'They drink and watch films. I creep out of my room and watch them from the doorway. I thought they were just normal dirty movies, but then I saw it was you.'

'Oh Friedrich. How can I—'

He interrupted her. 'You *disgust* me. I'm going to tell Mama. Now get out of my room.'

When Steiner returned home, she told him that Friedrich had seen the movie showing and had threatened to tell his mother. A brief expression of alarm crossed Steiner's face, but he gathered himself quickly. The boy would get a whipping, he said, and Alicia would never hear a word. Meanwhile, he had good news. Her father would be released at the end of the week.

'But do not imagine for a minute that this is the conclusion of our deal, young Rosa. I have grown too fond of you to give you up so soon. My friend in the police tells me that all Jews are now under constant surveillance, and he is going to keep a special eye on your family from now on. You understand what this means, don't you?'

She understood only too well.

12

When Papa returned home the following weekend, the look of joy on his face and the warmth of his embrace made Rosa feel that perhaps all her suffering had been worthwhile. He was thin and weak, covered in livid scars and fading yellow bruises, but he managed to eat at least some of the feast that Rosa and her mother had lovingly prepared. He swallowed three glasses of wine and fell asleep in his chair almost immediately. When they lifted him into bed, his body, all six foot two of it, felt light as a feather.

'At last we are a family again,' her mother said, pulling up the covers and smoothing his hair tenderly. So long as I continue to submit to Steiner, Rosa thought grimly. But as it turned out, not even that was enough to save them.

Hans would not speak about what had happened to him. But there was a new wariness in his eyes. 'We must get out of this city,' he whispered to Miriam that night.

'But where, sweetheart?' she asked, hoping that he would have a plan.

He did, but it was only half a plan. He wrote to friends

asking whether their holiday home on the Baltic coast might be available to rent.

At last there was a glimmer of positive news: a new scheme by which children could leave for England. The British were waiving visa requirements and a Jewish organisation in Berlin was responsible for prioritising requests: those children whose parents had been imprisoned, or who were too impoverished to keep them. Hans said they should apply for both Rosa and Willi.

'Are you mad? We go as a family or not at all,' Rosa said. 'And that's that.'

'And that's that,' her brother echoed. But as news reached them that whole families were being arrested, Rosa and Willi relented.

The reply to their application was prompt. At nineteen, Rosa was too old. Willi was accepted. 'I'm not going on my own. Not never,' he said.

'You'll be fine. It's only temporary.'

'How can I possibly go without my family?'

'We will all join you as soon as we can,' Hans said. 'We will be a family again in England, just you wait and see.'

'But where will I live, and what about school?'

'You will be fostered with an English family until we get there, and they will send you to school. Your English is already quite good enough,' Rosa tried to reassure him. 'You will soon be speaking it better than me.'

Later, when she went to bed, she heard him crying.

'I can't go, I won't,' he sobbed. 'Not on my own.'

'I know it's hard,' she said, holding him. 'I would feel just the same. But you have to be brave. Think of yourself as the leader of an exciting expedition, the first to discover our new country. When the rest of us get there, you will be able to show us around.'

He was not convinced. 'How do I know you actually will follow me, and not leave me there on my own for ever?'

'You know we cannot stay here much longer, my darling. Every day we hear more horrible news. We have to leave as soon as possible. And by taking this opportunity, you will be helping us all get out – it will cost less for three than it would for four.'

It was this argument that persuaded him at last. At fifteen, he was old enough to understand that he must be brave for the good of the family, and the next day he told his parents that he would accept. The ticket arrived just a week later. The train would leave from Berlin on 1 December, and Willi was to travel there with an escorted group from Hamburg.

They went together to the train station late at night, clutching a small suitcase and an envelope of travel documents, visas and identity papers supplied by the Jewish refugee organisation. All of them were trying to hold back tears, and Miriam was the least successful of all.

There was a long queue at the barrier, where officials were checking tickets and papers. As they waited, Willi began to whisper that he'd changed his mind, trying to drag them away.

Miriam held him close and whispered in his ear. 'Be a brave boy and we will see you there in few months' time.'

'Promise?' he asked, his face a pale moon in the dim lights of the station.

'I promise,' she said.

But when they reached the front of the queue, there was much consternation among the officials checking the papers. After a long and terrifying pause, they told Willi that his name was spelled wrong on the UK visa: Wilhelm Coffman. It didn't match his identity document or the train tickets.

'The visa is invalid,' they said, shrugging. 'He cannot travel.'

'This is ridiculous,' Hans railed. 'Just for a few wrong

letters, my boy cannot go to safety. Do you realise what you are saying?'

The officials called a supervisor, who studied the papers. Then he too shrugged.

'We are sorry, sir. They will not accept him onto the train in Berlin and then where would we be? Your boy would be stranded in the city without an escort and no ticket home.'

'Then I shall go with him to Berlin. Make sure he gets on that train.'

'We are sorry, sir, but the train here is full. And you do not have a ticket.'

'I can buy one.'

'You cannot, sir. It is a special train. The tickets are restricted to Kindertransport only.'

Willi stood by with round, bewildered eyes as Miriam collapsed to the cold concrete in tears. 'It is my fault, I should have checked,' she moaned as Hans continued to berate the guards and anyone else who would listen.

Rosa took charge of the situation. 'Come on, Papa. It's no good shouting at them, and Mama needs to get home. We can sort this out. He can always catch another train.'

Every day the net seemed to be tightening, with more restrictive laws announced and visas to America, Great Britain, Denmark and Sweden more and more difficult to obtain. Even as people tried to find ways of leaving the country, they clung to the chance that the opposition parties would rise up, or a foreign army might intervene. But any hope evaporated that terrible November night when Hitler's thugs rampaged through the streets, breaking windows, setting fire to piles of books. The synagogue was razed to the ground, the Torah scrolls burned and trampled into the dust; the rabbi who scrambled to save them was kicked to death in the street.

The family huddled together in the kitchen at the back of the building, too terrified to speak as they listened to heavy boots tramping the cobblestones outside their block, the sounds of violent shouts, heart-rending screams and breaking glass.

Papa was all for going out to confront whoever was causing the mayhem, but they held him back.

'Do you want to get yourself arrested again, or killed? And anyway, what can you do against those bullies, in your state of health?' Mama whispered.

Convinced that the next sound would be a knock on the door, they were too afraid even to look out of the window. At last they slept, fitfully, wrapped in each other's arms on the kitchen floor.

The following day, they tried to dissuade Rosa from going to work, but it was a Thursday, a 'Steiner day', and she was terrified about what would happen if she failed to turn up. As he loved to remind her, he had friends in high places. He could make people disappear.

Her walk to work took her through the centre of Hamburg, and the chaos and destruction was worse than she could have imagined. It was hard to comprehend: shop windows broken, merchandise thrown into the streets and destroyed with daubed paint and water. Vile graffiti was everywhere: 'Filthy Jews', 'Kill the Jews', alongside scrawled yellow stars.

'Why would people want to do this?' she muttered to herself as she hurried past. 'Whatever happened to live and let live?'

The air was filled with smoke, and as she passed the street leading to the synagogue, she soon saw why. The ruins of the building were still smouldering. Crowds of people were gathered in the street before it, some even braving the rubble, attempting to save what they could.

'You've come. I didn't expect ... Are you okay?' Steiner asked. Was that a look of concern on his face?

'Not really,' she said. 'What I saw ...' Only now did she realise how shocked she was, her head starting to spin. 'I need to sit down,' she murmured, and the next thing she knew, Steiner was kneeling beside her on the floor, cradling her head and urging her to take a sip from a glass of water.

'It is quite shocking,' he said. 'Those hooligans. Even the police couldn't stop them.'

The police didn't even *try* to stop them, Rosa knew. A neighbour had watched them just standing by as the so-called hooligans rampaged through the streets. In other words, the destruction was sanctioned by the government. Later, she read in the newspaper that the attacks were in response to the murder of a German diplomat in Paris by a young Jewish boy. Paris? What on earth could that have to do with Hamburg?

Steiner informed her that he'd decided not to send the children to school that day because it was too dangerous, but that he needed to go into the office to sort out some urgent legal matters. Rosa was to stay in the apartment, entertain the children, supervise homework, cook and clean. He said all of this with surprising tenderness, and she felt almost grateful towards him.

'And by the way, how is your father?'

'He is home now,' she said. 'Thank you.'

He smiled, and leaned over to stroke her hair. 'I am pleased that our arrangement has worked, my little one. I spoke to my wife at the weekend. The doctors say she still has some weeks of treatment ahead, but she aims to return home for Christmas, come what may, even if she has to return to the sanatorium afterwards. But that still leaves us time for some private enjoyment, wouldn't you say?'

Rosa did her best to paste on a smile. She could bear it so long as there was an end in sight. The money she earned just about kept the family from starvation, though there was nothing left over for travel documents, train fares or bribes.

Although her childcare services would not be required

during the school holidays, Steiner told her (nor, of course, the 'personal' services, he added with a sickening wink), he hoped she would continue to do the shopping, cleaning and cooking, since Alicia would not have the strength for chores.

Despite her misgivings about meeting the woman whose clothes and underwear she had been wearing and on whose bed she had been raped so many times, Rosa warmed to Alicia. She was funny and shrewd, and so clearly filled with love for her children that the two women clicked immediately.

At first Alicia spent most of her days in bed, and Rosa would bring her drinks and meals, but after a while she gained strength, the colour returned to her cheeks and she asked Rosa to help her get dressed. Thereafter she would appear each day, resting on the couch or sitting on the window seat, watching the crowds in the park beyond. She seemed delighted to have female company. 'It is so dull in the sanatorium,' she would complain. 'And some of them are so sick, it's hard to have fun.' As for her own health, she said that the doctors hoped she would be ready for permanent discharge within a couple of months.

With the threat of the 'Steiner days' lifted, Rosa could relax. Alicia was always ready to share a joke or two, and often told her to put down her duster and join her for coffee and cake. She took the mickey out of her husband's pomposity, and it amused Rosa to hear her answering back to him when he spoke too imperiously. The movie camera and other strange pieces of equipment had mysteriously disappeared.

One day after Christmas, Rosa overheard Alicia arguing with Steiner, pleading with him not to send her back to the sanatorium in Switzerland. She crossed her fingers: while Alicia remained, there would be no sex with Steiner. For a further week there was no news, and she held her breath. But one

Monday, she arrived at work to discover that Alicia had gone. There was an envelope addressed to her, with three ten-mark notes inside, and a letter.

Dear Rosa,

It pains me so much to leave my family, but Erich insists, and the doctors back him up. Please accept the enclosed as a thank you for the support and friendship you have shown me. We had fun, didn't we? It means a lot. I do hope you will still be there when I am finally allowed to return, probably at the end of February.

Best regards,

Alicia

Meanwhile, there was another distraction: a marriage proposal.

A couple of years previously, Rosa had briefly dated a young man named Daniel Levy. He was tall, dark-haired and reasonably good-looking, with straight white teeth and clear skin; polite, quite bookish and modest, and so much more mature than boys of her own age. Neither family was overly religious, and the two sets of parents had already met through mutual friends. It seemed the perfect match.

Except that after the excitement of the first few dates, Rosa found Daniel rather dull. 'He has no conversation,' she complained to her mother. 'Honestly, I've tried literature, poetry, sport, cars, everything. The only things he's interested in are machinery and money. That seems to be the limit of his ambition, to join his father's company and make money out of machinery.'

'You are only sixteen, darling, don't feel any obligation to the first boy who makes a pass at you,' her mother said. The following week, Rosa had plucked up the courage to tell him, and hadn't seen him since.

Now, two years later, there he was with his family at a discreet gathering organised by another Jewish friend. He seemed to have grown in confidence in the intervening years. He was chatty and even amusing, and Rosa was flattered when he asked for her address. The next day, he turned up with a bunch of flowers, and invited her to go for a walk.

As they got to know each other, he began to share his worries. His family were also in trouble. The company he had hoped to inherit from his father, the machine tool manufacturers that had been in the family for three generations, had been taken by the government. It had started with an unannounced visit from three men in sharp suits: they had asked for a tour of the premises on the pretext of checking whether the company was complying with safety laws. Then an official letter arrived saying that the business had been valued at an absurdly low sum – a fraction of its real worth – and giving Daniel's father two weeks to agree the sale.

Although the family were at first incredulous, reality soon began to sink in. Other Jewish business owners had received the same type of visits and letters, and one by one had been forced to sell. New legislation meant that within a few weeks, Jews would be barred from owning businesses. All capital would be seized.

The date for relinquishing the company was set for the end of January. Daniel's father had fallen into a depression and stopped going in to work: the family were very concerned for his mental health. Daniel had applied for jobs abroad. Rosa listened sympathetically: the furrier's shop her father had worked for was also closed now.

They were unable to date in the usual places: cafés, restaurants and cinemas. Many now carried bold notices: *NO JEWS*, and in any case, neither she nor Daniel had money for such things. Instead they walked, and talked about how they would get away from Hamburg and find a new future. It was when he came to collect her for one of those walks on a chilly Sunday in January that he told her.

'I've got exciting news,' he whispered. Hardly anyone was around, but they had become used to being discreet. 'I have been offered a job and sponsorship in England. It's a company that makes fans, you know, for air cooling. They are customers of ours and good friends of my father's. They've offered to give me lodging, too, until I can get myself set up.'

'What a wonderful opportunity,' she responded, surprised to find herself actually feeling a little bereft. She wasn't in love, far from it, but she had been growing quite fond of him lately, coming to rely on him as a steady hand in the gathering storm, a place of calm after her ordeals with Steiner. Beyond the occasional kiss, he made no demands for intimacy, and he had been particularly kind to Willi while they waited to see whether he would receive a new ticket for the Kindertransport.

'I shall be leaving in the next few weeks.' He reached forward and took both of her hands in his. 'And the thing is, Rosa, I don't want to leave you behind. Will you come with me?'

She was confused. 'But how? I don't have a visa.'

It took her a few seconds to cotton on, and then she burst out laughing. 'Daniel Levy, is this a roundabout way of asking me to marry you?'

A blush rose to the roots of his hair. 'I suppose it is.'

'Daniel's asked me to marry him,' she blurted out at dinner, feeling her cheeks flushing crimson. 'And go with him to England. Oh Mama. I don't know what to do.'

Miriam gaped. 'Do you love him?' she asked, recovering from her astonishment.

Rosa nodded, not wanting to lie. 'But it's all so sudden. And how could I possibly leave you?'

Miriam hesitated for the barest fraction of a second. 'You must accept him, my darling. Go to England, where you will be safe. From there you can get us all visas to join you. This could be the answer to our prayers. And perhaps we will get Willi on to the Kindertransport after all.'

But Willi never did get the chance to travel to England. By the time they got the spelling on his visa changed, there were no more places.

Rosa would never forget the day she told Steiner she was getting married and would be resigning her post. She'd left the door open to the kitchen, where the children were eating their tea, in the hope that this might offer her some protection. How wrong she was.

He grabbed her arm with a hand like a vice, pinching so hard that she could already feel the bruises forming, and dragged her into his study, closing the door. There he stood, his face just a foot away from hers, and whispered in a voice that could slice steel: 'Say that again.'

It took every ounce of her courage to look at him. Her face was numb with fear, and her lips would not form themselves around the words.

'Say it again, whore!' he shouted.

'I ... I am getting married, sir. In a fortnight. To a fine man. So I'm afraid I cannot continue working for you. It would not be right.'

He turned away and began to pace the short distance between Rosa and the desk, returning at last to face her.

'And what do you think I am going to do when you are

gone? Eh? Who is supposed to look after my children, cook and clean? Have you thought of that?'

'Yes, sir,' she said, gaining courage. 'If you advertise now, I am sure you will find someone to take my position. I am sorry—'

The slap was so powerful, it nearly knocked her off her feet. She steadied herself on the arm of a chair, and pulled herself upright again.

'How dare you answer me back like that, you deceitful Jewish bitch.' He slapped her once more. 'Now get out and never show your face here again.'

'But may I explain to the children? Say goodbye?'

'No, you may not. You will get your coat and leave at once. I will tell them what a traitor you are.'

She knew better than to plead, but as she turned to go she felt his grip on her arm once more, pulling her back. He crushed her face between his hands and brought it within inches of his own. She could smell his breath, rancid from too many cigarettes.

'And remember this, bitch. It is your greedy, worthless kind that has ruined this country, do you understand? And I will personally make it my business to ensure you and your family live to regret this day, just you wait and see.' He spat in her face.

She took her coat and ran out into the street, wiping away tears and spittle with her sleeve and walking home as quickly as she could, away from Steiner, away from that vile filming equipment, the disgusting graffiti and daubed yellow stars, into the safety of Daniel's arms.

13

Rosa and Daniel were married on the first of February.

Rosa wore a dress loaned by her friend Marta, and the cere-mony was followed by a modest celebration in the apartment attended by just fifteen people, close members of each family plus their neighbour Mrs Geller and Marta and her mother. Two weeks later, when their visa came through, the newly-weds boarded the train heading for Holland, and thence by ferry for England.

That night, and for several nights afterwards, Miriam sobbed herself to sleep. Would she ever see her beautiful daughter again? How would she fare with no friends other than her new husband in a completely unfamiliar country, with its own customs and cultures?

'She's strong, dearest,' Hans said when she expressed her fears to him. 'You know this. We have to focus on keeping ourselves and Willi safe now.'

Soon after that, events happened so fast that Miriam barely had time to think, let alone miss her daughter. The three of them were returning from an evening stroll when Mrs Geller appeared at her door, beckoning them into her apartment.

'The police came for you,' she whispered, her tone furtive, urgent. 'They were very aggressive and told me to tell you that they will come again tomorrow. You must leave tonight.'

They packed hastily, taking only as much as they could carry, and by daybreak they were on the first bus westwards out of Hamburg to Bremerhaven, which was where Hans's old friends lived. He hadn't received any reply to his earlier letter, and the reception they received was cautious – everyone knew that the punishment for concealing Jews was imprisonment, even death. But seeing their distraught state, the couple agreed to put the family up for a few days while they tried to find someone with a boat to take them north to Denmark. Sadly, this proved impossible. Offers of generous cash payments were turned down with a frown, a turned-away glance, or sometimes even a filthy curse.

'It's come to a pretty pass when a fisherman is too frightened to accept the price of a week's catch for a simple favour,' Hans said after several dispiriting encounters. 'It makes me feel like shop-soiled goods, or something the cat brought in.' That is what they think of us Jews, Miriam thought to herself. But she knew it was more than that. German people were usually kind and generous to a fault, but the Nazi rule of fear had already infected even these remote coastal areas.

After several days, and just as they were becoming desperate, Hans spied an advertisement in a shop window: *Farm labourers required.* The farmer, Herr Schmidt, greeted them with incredulity: a family who looked like intellectuals, who had never done a day of manual labour in their lives, applying to work on his farm? But all his workers had left to join the army, and his fields were in desperate need of preparation for the coming seasons. They were invited in for coffee.

'Why would city folk like you want to work on a farm?' he asked, with a typical countryman's bluntness.

'We may have little experience, but we will be good, honest

workers, that I can promise you,' Hans said, exchanging a glance with Miriam. She gave the slightest of nods. 'But the truth is, we had to flee Hamburg because our lives were in danger. '

There was a long pause, the air weighted with unsaid implications. The old man frowned, stroked his beard and nodded. At last, he spoke: 'My dear wife's father was one of your kind,' he said simply. 'She's dead now, alas, although I sometimes wonder whether it is a blessing that she didn't live to witness these terrible days.'

Hans and Miriam sighed silently with relief. The man understood; there was no need to say more. Willi took his mother's hand. He understood too. The farmer would not betray them.

'So here is the deal,' he said. 'You can live in my barn and work on the farm. I will give you food. I have a contact who can provide you with false papers, just in case, but even so, I suggest you remain concealed. You must not go into the village, or the town. And if your work is not up to scratch, I will have to let you go.'

All three of them worked twelve hours a day for the first few months. Their faces browned in the sun, calluses grew on their fingers and feet, muscles developed in places they'd never had them before. They slept in surprising comfort on hay mattresses in the roof space of the barn, and ate their meals in the farmhouse. Food was relatively plentiful, what with chickens and rabbits breeding abundantly, and as the summer went on, the vegetable fields proved wonderfully fertile. Herr Schmidt frequently complimented Miriam on the tasty meals she cooked each night.

She wrote to Rosa regularly, and was pleased to receive her daughter's replies telling her all about her new life. It sounded quite idyllic, what with the gardens and the church flowers and the music concerts and the charming family of four boys. But what is my clever daughter doing with her brain? Miriam wondered, in the rare moments when she found time enough to speculate. And she wondered whether, in fact, there might be a grandchild on the way.

Apparently Daniel was doing well at work and with the assistance of their hosts had written dozens of letters to people who might, just might, be able to help the two families gain visas for Britain. But so far they'd had no luck. There must be tens of thousands of people trying to get out, Miriam knew. Hitler seemed hell-bent on war, and it was becoming apparent that it was only a matter of time. She tried not to dwell on these things too much. It made her sad, the very real possibility that she might not see her daughter, or meet her grandchildren, for some years.

In September, when news came that Germany had invaded Poland, followed by the declaration of war, they knew their chance of getting visas was gone. The flow of letters from Rosa stopped overnight. Miriam's only consolation was that her beloved daughter was safe and happy.

Following the apple harvest, when the cold weather arrived, they worked on fencing, hedging and ditching, while trying to continue Willi's lessons as best they could in the evenings. Apart from missing Rosa – and unable to exchange letters now that war had been declared – they were almost content. As the winter passed and spring arrived, Miriam began to imagine that they might be able to survive the whole war in this way.

But it was not to be. The news they heard on the farmer's small radio after the evening meal became more and more distressing: the noose was being tightened, with new bans and curfews, the requirement for all Jews to wear a yellow star and, most terrifying of all, mass deportations to the East for 'forced labour'.

Months passed, then years – two more summer harvests, apple seasons, another Christmas – and they continued to keep their heads down. Even though they now had false papers, they avoided visiting the nearby town or fraternising with anyone they met. Unfortunately, Herr Schmidt was not so cautious about expressing his disapproval of the Nazis, especially when he'd had a beer or three. Word soon got round, leading inevitably to a visit from officers of the local branch of the party. Although the family were safely tucked away in their loft, the officers noticed that the supper table had been laid for four, and returned a week later with dogs.

They managed to pull up the ladder just in time and closed the trapdoor so that the dogs were unable to sniff them out, but it was now clear that it was too dangerous to stay. The farmer had a plan: he would drive them concealed in his pig trailer to a small port fifteen miles away, where he knew a fisherman who might agree to take them to Sweden, which was still neutral territory. The fisherman wanted hundreds of marks for his trouble – nearly all of their savings – so they would arrive with barely any money to support themselves. But it was worth it, Miriam and Hans agreed. There was no other option.

They waved goodbye to Herr Schmidt at the edge of the village, promising to keep in touch, and walked through deserted streets to the meeting place – a small area of scrubby woodland not far from the port – feeling horribly conspicuous. What if someone saw them and reported them? They were carrying their false papers, but even so, they could hardly pass as locals. It was a cold February morning, with a bitter wind slicing off the Baltic Sea, whipping up a freezing drizzle that seemed to scour their cheeks like sandpaper.

They reached the designated point and waited. Half an hour passed, and then an hour.

'What if he doesn't come at all?' Miriam asked.

'He'll come,' Hans said, patting the inside pocket of his jacket. 'That kind of money will be too much to resist.'

Ten minutes later, they saw three men emerging through the trees. They were not in uniform and looked like ordinary citizens, but Miriam though it strange that they were all wearing the same style of grey overcoat, and their shoes were too shiny to belong to locals. These men were city types.

'Are you waiting for Herr Kramer?' one of them asked.

'We know of no Herr Kramer,' Hans said. It was what they had been told to say, if challenged.

'He has been held up, unfortunately, and has asked us to take you to the ship.'

'I ... I don't think ...' Hans stuttered.

But the men were surrounding them now. 'We will take you to him,' one of them said. 'You must come now, though, or things may get more difficult.'

They knew then that their plan had been intercepted. Herr Kramer had betrayed them, or worse, he had been betrayed himself and was already under arrest. They had little choice but to go with the men.

Hans played his last card. 'I have money for Herr Kramer, here in my pocket. Perhaps you could give it to him.'

It was a mistake. The tallest and broadest of the three – clearly the strong-arm man – took two steps towards him and slapped his face so hard that he only just managed to stay on his feet. 'Are you trying to bribe us, Jewish pig?' he snarled. 'But you might as well hand it over now anyway. No amount of money is any use where you're going.'

This is it, Miriam said to herself. The beginning of the end. They had no idea who had betrayed them and nor were they ever likely to learn, but it was of little import. It seemed inevitable they would be sent to one of the now infamous work camps. No one knew of anyone who had returned.

They were taken to a car, driven to a remote railway depot north of Hamburg and herded onto a crowded cattle truck, heading east. They arrived at the camp dazed and exhausted after a terrible two-day journey during which they had nothing to eat and very little to drink. It was freezing, and there were no sanitary facilities. Willi was doubled up with stomach pains and cried out so loudly that the other occupants yelled at him to shut up. The normal courtesies and kindnesses between fellow humans were already being eroded by suffering, and life was cheap to the guards. When someone died, their body was simply thrown out onto the track.

At the camp, they were herded at gunpoint into two lines, men separated from women. They weren't even allowed the opportunity of a farewell embrace. The sight of Willi's distraught face as he and his father were led away was so devastating that Miriam would have collapsed entirely had the women on either side of her not held her upright. 'Shut up or they'll shoot you,' one of them whispered.

'Don't worry, you'll see them on the other side,' the second woman added.

The thought comforted her, for the moment. Miriam's entire adult life had been focused on protecting her children from harm, and she had tried her best for Willi, but now his fate lay with Hans and there was nothing more she could do to protect them. She could not have known that within twenty-four hours they would both be dead. The 'other side' was the other side of death.

She was all alone. The horrors of the journey, the brutal separation from Hans and Willi, and the humiliation of being stripped, shaved and tattooed seemed to sap her mental and physical resistance, and she resigned herself to whatever fate intended for her.

At this point, however, fate threw Miriam Kauffman a lifeline.

Standing in yet another queue, now dressed in striped pyjamas already well-worn and several sizes too big for her, she noticed that up ahead some individuals were being pulled aside and sent towards another hut. Fear gripped her chest – surely this meant further punishment about to be meted out? As the line shuffled forward, she kept her head down and turned away, praying that she would not be chosen. When the touch on her shoulder came, she nearly fainted with terror.

But it was not punishment. In fact, it was reward of sorts: the chosen women were to become a work detail, part of what the guards called the 'clearing-up commando', and at the time, Miriam did not appreciate that it would save her life.

Next day, after a restless night on a hard bunk shared with another woman, she reported for duty. They were taken to a vast warehouse filled with bundles piled several metres high, and told to start opening them, separating the contents into large wooden containers: men's clothing, women's clothing, children's clothing, jewellery, foodstuffs, small household items, medicines, valuables, and professional tools. The smell of mildew and rotting food was overpowering.

'These are other people's belongings,' she muttered to her neighbour as they began work, ripping open the sheets in which the pitiful bundles were wrapped, or releasing catches on suitcases and holdalls and tipping the contents onto the floor. 'Surely they should be returned to their owners?'

'They won't need them where they're going,' the woman whispered tersely.

'Whatever do you mean?'

'They're already dead, my friend.'

Dead? All these people, the owners of these thousands of bundles? Some of the weaker ones might have succumbed to illness on the train, but surely that could not account for all of these belongings? But there was no time to think. A harsh voice barked, 'Work faster or you'll feel my whip,' so Miriam stopped speculating and began to sort.

It was exhausting, back-breaking work, lifting the heavy bundles from the vast pile, stooping to the floor to open them, straightening up to throw items into the relevant boxes. They were allowed just half an hour's break for lunch – a bowl of weak soup with a few vegetables floating in it. By mid-afternoon, when Miriam feared she might simply collapse with exhaustion, a woman a few rows away keeled over and fell headfirst onto the bundle she was sorting. Women rushed to help as she lay there, apparently out cold, but were roughly pushed away by the guards. They shouted and kicked her, and then, when she did not get up, simply dragged her away.

'That'll be it for her, then,' Miriam's neighbour said.

'What do you mean?'

'She'll be off to the ovens tomorrow, mark my words.'

'The bakery? Doesn't sound too bad.'

Her informant stifled a harsh, humourless laugh. 'You poor innocent thing. Ask the others when you get back to the hut. They'll tell you.'

She didn't believe them at first. This place was a killing factory, they said, and most new arrivals would be dead within twenty-four hours. People were told they were going for a shower, but once they were locked inside the 'shower room', it would be filled with poisonous gas. The men who removed the bodies related the story and it spread in horrified whispers throughout the camp.

Surely this was just scaremongering, rumours exaggerated with every telling? The very notion was unimaginable, defying all reason. How could people do such a thing to their fellow human beings? So the Nazis didn't like Jews, but could they really be trying to eradicate them entirely? And if so, why wasn't the rest of the world rising up in protest?

But everyone she asked confirmed it. Now she knew for certain that the bundles they spent their days sorting were those of people who had already been murdered: Jews mostly, but also gypsies, communists and anyone else the authorities deemed undesirable. These once precious belongings had been packed by thousands of individuals in desperate hope, but now they would be sold or otherwise to support the evil regime that had so callously killed their owners.

The thought appalled her but, as the weeks and months went by, she became hardened to the horror: all she knew was that she had to go on living by whatever means available, so that she could be reunited with Hans, Willi and Rosa when it was all over. She had a duty to survive so that they could tell the world what had happened.

A year passed, and to Miriam's astonishment she was still alive, thanks mainly to the food and medicines they managed to steal from the warehouse for barter with other prisoners. It was a risky business. Those who were caught were whipped and sent to solitary confinement, some never seen again.

Miriam stole only occasionally, when in greatest need. But she knew in her heart that she would never be able to admit to anyone, not even her family, how she had survived. A Nazi lackey, sorting through the belongings of fellow human beings who had been brutally murdered for the sole reason that they held other cultural or religious beliefs. Because they were not, in the main, blonde-haired and blue-eyed.

The shame ate into her, making her feel dirty and degraded both inside and out, a stain that could never be washed away. During the day, as she worked, she managed to put the thoughts aside, but each night the visions flooded her mind again: the trains arriving, spewing out terrified people forced to queue with their cases and bundles of precious belongings, little knowing that they would have no use for them where they were going. But what good would it do them or her now if she refused to do the work? She would probably be dead within hours.

Each night she spoke to Rosa. When there was a moon to be

seen through the hut window, she imagined her daughter looking up at it in England.

We may not be able to write to each other, she said silently, but I am still here, my darling girl. You are my reason for living; the reason I go to that foul place every day, among the souls of the dead. I pray that you are well and staying away from German bombs. Just as soon as this is all over, I will be coming to you. We will be together again, that is my promise.

14

SUFFOLK, ENGLAND 1939

The chain of events that led to Jack's first meeting with Rosa had begun before Christmas. Daniel Levy and his father ran a factory making machine tool parts in Hamburg, which was a supplier for W. H. Preston and Sons. Jack's father had taken the ferry to Hamburg several times and had always received generous hospitality at the Levy home. He'd known Daniel since he was a young boy.

Lately Herr Levy had been writing in increasingly desperate tones about what was happening to the Jews: the way they were being hounded, excluded, their businesses closed or sold from under them. *We are at our wits' end*, he wrote, describing the terrifying attacks on homes, businesses, shops and synagogues in November, and how they waited each night, terrified, for the knock on the door.

John Preston did not hesitate. After checking with his wife, he wrote back: *We can find work for Daniel and provide him with a place to stay for as long as he needs.*

Shortly afterwards, Herr Levy's reply arrived, bursting with effusive thanks: *We are so grateful for your offer to help Daniel. We hope you will not mind welcoming an additional person to*

your house for a short while, as he has recently married a
charming young woman. Her name is Rosa.

Jack's mother had spun into action: the twin beds in the
spare room were pulled together, their legs tied securely with
string, and kitted out with double sheets, blankets and eider-
downs with the prettiest floral coverlets. The bathroom next
door was cleaned from top to toe and equipped with sweet-
smelling soaps and shampoos.

'I am woefully ignorant about what Jewish people can and
can't eat,' she muttered to Jack's father, scouring cookbooks for
recipes that avoided pork, ham, bacon and seafood. 'What if
they're properly kosher? And what does that mean anyway?'

'Too bad if they are,' he'd declared. 'They'll have to bend
the rules, won't they?'

'Why didn't they tell us he was planning to be married?'

He shook his head. 'It does seem a bit sudden, but these are
strange times in Germany,' was all he would allow.

And now they were here. The most beautiful woman Jack had
ever seen was sitting opposite him at the supper table, and his
usually robust appetite had completely disappeared. His
mother passed around plates of delicious-looking meats, beauti-
fully arranged salads and a pile of new white potatoes glistening
with butter and parsley, and he dutifully helped himself, but
could not eat a single mouthful.

Father brought out some bottles of beer and began a discus-
sion with Daniel about the differences between German and
English brewing techniques. Jack, who had taken a couple of
mouthfuls and discovered that everything tasted like cardboard,
sneaked glances over the table at Rosa whenever he sensed that
she was not looking in his direction.

She had released her mane of thick auburn hair from its
plait and it cascaded across her shoulders in a glorious waterfall.

Jack's palms began to itch: he imagined clasping bunches of the hair in his hands, combing his fingers through it. He studied her face, taking in the eyes that appeared to smile even when she was serious, the delicately arched eyebrows that contributed to her expression of mild amusement, the high colour on her cheekbones. She lifted a small forkful of food to those red lips, chewing it thoughtfully. Observing her immaculate table manners, he checked himself, placing his knife and fork down carefully between mouthfuls, keeping his elbows well away from the table.

She seemed to follow the conversation with lively attention but said little, occasionally glancing towards her husband. Jack tried to think of ways to break the spell, but his mother beat him to it. 'And what part of Germany are you from, Rosa?'

'Hamburg, like Daniel,' she replied. 'We have known each other from our childhood.' Her voice was gentle and lilting, with only the slightest German accent.

'Childhood sweethearts, how charming.' Jack cringed at his mother's presumption.

Rosa smiled, showing those astonishingly white teeth. 'Well, not exactly. But we are from the same community, you know?' She prepared a further forkful of food, a little piece of each item carefully placed and then speared. 'This is a delicious supper, Mrs Preston. You and your family are most generous in inviting us to stay with you.'

'It is a pleasure, my dear,' his mother said, blushing at the compliment. 'What with everything you have been going through, the least we can do is provide a safe haven until you can set yourselves up in your own home.'

'And Daniel is so grateful for the sponsorship,' Rosa went on. 'We cannot imagine ... without that ... what ...'

She stopped suddenly, lowering her eyes, distress written in her face. When Daniel reached out to touch her arm in reassurance, Jack felt a sharp pang of envy. He wanted so much to lean across, put a reassuring hand on hers. He racked his brains to think of something interesting to say, to distract her, to make her smile again. Plenty of ideas came to mind, but he dismissed them all as too frivolous, or too serious, or too pretentious. What could he possibly say to this young woman – a wife, with her husband by her side – with whom he could already feel himself falling in love?

Jack had never had any trouble chatting up girls. He was well aware that he was not classically handsome – no broad shoulders or chiselled jaw – and at five foot ten he was certainly shorter than he would have preferred to be, but his natural confidence and easy sense of humour seemed to make him attractive to the opposite sex. His only serious relationship to date had been with Gretta, the sixteen-year-old daughter of the Austrian family with whom he'd stayed when doing his work experience. Although their friendship had been relatively chaste, he'd found himself captivated, desiring her by day and by night, often at very inconvenient moments. Before he'd left to return to England, he'd declared his love for her, and truly believed it at the time. They'd both cried, vowing to stay in touch and visit as often as possible.

But Rosa was different. She was so beautiful, so unattainable, so exotic, her dark eyes flashing and her auburn hair glinting in the light. Her lipstick accentuated the fullness of her lips and the generosity of her smile. She was infinitely desirable, but in her presence he felt overwhelmed, like a tongue-tied kid. She was probably only a year or so older than him, if that, but she was most definitely a woman, not a girl. Way out of his league. And married, he reminded himself. Get a grip, boy.

They moved into the living room for coffee; his father took out the brandy decanter and the conversation drifted into politics. Daniel had already drunk several glasses of beer, and what he lacked in fluency, he made up for by speaking loudly and at great length. Mother was still pottering around in the kitchen and the other boys had excused themselves, claiming the need to finish homework and music practice, but Jack could not tear himself away.

His father was listening politely to their guest, although Jack could see his attention wandering from time to time. At this point in the evening he would normally have been quietly finishing the *Times* crossword – it was matter of pride that he completed it each day, and he was probably itching to get back to it.

'Why no one see what happens to our country?' Daniel was saying. 'Why not they take action? Your man Chamberlain is weak, and the rest are also the same.'

'It is very frustrating, but politicians have to listen to public opinion. No one wants another war—' Jack's father started.

Daniel talked over him. 'Public opinion,' he scoffed. 'Will that man Hitler be satisfied with Austria and Czechoslovakia? He will stop at nothing, I say. A little puddle like the Channel is not going to be a problem.' As he thumped the chair, Rosa placed a calming hand on his wrist, but he brushed her away, hissing something in German.

She stood up to leave, just as Mother returned with a stack of clean towels. 'The bathroom is all yours,' she said, holding them out to Rosa. 'You must be weary after your long journey. Is there anything else you need?'

Rosa looked relieved. 'Come, husband,' she said. 'I am tired. And it is time to let these good people have a rest from the woes of the world.'

As they left the room, she once again blessed Jack with that glorious smile. The image of her face stayed with him throughout the long, restless hours of the night.

Two months passed and spring finally arrived. For Jack, being close to Rosa was a kind of delicious torture, leaving him feverish with desire. More than once he'd had to find some excuse to leave the room, fearful that his flushed cheeks would give him away. His sleep was invaded by vivid dreams of her hair tumbling into his face.

He tried to contrive moments to be alone with her. If only they could talk, he thought, so that they could get to know each other. He longed to find out all about her, her family, her childhood, what sort of hobbies she enjoyed. But his mother held the view that their guest would only be happy if she was kept busy.

'Poor thing, she must be so worried about her family back in Germany,' Jack overheard her saying to his father. 'Still, I try to make her feel useful. It's half the battle, don't you think, keeping occupied?'

'Very good, dear, very good,' John Preston responded. 'Lively young woman like that needs to be kept out of mischief.'

Mrs Preston was a pillar of the village community, constantly engaged in good works: raising money for the local old people's home and the village hall restoration fund, and making sure the church cleaning and flower rotas were efficiently maintained. Most time-consuming of all was organising concerts in Westbury Town Hall for the airmen stationed nearby – 'morale-raising, that sort of thing'.

Meanwhile, with all four sons at home plus two extra guests, there was much to be done around the house. The gardener had joined the army, cook had left to care for her ageing mother, and the daily help came only twice a week, so Rosa and the boys were pressed into a never-ending round of shopping, cleaning, cooking, laundry, mowing lawns, digging, watering and weeding vegetable patches, stuffing envelopes, delivering newsletters, putting up flyers and collecting this and that from suppliers in Westbury.

It was late April by the time Jack found himself alone with Rosa. He hadn't even contrived it; the moment just happened. Supper was ready on the table – a spread of cold cuts and salads

– and everyone was waiting for his father and Daniel to return
from London. Jack was in the garden, sitting on the bench in the
dell, a steep dip in the land probably left from the time when it
was a sand and gravel quarry. His mother was an imaginative
and industrious gardener and had chosen to turn this feature of
the landscape into a secluded terrace with an arbour arched
with roses. Spectacular views westwards across the valley made
it perfect for enjoying sunsets. He was enjoying a quiet smoke
in anticipation of a good display when Rosa appeared, silently
and apparently out of nowhere.

'Can I join you?'

'Of course.' He shifted along. 'Would you like a cigarette?'

'Yes, please. Daniel doesn't like me to smoke, but he's not
here, is he?' He had not seen this rebellious, mischievous smile
before, and it melted his heart with its delicious complicity. He
cursed the way his hand trembled as he held up the burning
match.

And now here they were, just the two of them alone,
enjoying a moment's peace on this golden evening, with early
bees buzzing among the fruit blossom and sparrows bickering in
a nearby bush. Down in the valley, the little train trundled
along its single track from Marks Tey, carrying Daniel and his
father back from their day in London. Somewhere in the background he could hear his two youngest brothers arguing and
Matthew practising the flute.

As a moderately accomplished pianist in her own right,
Grace Preston had insisted that her four boys should all learn
musical instruments. Jack had played the violin for a few years
before giving up, discouraged by the unpleasant screeching his
bow produced despite the best efforts of his teacher. The
youngest two, Mark and Michael, had flatly refused to do
anything so 'girlie'. Only Matthew had persisted, and now, aged
sixteen, he was preparing for his first public performance, in
Westbury in a week's time.

'He plays well, your brother,' Rosa said. 'I am looking forward to the concert.'

'I don't think he is,' he said. 'Looking forward to it, I mean.'

She sighed, gazing into the distance, where the sun was sinking towards the horizon. Pink and orange tinges suffused the wispy clouds above and the landscape below. 'You are lucky to live in England. It is so beautiful.'

'I am sure Germany is, too.' As soon as he said it, he knew how stupid it sounded. 'I mean, before all of this ...'

A long silence. And then, 'Yes, I miss it. Well, I miss how it used to be. Have you ever travelled in Europe, Jack?'

'*Ich habe für ein paar Monate in Österreich gelebt und ein Praktikum gemacht,*' he said in a fit of bravado, and then blushed deep to the roots of his hair. What on earth was he thinking of, displaying his ineptitude to this beautiful woman? What a fool she must think him.

'I didn't know you spoke my language. You kept that very quiet,' she said, laughing.

'My engineering vocabulary is second to none. Ask me about *Schwungräder* and *Beschleunigung*. Took me ages to get my tongue around that lot.'

'You are full of surprises, Jack Preston.'

'No, no, I speak only a few words really.'

'But I'm sorry to say you have an Austrian accent, like an ignorant country boy, a cowherd, we sometimes say.' She giggled and then paused for a second, her face becoming serious. 'Like that terrible man, our Chancellor.'

'Hitler?'

'We never speak his name. He is too wicked.'

'I'm sorry. I shall never say it again.'

'But perhaps I can teach you the proper way to speak my language. Repeat after me: *So sprechen wir in Hamburg Deutsch.*

'That is the way you speak German in Hamburg,' he said,

repeating it in English. 'It is much prettier than the Austrian accent.'

Now it was her turn to blush, turning her gaze to her feet. For a few seconds they sat in silence, listening to the birdsong.

'I wonder,' she said after a while, 'where these accents come from in the first place.'

'I shall have to take a degree in languages so I can tell you the answer.'

'You would do that just for me?'

'Anything to avoid working in a fan factory.'

She turned to look at him, a small frown creasing her forehead. 'You don't want to join your father's company? It is a good business, no?'

'No, I want to learn how to fly.'

'Would you join the air force?'

He shrugged. 'Perhaps, if they'd have me. But mainly I want to travel the world and see great cities like Rome and Delhi and Istanbul.'

'And I want to live on a tropical island with blue seas and coconut palms,' she said, joining in the game.

'Seeing kangaroos in Australia ...'

'And lions and elephants in Africa ...'

'Polar bears in the Arctic ...'

'And penguins?'

'They live in the Antarctic, don't they?' he said, unsure.

'Hmm, maybe you are right. Let's go there too, then. I love penguins. They are so comical.' She pulled a face and waggled her shoulders in imitation of their walk, making him laugh out loud. This woman was full of delightful surprises.

'Have you been to the Antarctic?'

'Of course not. Now you are being silly, Jack.'

'Then how do you know so much about penguins?'

'We saw them in Hamburg Zoo,' she said. 'My brother,

Willi, he used to imitate them like that, and it always made us laugh so much.'

'I never knew you had a brother,' he said. 'How old?'

'Fifteen.'

'Same age as Mark. He's a little terror. The worst of the bunch.'

'I miss Willi very much,' she said, lowering her voice.

'He will be able to join you soon, I'm sure,' Jack said. He'd heard that his father was helping Daniel obtain visas for their families.

'It is so difficult,' she said. 'They are trying to get him on to the Kindertransport, but there are quotas, you know. Also for the visas. So many people want to get out of the country. So many people are afraid.'

'It's horrible for you,' he said, reluctant to pursue this obviously painful topic. As he finished his cigarette, carefully stubbing it out on the leg of the bench and concealing the stub beneath a divot of grass at their feet, he glanced sideways at her face, and once again her beauty took his breath away.

Leaning back, he casually, oh so casually, rested his arms along the bench. His fingers touched her shoulder and it startled her. He pulled his hand away sharply. 'I'm sorry,' he said, feeling the blush already burning his cheeks. 'That was an accident.'

'Don't be,' she said. 'It was nice. Just a surprise, that is all.' She smiled, catching his eye, and making him blush even more. 'You are very sweet, Jack.'

In that split second, he suffered an irresistible urge to kiss her. But before he could act, his mother's strident call echoed across the garden: 'Hellooo? Where is everyone? I need some help.'

. . .

A week later, Jack found himself sitting beside Rosa in Westbury Town Hall, along with a three-hundred-strong audience of airmen from nearby bases. The chairs were packed in so closely that their upper arms were touching, their legs just an inch away from each other. Jack found this proximity so arousing that he was glad of the paper programme unfolded on his lap, and forced himself to concentrate on the music to stop his thoughts straying.

His mother had created a varied programme, with local amateurs playing everything from Bach to ragtime, and a small girl who melted hearts with a surprisingly tuneful rendition of 'Daisy, Daisy'.

In the interval, he'd found Matthew throwing up in the gents' toilet.

'I can't do it, Jack.'

'Of course you can, you're the dog's bollocks. And everyone will clap even if you're awful.'

Matt wiped his mouth and stood up with a weak smile. 'Thanks for the encouragement, brother.'

'Here, have a mint. You smell disgusting,' Jack said.

Despite the last-minute attack of collywobbles, Matt played flawlessly, accompanied by his mother. They acknowledged the applause, then his mother went off stage and Matthew took up his flute again to play a haunting solo full of falling phrases. Jack had asked, after listening to endless repetitions at home, what it was about. 'A god falls in love with a nymph, who hides from him by turning herself into a water reed. He cuts the reed to make himself a flute and so kills her.'

'Bloody hell, he kills his lover by mistake? Cheerful stuff, then.'

'All the best flute music is sad,' Matt had said.

The audience was spellbound. Jack glanced sideways at Rosa and was shocked to see tears streaming down her face. He pulled a handkerchief from his top pocket – clean, for once –

and passed it to her. She took it silently and gave him a weak smile. How his arms ached to comfort her.

As the piece came to an end, the audience erupted with rapturous applause, cheers and shouts of 'Encore!' His brother bowed, blushing, and his mother returned to the stage, bringing with her all the other performers. The evening had been a triumph and she was radiant. 'We've raised three hundred pounds for the Red Cross,' she said as they filed out.

'It was a most delightful evening, my dear,' Jack's father said, putting his arm around his wife's waist and giving it a little squeeze. Physical intimacy between his parents was so rare that Jack squirmed with embarrassment. Then he noticed Daniel taking Rosa's hand and leaning down to whisper in her ear, which made him almost nauseous with envy.

15

———

It was difficult and exhausting living with another family in a strange country. Daniel was at work every day and Rosa was glad that Mrs Preston kept her busy, helping the time to pass. But playing the meek, obedient wife was harder than she could have imagined, and this country life with its never-ending round of chores was very dull. Daniel was so serious: he hardly ever laughed, and conversations always felt as though he was lecturing her. She'd almost given up trying to talk to him.

Even as she'd married him, Rosa had known that she would never love Daniel, but she'd hoped that a mutual affection and respect might grow into something deeper, though she feared that Steiner had ruined any chance that she might enjoy intimacy. On their wedding night, in Daniel's childhood bedroom, with his parents sleeping next door, she'd steeled herself to accept his clumsy approaches. She could tell that he was doing his best to be tender, but felt nothing for him other than gratitude. Everything she gave to the marriage – including his nightly invasions of her body – was out of duty. There was no meeting of minds.

She'd begged him to take a weekend off so that they could

explore their new country, to go to London or to other famous places that she had read about: Cambridge, Edinburgh, Canterbury, the hills of Wales. But he appeared strangely reluctant. 'Just wait until we get settled in a place of our own. Then we shall do a grand tour of the British Isles.' She missed her family and felt constantly anxious about their welfare. All the fun seemed to have leached out of her life.

And then came that moment in the garden with Jack. He was such a contrast to Daniel: young and lively, genuinely interested in what she had to say, and even more importantly, he'd listened sympathetically when she'd expressed her concerns about her family. He was easy to talk to and they had chatted so easily during those few sunset moments that almost for the first time since she'd arrived in England, she had felt genuinely happy.

Not only that, but somehow this boy, at least a year her junior, seemed to spark something inside that she feared had been killed off forever by Steiner. Something about his sweet freckled nose, that curly brown hair and the eyes that crinkled with amusement made her feel warm and safe inside. And she wanted more. She'd shocked herself by wanting to kiss him.

No, she would not allow herself to be tempted, she told herself firmly; it was too risky. She knew that she could be impulsive, hot-headed. It had often got her into trouble in the past, at school and at home. She must get a grip on herself. Daniel had saved her life – and possibly the lives of her family – by marrying her and bringing her to England. Her permission to remain here was conditional on being married to him – it was his name on the visa. If she was unfaithful to him, she could be sent back: to what?

But living with him was becoming increasingly difficult.

. . .

It was the pettiest of arguments, something to do with him objecting to the fact that his wife had the temerity to express an opinion about the latest round of negotiations between the British government and Hitler. When she said that no amount of talking would change that monster's mind, she felt him tensing beside her. Then he went on to drink three whole bottles of Mr Preston's India Pale Ale and became increasingly argumentative. It was embarrassing, and impolite, she felt, to take advantage of their kind hosts in this way.

When they reached their bedroom, he told her to sit down on the little three-legged dressing table stool. 'Now listen to me, wife.'

She sighed, sensing a lecture. 'It's late, Daniel. I am tired. Can't we just go to sleep?'

'Not until you learn what is expected of you.'

'And that is?' She shouldn't have been so cheeky, perhaps, especially when she knew he'd had a bit too much to drink, but really he was being quite obnoxious. The slap came out of nowhere.

'A woman should not have political opinions,' he said. 'Say it, Rosa, say it.'

Even as her cheek burned, and she was finding it hard to breathe from the shock, Rosa thought he was being ridiculous. 'Why not?'

The second slap was harder, the stool overbalanced and she fell to the floor, hitting her head on the side of the dressing table. 'That's why not,' he hissed. 'You are my wife, and you will do as I say. Is that understood?'

Rosa struggled to her feet and ran downstairs to the kitchen, anything to get away from Daniel for a few moments and calm her shredded nerves. She moved around as quietly as possible and was shocked when the door opened and Jack appeared.

'Hello,' he said. 'Can't sleep?' And then, as she turned her face towards him, 'What's happened to your cheek?'

She put her hand to the place where Daniel's slap had landed and felt the skin hot, and probably reddening. Jack reached forward and stroked her hand gently with the tip of a finger, as though his touch could heal.

'Did he do this to you?'

'I am not a good wife,' she muttered to the floor.

'What? For goodness' sake, Rosa. It is not your fault.' He reached his arms towards her.

'No, Jack. You must go,' she said, pushing him away. 'He will come looking.'

'Then let him. He needs to know that he can't get away with this.'

'No, please. It will only make things worse. You must let me fight my own battles. Now go upstairs,' she urged. 'For me. Please.'

By the time she returned to the bedroom, Daniel was already snoring. She crept into her side of the bed with as little sound or movement as possible, terrified of disturbing him, and curled up into a tight, protective ball. First Steiner, and now Daniel. Is it something about me, she wondered miserably, that makes men want to hit me? Something I say, or the way I look at them?

Next day, he apologised. 'I don't know what came over me. I am under such a lot of strain at the moment, because of this difficult situation – the new job, living with the Prestons, the worry about the visas for our families.'

She forgave him, of course. It was her duty, the price of being allowed to leave Germany, to get visas for her parents and Willi, and nothing must get in the way of that. 'I know you are doing your best, Daniel. I am worried for our families too.'

'I am doing everything I can, my darling. Mr Preston has also written to contacts he has in London. Leave it to me, dearest. There is no point in making yourself ill with worry.'

So she never mentioned to him the letter that arrived from

her mother a few days later: *We hope you are well? We are doing fine, don't worry. We wonder how Daniel is getting on with his enquiries about visas for us? Enclosed is a letter for you, hand-delivered to our Hamburg address. Frau Geller forwarded it to us.*

The letter enclosed was addressed to her by name, and in Erich Steiner's handwriting. She opened it with trembling hands, her eyes skittering across the words. He congratulated her on her marriage, and said that the children were missing her, with only the mildest hint of rebuke for failing to give suffi-cient notice of her resignation. It ended with the request to pass on his best wishes to her parents, Hans and Miriam Kauffman, and her young brother, Wilhelm Kauffman, as well as to her husband, Daniel Levy.

The message appeared oddly benign, conveying nothing particularly sinister, except for the deliberate, purposeful naming of each member of her family. Most ominous of all was the signature: *Erich Steiner, Ortsgruppenleiter, Hamburg Central.*

He once told her that he'd only joined the Nazi party because his position as the head of a major law firm made it obligatory. 'There are things you cannot refuse these days,' he had said. But he claimed to have resisted applying for higher office, even though they had invited him to do so. 'If I was truly ambitious, I couldn't risk consorting with a Jewish woman,' he'd told her as he stroked her body. 'And how could I possibly relin-quish this delight?'

She could see now that the main purpose of the letter was to inform her that he was now a local group leader for the Nazi party, rising up through the political ranks. He would be keen to prove his credentials by rooting out Jews. He was also making the point, in case it was not already abundantly clear, that he knew all the details of her family, their names and where they lived.

And now, like a cold shaft of ice slicing into her heart, she heard again Steiner's words on the day she told him she was leaving: 'I will personally make it my business to ensure you and your family live to regret this day, just you wait and see.'

She was gripped by a terrifying knowledge: her family were in imminent peril and she was too far away to do anything to protect them. Thank goodness at least they had now left Hamburg.

16

After a long period of unseasonably gloomy weather, the sun reappeared.

It was Michael's suggestion that they take the canoes to the river. 'There'll be plenty of water after all that rain.' They had built the two kayaks the previous year from mail-order kits, of wooden batons covered in varnished canvas, which meant they were light enough to be carried between two people the half-mile down the hill.

As the boys went around the back of the house to the shed where the canoes were stored, they came upon Rosa sitting on the kitchen step reading a book.

'Where are you off to?' she asked. 'Up to mischief, no doubt?'

'We're going to the river,' Jack said. 'Canoeing. Do you want to come with us?'

Her face lit up, then fell again. 'I'll have to ask your mother. She may need me here.'

He followed her into the kitchen. His mother demurred at first, but he protested. 'Poor Rosa, she hardly ever gets any time off, Ma. Hasn't she earned some fun?'

Finally she gave in. 'You'll look after her, won't you? Don't go dumping her in that dirty old river.'

Jack said he would do his best but the canoes were notoriously unstable and part of the fun was getting wet. There was a new spring in his step as they set off down the hill.

Michael was right, the often sluggish river was flowing faster than usual, and the water had risen high up the banks so that launching the kayaks was relatively easy. Jack declared that the three other boys should share the larger of the two craft, and he would take Rosa in the smaller one. That way she was less likely to get tipped into the water. 'Although no promises, mind,' he said, with what he hoped was a teasing smile. It also meant he would get her all to himself.

'Take the middle seat,' he said. 'It's the most comfortable.' Of course it wasn't any more or less so than the ones in the bow or stern, but it sounded more gallant that way. He leapt into the boat overenthusiastically, making it rock and causing her to shriek with alarm, before taking the seat behind her in the stern.

'Would you like to paddle with me?' he said, offering her the second paddle.

'Of course,' she said. 'In Germany we have the best lakes and rivers in the world.'

Jack was momentarily disappointed – he'd envisaged being able to teach her, sitting close behind and holding her arms to demonstrate the correct action as his father had once shown him – but that quickly passed as they began to paddle in harmony, slipping through the water at thrilling speed, aided by the faster-than-usual current. They soon left the three boys – who were larking about – far behind.

The sun glittered on the water, dappled by ancient willow trees overhanging from the banks. Curious cows at the river's edge huffed their grassy breath towards them, fierce-looking dragonflies patrolled the air, families of mallards squawked raucously as they scattered in their path, and he could swear he caught a glimpse of vivid blue: a king-fisher. A swan peered at them from her nest in the reeds; her partner circled menacingly close by, puffing up his wings in warning.

All these sights were familiar to Jack, but today, he decided, this was as close to heaven as he could ever have imagined. Rosa's back was just a few inches away from him, her thick plaited hair pinned up to reveal the pale, tender skin of her neck, the muscles in her shoulder blades working as she powered the paddle through the water, creating little eddies that arced into their wake.

'Hey, come on. You're not keeping up,' she said, turning to look at him.

'I'm enjoying the view.'

'You cheeky thing.' She giggled. 'I suppose you mean the cows?'

'Of course, they are beautiful cows, don't you think?' he said. 'And the kingfisher, did you see it?'

'*Fischer der Könige?*' she said. 'Someone fishing for kings? What is that?'

Her English was so fluent he sometimes forgot. Just for fun, he spoke in German. 'It's a little river bird. Very shy. Bright blue.'

'Ah, we call it *Eisvogel*,' she replied.

As they paddled onwards, Jack began to feel that this was turning out to be one of the best days of his life.

'I have another surprise for you,' he said. 'Have you ever been to an English pub?' He'd calculated that it might be nearing noon, opening time, when they reached the next village, and had pocketed a handful of change just in case.

'No, is it nice?'

'Wait and see.'

'You're teasing me. What about your brothers? They are too young to drink alcohol, no?'

'They can sit outside,' he said. 'They're used to it. We can bring them lemonade.'

A quarter of an hour later, he and Rosa were sitting inside the cosy public bar while his brothers outside wrangled over who was going to take charge of the little blue sachet of salt in the packet of potato crisps.

Rosa took a tentative sip of the half-pint he'd bought her.

'Ugh,' she said, wrinkling her nose and puckering her lips so comically it made him laugh. 'Now I know why you call it bitter.'

They chatted easily about what kind of social life each had enjoyed as youngsters – youth clubs and trips to the lakes for her, tennis clubs and hanging out with school friends for him – until their glasses were empty and he invited her to try a shandy, explaining that it was beer mixed with lemonade.

After she'd tasted it and approved its sweeter taste, they fell into a short silence. And yet it did not feel awkward sitting there and not talking, Jack thought, just comfortable and companionable, like good friends. And then, quite out of the blue, she asked, 'Have you ever been in love, Jack?'

He found himself laughing too heartily to cover his confusion. Was what he'd felt for Gretta, love? Whatever it was paled into insignificance against the magnetism he'd felt towards Rosa since she walked into his life.

She was speaking again. 'I am so sorry. This beer is stronger than it seems. I should not have asked you such a personal question.'

'No, it is fine,' he said, clearing his throat. 'I have been in love just once. At least I thought so at the time. But it was puppy love. It didn't mean anything.'

She nodded, her face down. The smile had disappeared.

'Tell me ... about Daniel. Are you okay now? After that night, I mean.'

A further long silence. 'I do not really know,' she

murmured, at last. 'He apologised to me and I forgave him. He is a kind man, but I do not think he loves me.'

'You deserve better,' he said.

'But he has been my saviour. It is because of him I was able to get a visa, and we may be able to get our families out, too. It is so complicated.'

What could he say? How he wanted to draw her to him, to hold her, to help her. Her beautiful face was so sad.

Paddling against the current made the return journey harder work, and with their greater forces his brothers surged ahead and were soon out of sight. When Jack and Rosa arrived back at the landing stage, there was no sign of the other canoe. Jack lifted the boat from the water and was about to ask Rosa if she minded helping him carry it up the hill when he caught her looking at him.

'What? Have I said something funny?'

'Not at all,' she said. 'The way you lifted the boat – you made it seem so easy.'

'It's not heavy,' he said, blushing.

'It has been a wonderful day,' she said. 'You have made me forget about Germany, and my worry for my family. I think, for the first time since we got here, I have been able to be myself.' Her face became serious, and then, to his astonishment, she turned to him, placed her hands on his shoulders and reached up to press her lips against his. It was brief, and innocent enough, but there was no mistaking the rush of electricity that surged through his body.

'Thank you,' he croaked, flooded with desire.

'It is for me to thank *you*, Jack. You make me feel happy.' They looked at each other in a long moment of deep under-standing, then she turned away and went to the other end of the canoe to help him carry it up the hill.

As they were putting the boat back into the shed, she moved to him in the gloom and kissed him again, more deeply this time. Her lips were so soft, so yielding. Once more his body became consumed with the intensity of his desire. Again she pulled away, apologising.

'We must not be doing this.' Her fluency in English seemed to falter. 'It is wrong. And I am leading you on. We must not be alone again.'

The days and weeks passed, and while Jack did his best to avoid being with alone with Rosa, he sometimes caught her looking at him. When he met her eyes, she looked away suddenly, as though nothing had happened. Until it did.

She met him on the stairs. There was a small half-landing on which you could stand to allow people past, and he was heading up the first leg, without looking ahead, when he encountered Rosa waiting there.

He smiled at her and she smiled back and, as he passed, she reached for his hand.

'Jack?' she whispered. 'Can we meet?'

'Are you sure?'

She nodded. 'Somewhere safe.'

'Let me think,' he said.

After an agonising few days, the opportunity arrived.

Jack's mother had gone shopping, leaving a mound of vegetables for Rosa to prepare, and his brothers had gone down to the river again. They were alone.

'It is such a beautiful day,' he said, trying to sound casual. 'Would you like to come out for a picnic?'

'I must finish these vegetables and hoover the hall before your mother gets home,' she said. 'There is not time.'

'Did she say when she would be back?' he asked.

'Before teatime, I think.'

'Then we have at least three hours. I'll help you with these later. I want to show you a special place of mine.'

The stretch of beech woods had been long neglected by the local farmer, and could be reached only by walking through abandoned gravel workings once used by a now defunct brickworks. Jack had never seen anyone else there, even when the woodland floor offered glorious displays of springtime aconites, followed by bluebells and now, at this time of year, a brilliant field of tall foxgloves, spikes of purple bells that hummed with bees.

The sight made Rosa gasp. 'Oh, what are these flowers, Jack?'

'Foxgloves,' he told her.

She went up to examine them. 'We call them *Fingerhut*, which is like a cap you use when you are sewing to save your fingers.'

'A thimble?'

'The English name is much more poetic, I think.' She turned and looked around. 'You are right, it is very beautiful here.'

He unpacked a rug, a bottle of lemonade and some biscuits stolen from his mother's hidden tin.

'How are you, Rosa?' he asked. 'How are things with Daniel? Has he made any progress on the visas?'

'Oh, I don't want to talk about any of that today. Today is a time for forgetting.' She lay back on the rug, looking up into the canopy. 'Tell me about these wonderful trees.'

He explained how beech trees came in different varieties, some of them with copper leaves, and how they had both male and female flowers on the same plant.

'That's convenient,' she said, giggling. 'They don't have to bother with a husband or a wife.'

'It's called monoecious,' he said, 'though that's not a word you're likely to use in normal conversation.'

'And how are you, Mr Monoecious?' She stumbled over the word. 'Have you been to bed with yourself recently?'

By now he was laughing so much that he failed to notice she was leaning up on an elbow, looking into his face. The kiss came as a complete surprise.

'Are you sure, Rosa?' he whispered, shocked.

She didn't answer in words, but pulled him close again, kissing him even more passionately. After that, instinct seemed to take over. Several times he asked her whether this was what she really wanted, and each time she nodded.

Although he considered himself to be relatively experienced in sexual matters, Jack had never been 'all the way' before, and he could not believe how natural it was, as though their bodies were perfectly formed for this very act. There was no fumbling, none of the awkwardness he'd experienced with other girls. At the end, when she threw back her head and moaned like an animal, he was totally overwhelmed; he could not believe he had caused her such intensity of feeling, nor that this could have brought him such a sense of utter bliss.

Afterwards, as they lay in their dell of purple foxgloves, the birds chirruping away just as before, the sunshine glittering through the leaves of the beeches and great oaks above them, and gentle breezes carrying the sweet smell of new-mown hay, Jack felt as though his world had been turned upside down. He turned and looked into her face. There were tears in the corners of her eyes.

'Rosa. You are crying. I didn't hurt you, did I?' he asked, fear gripping his stomach.

She shook her head. 'No, not at all. It's just that ...' She took a breath. 'Just that I never thought it could be like this.'

He lifted a hand to her cheek. 'It was okay?'

'It was so much more than that,' she said, smiling now.

17

Looking back on that golden afternoon, Rosa could hardly believe what she had done. It felt like a dream.

Am I crazy? she asked herself, more than once. Did it really happen?

She'd been nervous at first, of course. Sex with Daniel – she could never bring herself to think of it as 'making love' – was such a serious, almost mechanical affair, predictable, the same every time. In some respects, this was helpful, because knowing what to expect had helped to erase the horrific memories of Steiner. But although she had learned to tolerate the act, she had never actually experienced desire with her husband.

But somehow she had known that it would be different with Jack, and so it proved. He was respectful towards her at every stage, asking her whether she was sure, and each time the power of her desire for him made it completely impossible to resist. She had never known what it was like to feel such an over-whelming need. Making love with Jack was fun, playful, and completely disarming, totally without embarrassment or inhibition.

Perhaps most importantly, she came to understand in the

many hours she spent reflecting on it afterwards, it was a delightful game in which both partners felt equal. There was no expectation, no sense of duty or fear. And being in the open air, in that beautiful place, had simply made everything more thrilling, exhilarating. In the end, she had abandoned herself completely to him in a way she could never have believed possible. She felt as though she had been brought back to life after a long, frozen winter.

The weather stayed warm and they met twice, three times, whenever they could, discovering more about each other through gentle, playful conversations and opening her eyes to the astonishing possibilities of mutual pleasure.

'I love you.' The words sprang so easily to her lips, and he responded in kind, although deep down she knew they were living in a fantasy.

'I want to be with you for ever,' he said.

'But how can that be, Jack? I am a married woman.'

'I don't care. I just want you. We could run away somewhere no one would know where to find us. There must be somewhere. What about a remote Scottish island. We could keep sheep and grow our own vegetables,' he said. 'And make love by a roaring fire.'

How she wished that could be possible. She found herself infatuated, and it was clear he felt the same. But their moments together were always too short. Each time they were forced to part – taking separate routes back to the house at carefully timed intervals – it felt like a small death.

The opportunities became still fewer after Jack's father insisted that he begin his apprenticeship at the factory. 'You've had enough time gallivanting, lad,' he said at supper one evening. 'Time to earn your living.'

'But it's the summer holidays. Surely I can have a few weeks off?'

'You've already had a few months and more. You'll be coming into the factory with me next Monday morning, and that's final.'

With fewer opportunities, Jack began to take greater risks. 'I love you,' he would mouth silently, catching her eye across a room, and when they passed in the corridor he would reach out to touch her hand. It was exciting, but began to feel increasingly dangerous.

One day he crept up on her as she was hanging out the washing, pulling her into his arms. 'No, Jack,' she whispered, wriggling free. 'Let me go.'

'I'm sorry. You are impossible to resist.'

'It's not a game, Jack. What if your mother had come round the corner at that moment?' She felt angry and tearful all at once. 'It is too dangerous. What if Daniel or your parents find out? We would be sent away, and Daniel would divorce me. Then what would happen to my family? Any chance of getting them out of Germany would be lost. You understand, don't you?'

He retreated, apologising, and slouched away like a scolded child, making her feel guilty for having been so harsh. Later, as he passed her in the corridor, he whispered, 'We have to talk. Ma is doing the flowers in the church tomorrow morning.'

'She's already said she wants me to go with her.'

'Find an excuse. A headache, anything. Meet me in the woods around eleven.'

She considered not going, but he sounded so urgent.

'Another headache? Are you unwell, my dear? Or do you have happy news to impart?' Jack's mother glanced meaningfully towards Rosa's belly.

'Oh no, nothing like that. At least not as far as I know,' Rosa stuttered. 'Perhaps I took too much sun yesterday, hanging out the washing.'

Mrs Preston's expression was sceptical. 'But it was cloudy, my dear, have you forgotten? The washing was still damp when we gathered it in.' She sighed slightly, reaching into the kitchen drawer. 'Still, I expect I'll manage without you. Here are some aspirins. You had better get yourself off to bed. Put a cold flannel on your forehead.'

Rosa arrived at the woods half an hour late, having run most of the way. 'Your mama wasn't very pleased, Jack. Do you think she suspects something?'

'All that matters is that you are here with me now.' He took her hand and drew her down onto the rug beside him. 'Who cares if they find out, anyway? They will have to know sometime.'

'What do you mean?'

'I love you, Rosa. I want to spend the rest of my life with you.'

She pulled away. 'No, Jack. It is not that easy. I am a married woman.'

'I know that, silly.' He sat beside her, looking at her, lifting a strand of hair from her cheek. 'But you said yourself it was a marriage of convenience.'

The silence that followed was almost unbearable. Even the birds seemed to mute their song. It was no good. She felt torn apart.

'Oh my dearest. I did not mean to make you cry,' he said, wrapping his arms around her.

'I am married to him and that is that,' she sobbed. 'There is no changing it.'

'But when war is declared—'

'When *what*? Are they declaring war?' She gaped at him, face pale and tear-stained.

'We have to be realistic, my love. It's not looking good. But at least there'll be no sending you back then.'

'Then whatever will happen to my family?' she whispered. 'There will be no hope of getting them out. What if they are killed? I might never see them again.'

'I'm sure that won't happen, my darling.' But his words sounded hollow.

That night, she wrote to them, wondering whether this letter might be the last to get through.

Dearest family,

Everyone here seems to believe war is coming soon, and if that happens, it will be very difficult for us to correspond.

I am so sorry that the combined efforts of Daniel and Mr Preston have not resulted in visas for you, or for Daniel's family. Believe me, they have written to everyone they can think of, but it seems the visas are being so carefully controlled there is nothing to be done.

I hope that you are still safe on the farm. Please do not worry about us. All is well here. Daniel is enjoying his work and we hope to find our own accommodation soon.

Your loving daughter,

Rosa

18

Working at the factory was more interesting than Jack had ever imagined.

He began on the bottom rung, shadowing the engineers as they fixed mechanical and electronic problems of all kinds. It was strangely satisfying to see a system restart with a healthy whirr, knowing that the small adjustments you made had avoided the expensive loss of working hours and ensured that a contract could be fulfilled on time.

During that first fortnight, a new lathe was delivered and he was part of the team installing it. To see the machine in operation, turning out metal parts precision-engineered to tiny fractions of an inch, was so rewarding. He joined the team in the pub afterwards to celebrate. 'You're one of the boys now, Master Jack,' they said, raising their glasses to him, and he began to see that the work could be hugely satisfying, and how his father, and his grandfather before him, had been content to spend the whole of their lives in this joint endeavour.

Although the company usually supplied fans to commercial organisations, a flood of orders from the army, navy and air force meant they had to hire and train two dozen more staff and start working double shifts.

What with the small but useful wage in his pocket at the end of every week, and the company of Rosa – if only for a few stolen moments in the evening or at weekends – he discovered a kind of happiness he could never have predicted. They would find a way of being together, he told himself, all in good time.

The bitter conclusion to that long, hot summer arrived abruptly a month later. His father was in London at some dinner for fan manufacturers, and Jack was heading for bed when his mother waylaid him.

'Come into the drawing room, Jack. Take a seat.' Her voice was chilly. Something was wrong. The grandfather clock in the corner of the room knew it too, seeming to tick even more slowly than usual, drawing out the agony of suspense.

She smoothed her skirt over knees clamped tight with tension, took a small breath, cleared her throat and, at last, began to speak.

'How long has this been going on, Jack?'

Whatever was she referring to? His recent tendency to swear a lot? His frequent requests to borrow the car? Worse still, had she noticed something between him and Rosa?

'Mother?'

'You know perfectly well what I am talking about, son.'

'Enlighten me, please.'

There was fire in her eyes now. 'Don't be insolent, Jack. You may be eighteen and consider yourself an adult, but your behaviour with our guest' – her lip curled – 'has been nothing short of utterly irresponsible. Don't try to deny it. Mothers see these things. I suspected something might be going on between you, but this afternoon my fears were sadly confirmed. I saw you with her in the dell.'

Jack's stomach gave a sickening lurch.

'Have you nothing to say for yourself?'

He shook his head. There was literally nothing to say. *I love her, I love her, I love her.* The words churned in his head until he realised, to his horror, that he was actually saying it out loud. 'I love her, Mother.'

'Pfft,' she scoffed, standing and starting to pace the rug in front of the fireplace. 'That might be what you imagine right now. But let me reassure you, there is no future in it. You should be ashamed of yourself, taking advantage of a young woman when she is so dependent on our help. A *married* woman, Jack. Whatever were you thinking of? I shall talk to your father when he gets home. They will have to leave.'

'You can't turn them out, Ma. They have nowhere else to go.'

'Well they can't stay here, can they, you stupid boy? Perhaps you should have thought of that before you allowed your head to be turned.'

He spent a sleepless night desperately trying to formulate a plan. In the morning, he lurked around the garden hoping that Rosa might break free from his mother's clutches for just a few seconds. She was being kept especially busy that day.

Just before lunchtime, she appeared with basket of laundry beneath her arm. The washing line was within sight of the house, so Jack waited until she had hung enough sheets to afford him cover.

'Psst.' He had to hiss twice before she turned and saw him.

'What are you doing hiding behind those sheets?' The playful innocence in her face was heartbreaking. He couldn't bear to tell her.

'Shh,' he said, finger to lips. 'We need to talk, urgently. Say you're going to the toilet or something, and meet me in the dell in ten minutes.'

She frowned. 'Is there something wrong?'

'I can't talk right now. Say nothing to Mother. Just come as soon as you can, my darling.'

She nodded, finished pegging the last sheet, and disappeared indoors.

Ten minutes later, she arrived at the dell.

'What is it?' she asked, joining him on the bench and taking his hand.

Her touch usually made his heart dance, but this time it felt forbidden, dangerous.

'My mother knows about us,' he blurted out. 'She saw us here yesterday afternoon, and confronted me last night. She says she's going to tell Father this evening.'

She gasped, hand to her mouth. '*Mein Gott!* They will tell Daniel.'

'It's worse than that. They're going to send you away.'

Her face was pale. 'But what if he divorces me? Will I lose my right to stay?'

'If he divorces you, we will be free to marry, my darling.' He reached for her, but she turned away.

'It is not so easy, my dearest Jack,' she said.

'But I love you. I want to spend the rest of my life with you. You said yourself that you don't love him ...'

She began to sob. 'Oh, I wish ... I wish we could just run away like we talked about. But it would never—'

'We can. We will do just that, darling. Here's the plan,' he said. 'You will pretend to be sorry and do as they say, leave with Daniel, then contact me just as soon as you have an address. Then we will run away.'

He drew her to him. The kiss was passionate, desperate, desolate. Both knew it would be the last, at least for a while.

That evening, when his father arrived home, Daniel and Rosa were summoned to the living room. Jack lurked behind the closed door, feeling the blood draining from his face as he listened.

'Are you aware,' his father started, 'of a ... let us call it a liaison, between your wife and our eldest son?'

Daniel's voice: 'I am sorry, I do not understand. What is this, Rosa?'

There was no reply. How humiliated she must feel, how defenceless. Jack couldn't let her face these accusations alone. He rushed in.

'I can explain,' he burst out. 'It is not her fault.'

His father took three steps towards him, his face like a thundercloud. 'Get out, boy,' he hissed.

For a moment, Jack thought he might punch him. 'No,' he said, standing his ground. 'This is about me as much as it is about Rosa.'

'Then stay, but don't say another word.'

Jack mouthed, 'I'm so sorry' in Rosa's direction, but she was gazing at the floor. Daniel shot him a murderous look.

'How dare you?' Pa turned to Rosa. 'How dare you take our generosity and hospitality and throw it back in our faces like this?'

She said nothing.

'If I had known ... I can only apologise for her behaviour,' Daniel stuttered. 'What do you say, wife?'

Rosa's soft voice – Jack had to strain to hear it – whispered just three words: '*Es tut mir leid, es tut mir leid.*' Sorry, I am so sorry.

But how could she be sorry for what they had had together? Jack thought. How could anyone regret the sublime magic they had woven? The melding of their souls, their minds and bodies; their professions of love, the plans to run away to a deserted island, perhaps somewhere in the Hebrides or off the Baltic coast where no one would know them and war would not reach them?

'You will leave this very evening, and you will not return, ever,' his father was saying. Do you understand me?'

Rosa and Daniel packed and left in a taxi as the sunset flooded the hills on either side of the broad valley with warm pinks and oranges: a landscape of such heartless beauty that Jack could no longer bear to watch it. He ran into the house, drew his bedroom curtains and punched his pillow until the feathers began to fly.

A week later, her letter arrived.

Dearest Jack,

We are in London, and quite safe at present, so please do not worry about me. I cannot leave him or I will lose my right to stay in this country. Daniel has now set his heart on going to America and plans to apply for visas as soon as possible.

Goodbye, my dearest boy. Forgive me. What happened between us was so special, but it is over. Please, for my sake, do not try to find me. Not now, not ever.

R

He crumpled it in his hand and ran all the way to the woods. Scenes flooded his head: the way his heart leapt like a fish on the end of a line each time she came into the room; Rosa looking up at him, her long tresses splayed out over the grass like Medusa; Rosa sighing, closing her eyes in bliss; the time she told him she loved him.

The past few months had been a beautiful dream, a dream he could never imagine ending. Blinded by passion, he had truly believed they would spend the rest of their lives together. But now she had abandoned him. She had left no address, and told him never to contact her again. It was over. His howl, a fierce, visceral cry like a wounded animal, shocked him as it echoed around the glade. And then he began to sob like a baby.

There was nothing else to live for. For a wild moment he imagined taking his father's car and driving it into a tree, or travelling to the nearest bit of coastline, walking into the water and allowing it to close over his head. What about jumping off a cliff? Or a high building?

After a while, he pulled himself together. He would not give up. He would do his best to find her, persuade her that their love was worth holding onto. But how? He didn't even know where they were living.

A week later, Chamberlain declared war.

Without telling anyone, Jack took the bus into town, doing his best to avoid talking to his fellow passengers, with their anxious eyes and strained faces, and queued with dozens of others at the recruiting office.

The previous summer, in Austria, a friend of his host family had taken him up in a biplane. It was a glorious day, the sky filled with puffy clouds, and they had flown over the foothills of the Alps, their white peaks glinting in the distance. He had been utterly entranced by the exhilaration of air rushing past his face, by the extraordinary sense of freedom, by seeing the world from an entirely new perspective. Ever since then, he'd been trying to work out how he could afford flying lessons. Here was his chance. He would place his life in the hands of fate, and if he didn't survive, at least it would have been in a good cause.

There were posters on the wall of the recruiting office: fierce-looking soldiers manning large guns, crisp-suited sailors peering at the seascape through binoculars, handsome airmen waving from cockpits. He envisaged himself as one of those airmen, brave and self-sacrificing. Dying young.

Although the officials were at pains to make it clear there were no guarantees about where he would end up, he specified his preference for the air force. Now he just had to wait and see.

His parents were horrified.

'You're going to abandon us?' his father spluttered. 'Don't you realise the factory is already at full stretch with orders for the Air Ministry? The call-up doesn't apply because ours is an essential occupation. What we're doing is just as vital as fighting.'

'And a lot less dangerous,' his mother added quietly.

Jack ignored their objections. Within six weeks he was on a troop ship to Canada with three hundred other young men, bound for the plains of Manitoba for basic pilot training. His chances of survival were slim, everyone knew that. But he hardly cared. If he died, so be it. What was the point of living without Rosa?

19

As they fled Suffolk on the train that evening, all Rosa could think about was Jack's dejected face. *The only man who ever made me feel like a real woman, and I will never see him again,* she thought miserably. She tried to engage Daniel in conversation, but he refused to respond.

Then, as they emerged from Liverpool Street station, she saw a newspaper billboard: *PARLIAMENT TO BE RECALLED – EMERGENCY POWERS BILL.*

'Look, Daniel,' she said. 'What does that mean?'

'It means they're preparing for war,' he said, taking hold of her arm with a vice-like grip. 'Come on now, we haven't got time for that.'

'But what about visas for our families?'

'It's too bloody late,' he bellowed. 'We'll be at war in days. And thanks to you and your little fancy boy, I have no job and we have nowhere to stay. If we go to war, there'll be no hope of getting visas for America. It's all going to hell.'

They tried the first place they saw advertising rooms for rent. The room overlooked a railway junction and smelled of cooked cabbage, and hot water was only available for an hour in the morning and two hours in the evening, to be shared between eight lodgers. But they had no other choice.

Throughout the train journey, Daniel had appeared preternaturally calm. Now, as the door to their room closed behind them, they were alone for the first time since leaving the Preston house, and his pent-up fury exploded.

She cowered in the corner as he swore at her for her infidelity, tearing open her suitcase and throwing her clothes, shoes, photographs and other precious belongings around the small attic room. There was no point in trying to reason with him. When she begged him to tone down his language, he swore some more before grabbing his coat and storming out, saying he was going to get some food.

Her reprieve was short-lived. An hour later, he returned with a bottle of whisky, already half empty, and ordered her to undress. When she resisted, he raised his fists. She could hardly believe it was happening again.

In the morning, he was contrite, apologising over and over. 'I am so sorry, my darling Rosa, so sorry. I should not have treated you like that. But I cannot bear to think of you with that, that … wretched boy.'

'It was only a kiss,' she lied. 'That's all it was. An innocent peck on the cheek. As a friend.'

'How can I believe that,' he scoffed, 'when you have been lying to me all this time?'

'It meant nothing.'

He sighed. 'I have little choice but to accept your word, I suppose. But let me tell you this, Rosa. If I hear you even so much as mention that boy's name, or discover that you have made contact with him, or catch you making eyes at another man, I will throw you out. When I divorce you, you will have no right to stay in this country. That is your choice. Now get dressed and smarten yourself up. We're going to the American embassy.'

By the time they reached Grosvenor Square, the queue stretched around the block. By midday, they had scarcely moved. It was raining, and Rosa's shoes were soaking, her feet numb with cold. When the embassy closed its doors that evening, there were still at least a hundred ahead of them in the queue. They went again early the next day, but people had been camping overnight and they still had to queue for most of the morning.

At last they got inside, where they were led to an interview booth and told that each of them would have to fill out a ten-page form. 'That's it?' Daniel said, as they returned them. 'When will our visas arrive? We need to know so we can book our passage.'

The man shook his head, a slight smile playing on his lips. 'Don't get your hopes up, pal. There ain't many visas for the mighty US of A, especially not these days. And if war comes, you can whistle for it.'

'That's that, then,' Daniel said as they left the embassy. 'What a fine mess you've created. No job, no money, nowhere to live, no chance of getting to America ...'

Rosa followed him meekly. What choice did she have?

The following day, Daniel declared that he was going out to find a job, but when Rosa suggested she might do the same, he scoffed at the idea: 'What skills do you have? And how do I know you won't fall into the arms of the next fancy boy who makes eyes at you?'

Their little room was so gloomy, and she couldn't bear to be alone with her thoughts, so she walked and walked, exploring London's East End. People here seemed terribly poor and ill-dressed, and the shops were small and poky. The houses were all crammed together, with no gardens, front or back. Washing lines were strung across the street, and there were hardly any trees. It was nothing like the London she had seen in picture books, with its wide streets, beautiful parks and imposing buildings. Where was that to be found? she wondered.

She discovered a library and read the newspapers, coming to understand that as expected, Hitler had reneged on all his promises and war really was inevitable. The news was like a cold hand gripping her heart. What would happen to her family? Hitler's armies seemed invincible. They had walked into plenty of other countries without apparent resistance. What if they should invade England, too?

Next day, sirens sounded, near and far, all over London. Rosa ran downstairs to join the other lodgers on the doorstep, peering up at the sky.

'What does it mean?' she asked.

'They've only gone and declared flippin' war,' someone said. 'Effing Krauts. That's our lives up the creek for the duration.'

Along with the other men in the boarding house, Daniel signed up for nightly fire- watching shifts, but there were no raids, and talk began of a 'phoney war'. Of course, it wasn't easy being regarded with suspicion by everyone they met. Rosa knew they would have to improve their English accents. While Daniel's grammar and vocabulary were greatly improved, he didn't seem to have the ear for inflection.

She tried to coach him. 'Repeat after me: "We have to live."'

'Vee hef to liff,' he would reply, oblivious to the difference.

Fortunately their landlady, Mrs Tanner, had been born to German Jewish parents, and treated them with sympathy. 'Ain't your fault that evil man – may his name be destroyed – got into power, is it?'

Daniel applied for war work, and within a few weeks he was travelling each day to a factory where they made parts for

cannons and guns. It was menial work compared with the
managerial role he'd enjoyed in his father's firm and the sales
post at the Preston's, but he was pleased to be contributing to
Hitler's defeat.

In early December, they learned that they would have to
register as 'enemy aliens', and read news of internment camps
being set up on the Isle of Man and elsewhere. Individual cases
would be considered by a tribunal, they were told. Six weeks
later, they heard to their enormous relief that they were regis-
tered as 'Category C', and not considered to be a risk to national
security. They would not be interned. Not yet, anyway.

The government announced that all women should sign up
for war work too, and again Rosa suggested she should do so, but
Daniel still refused to allow it: 'You are a married woman,' he
said. 'I will not have my wife going out to work. And you
wouldn't last a minute in a factory like mine.'

She couldn't help laughing. 'For heaven's sake, Daniel, this
is the twentieth century. We are visitors in a country at war.
And it's not as though we are rolling in money. Look at this
place.' She waved an arm around the small room with its splut-
tering gas fire, the dripping tap in the basin, damp stains
creeping up the wallpaper. At last he relented.

At the recruitment office, they enquired about her skills,
and when she mentioned her fluency in written and spoken
English, German and French, the man behind the desk asked to
be excused. After an alarmingly long wait, he returned with his
boss. She was taken to a closed room and quizzed further, then
told to wait some more while the boss made a telephone call.
Eventually she was sent away clutching a slip of paper.

'Report to this address on Tuesday next week, nine o'clock
sharp,' he said. 'Do not share this information with anyone else.'

A week later, she found herself traipsing along a bleak,
windy street in Whitehall, sick with nerves.

The interview was long and confusing. After asking her in

English what she was doing in London – accepting her explanation without question – the interviewer switched to German, in which he was equally fluent, and began to engage her in the sort of conversation you might have after being introduced at some polite social gathering. What was her home town? Ah, Hamburg. Beautiful city. Did she know the opera house? Who were her favourite composers?

He switched to French: had she ever been to Paris? What did she think of the impressionist painters? Had she read any Voltaire?

She sensed that her answers were woefully inadequate, but managed to muddle through. The written test – translating between three languages – was even tougher. But at last she was called back and invited to sit down. The man was reading through her scripts.

'Hmm. Not bad, Mrs Levy. Quite impressive, in fact.'

'Thank you.'

'I see you are a German national.'

'Yes, although we – my husband and I – have been classed as Category C.'

He smiled. 'You think I don't already know this? We know quite a lot about you already, Mrs Levy, otherwise we wouldn't be touching you with a bargepole.' Rosa was momentarily distracted. Whatever did a bargepole have to do with it? 'However, your skills are going to be very useful to us in the coming months.' He passed across the desk a single sheet of paper headed: *United Kingdom War Office: Official Secrets Act.* 'Read this carefully,' he said.

Although she still had no idea what she was being asked to sign, Rosa understood that she would never be able to talk about her work, or divulge the name of her employer or the title of her post. The punishment for doing so would be a criminal trial for treason and, probably, imprisonment.

'Fine with all that?'

She nodded, feeling slightly sick.

'Then sign it, please.'

She took a deep breath and accepted the pen he offered – a heavy gold tube with a signature along the side. Once she had signed, he leaned over the desk to shake her hand. 'Welcome to the War Office,' he said.

On her first day, she found herself in a large, noisy room filled with other women sitting in rows at typewriters. A plump, bossy matron in a tight navy blue suit showed her how the typewriter worked and instructed her to spend the rest of the day practising – in particular, how to use all of her fingers to hit the keys. 'You'll never type at any speed using two fingers,' she said, wafting away in a haze of lavender talcum powder that left Rosa feeling strangely queasy.

She watched the women around her tapping away at great speed. Some of them were not even looking at the keys, for heaven's sake. She would never be able to type that fast. Why was the keyboard arranged in such a confusing way? And the wretched heavy shift key never stayed where she wanted it, so that numbers came out as letters, and lower-case letters as capitals. But by the end of the second day, she was managing to type a little faster, with fewer mistakes.

'You're ready for your first translation,' the bossy woman said on the third day.

After a few weeks, Rosa was starting to feel at home in this unexpected environment, and at home, she and Daniel had reached a sort of accord. He demanded sex almost every night, and she tried to enjoy it, but failed. It was only after Christmas – a modest but jolly celebration hosted for the motley crew of boarders by their landlady – that Rosa realised her monthlies had not arrived. They had been so busy, so keen to establish themselves, that she hadn't even noticed.

How long had it been? She racked her brains. Life had been so chaotic, so stressful, that it was possible she'd missed two, perhaps even three months. Could she be expecting?

20

Baby Hans – named after Rosa's father – was born on 27 May 1940, just as thousands of troops from the British Expeditionary Force were rescued from the beaches of Dunkirk by a ragtag flotilla of fishing boats, barges and paddle steamers.

News of these alarming events passed Rosa by in the haze of new motherhood. She'd had to give up her job, of course, but that seemed a small sacrifice for the gift of the beautiful little boy with whom she'd fallen in love from the very first instant.

Mrs Tanner managed to negotiate for them to rent a slightly larger set of rooms on the first floor of the building next door. They moved in when Rosa returned from the maternity hospital, a week after the birth. It was hardly luxurious, and well overdue for a lick of paint and some new carpets, but it had a separate bedroom, a small kitchenette off the living room and, most exciting of all, their own bathroom. A terrifying gas geyser spat scalding water into the basin or the tiny tub, depending on which way you aimed the spout. The shared toilet was one floor down. Baby Hans was dressed almost entirely in second-hand clothes donated by Mrs Tanner's friends and neighbours; they found a broken pram in the street and Daniel fixed the wheel so that it worked almost perfectly.

From the start, the baby's thick shock of brown hair prompted everyone to remark that he was the spit of his father, and Daniel could not have been more proud. Not that he spent much time with the boy. Work at the factory was busier than ever, with three shifts now operating twenty-four hours a day, seven days a week. Daniel was promoted to floor supervisor, which meant he was often required to be there for up to twelve hours a day, sometimes even at weekends. He was exempt from conscription, for which they were both grateful.

As the weeks and months passed, Rosa developed a new level of affection and respect for her husband, especially when she saw him responding to his son with surprising tenderness. But the exhaustion of new motherhood and the increasing demands of Daniel's work schedule began to put a strain on the marriage once more.

When the Blitz began, they considered moving out of London, but Daniel wanted to stay within reach of the factory. The work had given him a new purpose in life, not to mention a decent income for once. And Rosa had come to depend on Mrs Tanner, who refused to be cowed even when German bombs fell close by, destroying houses in neighbouring streets.

They dreaded the 'Moaning Minnie' air-raid sirens warning of night-time bombing raids, which meant decamping to the crowded and dingy depths of the local Tube station. Hans was a fractious child, picking up on his parents' anxiety, and it was always a struggle to keep him from disturbing the sleeping throngs around them on the platform.

'What a sorry welcome for the poor little laddie,' people would comment, tutting and shaking their heads. 'What kind of a world has he arrived into?'

More often than not, Daniel arrived home late from work, stinking of beer. When Rosa challenged him, he snapped back:

'What's wrong with going out every now and again? There's precious little joy to be had from your gloomy face.'

'What about your son? Don't you want to spend more time with him?' she pleaded. 'I could certainly do with some help.'

'I can't think what you're complaining about. I go to work every day, slaving my guts out, while you sit around with the baby on your knee, yakking to Mrs Tanner. You don't even behave like a proper wife any more – I have to beg you for what is my right as a husband. And you have the nerve to complain about me enjoying a bottle of beer every now and again.'

She knew there was no point arguing: she would never love Daniel, and he would never be the husband she'd once dreamed of. She still yearned for Jack, and wondered whether he'd defied his father to join the air force. Was he in one of those small planes they frequently saw flying over London, heading for the coast to face the German bombers? She read something about the low survival rate of pilots and prayed that he would stay safe.

And now there was little Hans to consider. As she'd heard Mrs Tanner say of another couple: she had made her bed and now she had to lie in it.

What she missed most of all was her mother. In the dark sleepless nights and throughout the long, tedious days of feeding and endless laundry, she yearned for Miriam's comforting presence. How proud she would be: she could almost picture her cradling the boy, the look of devotion in her eyes. She could see her father standing taller with pride on learning that his grandson was named after him. Willi would be awkward, of course, reluctant to hold the baby and unable to admit that deep down, he too was proud of his new nephew.

She knew that no letters would reach them, but that didn't stop her writing. *Dear Mama, Papa and Willi, Hans smiled for the first time today! Such a sweet, gummy smile, my heart nearly burst with love for him. But it is also broken with sadness that you cannot be here with us ...* And, a few months later: *We are all safe and well despite the bombing. Don't worry about us. Hans is starting to eat real food, what a mess he makes! But at least he is now sleeping better ...*

The letters were never posted, of course. There was little point. She stored the envelopes in the back of a drawer, telling herself that she would keep them for when the family was reunited. In time, the little bunch tied with a ribbon became in her mind a kind of talisman. While the letters were safe, the family would be too, and they would all meet again, just as Vera Lynn promised, 'some sunny day'.

At the same time, Rosa blessed her good fortune in having met Mrs Tanner. Their neighbour and former landlady took a grandmotherly interest in young Hans, and frequently dropped in to help, bringing food and other supplies. She also brought news.

'Ain't it *meschugge*,' she would exclaim in her curious accent, part East End, part Yiddish. 'That drunken *schlemiel* Churchill can carry on all he likes about blood, toil, tears and sweat, but what exactly is he going to do about Hitler – may his name be destroyed – on our doorstep?' The war was not going well, whatever the newspapers said.

It was Mrs Tanner who suggested Rosa and Daniel should consider changing their surname – just as she had, from Tannenbaum – to something less German- or Jewish-sounding. Daniel, however, was reluctant. 'Levy is my family name,' he said. 'To change it would feel disrespectful, like abandoning my heritage.' But as news came of troops gathering on French and Belgian shores, he began to waver.

In the end, it happened quickly, the night Mrs Tanner offered to babysit while they went to the local fleapit cinema. 'Have yourselves a few hours off from the littl'un. You both deserve a bit of fun.'

The movie was *The Real Glory*, and Rosa was transfixed. It

was the first time she'd been to a film since Jews were banned from cinemas in Hamburg. The star, Gary Cooper, reminded her so much of Jack that she found herself smiling even through the sad parts. The way the corners of his mouth curled down in that wry smile, the way his eyes crinkled with amusement, the way he turned his head and looked sideways at his co-star, Andrea Leeds. Her heart ached for the kind of passion that was now so entirely missing from her life.

As they emerged from the cinema, passing the poster advertising the movie, Daniel announced: 'Cooper, that's a solid English name.'

'Rather dull, don't you think?'

'Dull is good,' he said. 'The last thing we want is to stand out. And who knows, it might help us get an American visa later, if it reminds them of their big movie star.'

So it was decided. Rosa felt certain that she would never get used to being called Mrs Cooper, but it was what Daniel wanted, and what he wanted was usually what he got. Besides, she thought, we can always change it back after the war is over.

PART 3

21

LONDON, MAY 1945

At long, long last the war is over.

Rosa had returned to work when Hans turned two. The War Office actually wrote to her: *Your skills are much in demand and we would be pleased if you were able to join us again.* Her first response was incredulity. What a ridiculous idea. She was a mother now, and anyway, she had nothing to wear for that kind of life any more. Her office clothes were threadbare, her shoes down at heel. Stockings were still in short supply, and she'd seen how girls had taken to drawing seam lines down the backs of their legs.

But she was flattered to be asked, and the more she thought about it, the more appealing the notion had become. Hans had been walking for months and, when she wasn't washing or ironing, her days were spent chasing him around the flat or through muddy parks. Much as she loved her boy, motherhood was definitely rather boring.

So when Mrs Tanner offered to look after him – 'he's no bother, dear little *bubbeleh*, and to be honest, I'd be glad of a few extra pennies' – and it suddenly looked possible, although

Daniel was reluctant. 'It's shameful and undignified for a new mother to leave her child,' he said.

'My work is just as important as yours,' Rosa retorted. 'We all have to do our bit for the war effort, don't we? And anyway, how are you going to stop me when you're out all hours of the day and night?'

After her initial nervousness she'd settled quickly back into the routine of work, her mind pleasingly absorbed by the task of translating technical documents relating to the German war machine. She had made a new friend, a brilliant young blue-stocking who had studied at Cambridge before the war and who spoke four languages to Rosa's three. With her long blonde hair and shapely figure, Paula could have been a model had she not fiercely despised anything so frivolous as fashion.

The pair of them clicked almost immediately, bonded by their mutual inability to control the giggles when addressing Mrs Sidebottom.

'It's hopeless,' Paula would say. 'I know it's juvenile, but I just can't help it.'

'Mrs Siddybertohm to you, young lady,' Rosa would mimic, provoking further bouts of laughter that they attempted to muffle in their sleeves.

Both of them expected to lose their jobs when the war ended, as many did, to make way for returning servicemen, but somehow they are still here.

So they are both at work that day when, just before 3 p.m., the typewriters fall silent. Mrs Sidebottom tunes to the Home Service on the radio in her lavender-scented office, and they all gather to hear the official announcement.

Everyone embraces, including Mrs Sidebottom, and they dance crazily around the office. No one suggests they should return to their desks, and the next day will be a public holiday, so they join the flood of office workers down the stairs and out into Whitehall, amid the clamour of a hundred church bells, and head for Buckingham Palace.

When the King and Queen appear on the balcony with the two princesses, Elizabeth and Margaret, a great roar of joy goes up from the thousands of people gathered there. It is a thrilling, exhilarating moment that Rosa will never forget. Britain has saved her, and her husband and child. And now, at last, she will be able to find her family in Germany.

She writes to them immediately, posting her letter to their last known address with the farmer near Bremerhaven. Although they may not still be with him, she hopes that Herr Schmidt will know where they are and will forward her letter.

But the days and weeks pass, and no reply arrives. There is no news from Daniel's family either. He doesn't even know whether they managed to leave Hamburg before the week-long Allied bombardment, which by all accounts has obliterated the city centre. They write to anyone for whom they have addresses from before the war – school friends, people from Daniel's father's factory – but receive no reply from anyone.

As the silence continues, Rosa's darkest fears deepen.

Horrifying reports begin to filter through: stories of concentration camps, the enforced transportation of Jews and other so-called enemies of the state, and rumours that thousands have been murdered by the Nazi machine. The first photographs of the liberation of Belsen concentration camp are published, so shocking that Rosa finds herself unable to focus on those living skeletons with their sunken eyes, those bodies so carelessly thrown into mass graves.

She wakes each day with a sinking feeling in her stomach. When so many have been imprisoned and brutally murdered, what hope is there that her family have survived, or Daniel's for that matter? They agree that they will travel to Germany as soon as possible to search for them, but quickly discover that no ferries are likely to be available for civilians for many weeks or even months, and are warned that travel within the country is severely restricted.

Rosa manages to pluck up the courage to ask Mrs Sidebottom whether anyone in the War Ministry might have access to German records, but is told firmly that all such information is strictly top secret and will probably not be available for many months, or even longer.

They are free from fear for the first time in years, she tries to remind herself, and it is summertime and the cheery wash of sunshine makes even the bomb-damaged city look fresh and bright. It should be a time for rejoicing, but her sadness is overwhelming. Watching Hans, now a lively five-year-old, running around the playing field in pursuit of his precious football sometimes brings tears to her eyes. He may never know his grandparents, never feel the love of a wider family of cousins, aunties and uncles.

As always, in her quiet way, Mrs Tanner offers a glimmer of hope. She arrives one day with a slip of paper on which is written the address of the Central British Fund for Jewish Relief and Rehabilitation, an organisation set up to help trace missing families. 'There is always a chance,' she says. 'You must try everything you can.'

'And if we can't find them even then?'

'Then you must console yourself with the fact that you have tried your very best. You have survived, and you have your husband and your boy, and there are many other people who love you, my dearest Rosa,' she says, giving her a hug.

It is early September when, after work, Rosa travels to the offices of the Centre in Bloomsbury and queues with more than a dozen other anxious-looking individuals before being admitted through the doors. The building is shabby, smelling of mildew and ancient paperwork. Inside, she is given a card with a number, and invited to take a seat in a waiting room. Most people are smoking; the air is blue, almost suffocating. She makes a couple of attempts at conversation, remarking on the weather in the English tradition, but they falter and she settles down to read the book she has borrowed from her friend Paula.

The book has just been published and is very controversial among the critics, Paula says. It is called *Animal Farm*, with the subtitle 'A Fairy Story', but as far as Rosa can see, it is not about farming at all, nor is it in any way a traditional type of fairy story. It is a strange tale about a group of animals who rebel against their farmer and end up being ruled by a dictator pig. Paula says it is a parody of the Stalinist regime in Russia, but Rosa thinks it could equally be a reflection of Nazi Germany, the way the animals bow and scrape before the odious pig even while hating it. The book is cleverly written and she is enjoying it, although Paula has warned her that the ending is bleak.

A woman with a strong European accent and heavy black spectacles calls out her name: 'Mrs Cooper? Come with me.' She leads her to a small interview room. 'Take a seat,' she says kindly. 'How can I help you today?'

Rosa explains.

'Sadly you are one among many, Mrs Cooper,' the woman says, tipping her head to the waiting queues. 'We are just a small voluntary organisation, and our contacts in Germany are already struggling to manage all our requests to trace people's families. As you can imagine, the records are in complete disarray. It is an enormous task, with many hundreds of thousands of people having been misplaced by the war. But we are doing our very best, and if you leave us your name and address, we will contact you as soon as we receive any news.'

She lowers her voice. 'Of course it is important always to retain hope, my dear. But you need to prepare yourself. This evil regime has murdered many of our kind. Not many Jews escaped the concentration camps, I'm afraid.'

Rosa is halfway home when she realises that she has left Paula's book on the table in the waiting room. She will have to go back for it another time. And in the meantime, all she can do is wait.

Her only distraction is little Hans, but as he grows, she sees new likenesses in his face to her father and to Willi, and the thought that her parents have died without ever meeting their beautiful grandchild makes her feel even more desolate.

The sadness settles over her like one of those dense London fogs, refusing to lift.

22

Miriam is cocooned in a cloud of white. Hushed voices float on the air around her, blurry faces loom into her vision like pale moons before fading away. She feels no pain, or even any other sensations: it is as though she is actually floating. This, surely, is what heaven feels like. She closes her eyes and drifts off again.

Later, although she has no idea how much later, she is startled by a voice close by: 'Can you open your eyes for me, Mrs Kauffman?' She feels the pressure of a warm hand on her bare shoulder and tries to lift her eyelids, but they seem strangely reluctant. A curious sound, a sort of moan, comes from nearby, and she realises from the vibrations in her throat that it is probably her, attempting to speak. *Entschuldigen Sie, bitte,* she is trying to say. Please excuse me.

'Never mind, my dear,' the voice says. 'All that matters is that you are back with us again. Don't wear yourself out trying to talk.'

They speak English in heaven, Miriam thinks to herself. I'd better do the same, or they might throw me out.

It is a man's voice this time, deep brown and resonant with authority. 'This lady was found collapsed in the street,' he says.

'She was suffering from acute pneumonia and malnutrition. From documents found on her person, we gather that she is Mrs Miriam Kauffman, of German extraction, with a recently issued English visa. As you see, she is painfully thin. But I think we can understand why when we see this ...' Miriam feels a hand on her arm, lifting it up. 'This number tattooed on her arm, my young friends, is a sign that this poor lady has miraculously survived incarceration in a German concentration camp. It is likely that starvation and ill treatment has caused her health to have been inevitably compromised, so it is hardly surprising that she has succumbed so badly to the pneumonia. However, thanks to the excellent ministrations of the sisters here, she is showing signs of turning the corner. Any questions?'

Another voice, lighter; a younger man, Miriam supposes. 'Have we tried sulphonamides? Like Winston Churchill?'

'No, my friend,' the older man replies. 'In the past couple of years, it's been proved that this new drug penicillin is far more effective, especially in the most severe cases such as this one. A few years ago, we would not have expected this lady to survive.'

Miriam manages to prise her eyes open and is amazed to discover that her bed is surrounded by faces, mostly of young men in white coats, except for the tall, imposing figure of an older man in a three-piece tweed suit, sporting a neatly trimmed beard. Also in the crowd are a couple of nuns in crisply starched white wimples.

'Good morning, Mrs Kauffman,' the tweedy man says. 'You have decided to join us, I see. These are my medical students, and your nurses. How are we feeling today?'

'*Durstig,*' she starts to say, before correcting herself. 'Thirsty.'

'Excellent, excellent. Bring this lady a glass of water, Nurse. And perhaps a cup of tea.'

The man and his acolytes sweep away to the next-door patient and disappear as the curtains are pulled around them.

But Miriam is fully awake now, and struggling to sit. One of the nuns comes to her aid, plumping up the pillows to support her, and within a few minutes she is holding a cup and sipping the most deliciously sugary tea she has ever tasted.

That evening, she manages to eat few mouthfuls of the meal they bring: a small lump of tasteless white fish in an equally tasteless glutinous sauce, and a bowl of sour brown sludge that turns out to be stewed apple. Hardly manna from heaven, she thinks, but far better than anything she received in the camps. And these sweet-faced nuns seem to have saved her life, at least.

Later, when they come to take her tray and are helping to settle her down for the night, she ventures to ask: 'Excuse me, please. But where am I?'

'Bless you, my dear,' the nun says. 'Has no one told you?'

Miriam shakes her head.

'This is the hospital of Our Lady and All the Saints, in the City of London. You were found in the street not far from here, in quite a bad way, I'm sorry to say. We are all delighted to see you looking so much brighter today.'

'How long have I been here?'

'Hmm, let me see now. Nearly three weeks,' the nun says.

Three *weeks*? 'What month is it?'

'It is August.'

How did she come to be in hospital in London? She struggles to remember. Then, like a floodlight being switched on, she remembers: the border, Jack Preston, who gave her the visa. She is here to find Rosa. How could she have forgotten? Her precious daughter could be in this very city. Perhaps even nearby.

Time is passing; time that could have been spent looking. She feels a sudden urgency, as though the opportunity to find Rosa might slip through her fingers if she waits too long.

. . .

Miriam's strength returns frustratingly slowly. The nuns help her into the chair beside her bed, but she is so dizzy that she feels nauseous and begs to lie down again. Another day, with two nuns supporting her, one on each side, they help her to her feet and encourage her to take a few steps. Her legs feel disconnected from her body. She understands what is required to make them move, but doesn't have the power to make them do it.

With the return of her physical strength comes the detail of her memories: her journey here on the ferry and then the train, the landlady, the rain, the doorway. That is the last thing she can remember. She asks what has happened to her clothes, her bag, her belongings. The nun brings a parcel, inside which are the coat, jumper and slacks, shoes and underwear that she was wearing, all now clean, dry and neatly folded. Also an envelope, crinkled from having been damp, containing her precious visa and identity card, and the money, untouched, as well as the slip of paper with Jack's address. She stored it, she now remembers, in the inside coat pocket for safety.

'My bag?'

'No bag, I'm afraid, my dear. Nothing else with you when they picked you up. Was there anything valuable in it?'

Miriam shakes her head, smiling. 'Nothing. Just some old clothes, my drinking bottle, some food.'

'The hospital almoner should be able to help you when you are ready for discharge,' the nun says.

She asks for paper and an envelope and writes to Jack at his parents' address, hoping that he might have returned home from Germany by now. She remembers him remarking on the 'difference of opinion' that led to Daniel leaving the fan company, and his view that now the war was over it would be easier for Daniel and Rosa to get visas for America. There is no time to lose.

23

Jack is home on leave and his father is pressuring him to stay for good. 'Enough gallivanting around Europe, my boy. The war is over. Time to face real life.'

He feels like a stranger in a familiar land, embarrassed at being made to feel like a hero at every turn, hating the way his mother introduces him to everyone they meet with the words: 'Remember Jack, my eldest? He was a fighter pilot, you know.' His brothers take every opportunity to mock him. 'Hail the conquering hero comes,' they chorus as he enters the room. When he goes to the local pub, the barman insists on standing him a free drink.

His father seems visibly to swell with pride as he shows Jack round the extension at the factory and the new equipment they have recently installed, and especially when one of the workers approaches to shake his hand. 'Good on yer, young Master Jack. Beat the bastards, didn't we?'

All the people in the village and the places they visit are so totally familiar, so deeply ingrained, an essential part of himself. And yet he feels oddly removed, like an actor playing a role. He left home at eighteen to join the RAF. Now he has returned six years later an entirely different person. But to his family he is just their Jack, son and brother. How could they hope to understand what is going on inside his head, to appreciate the experiences that have shaped him into someone they can never fully know?

He has seen sights that his brain will never be able to erase: his friend's plane going down in flames just ahead of his own; the look of abject terror in the eyes of the German pilot wrestling with the joystick of his fatally damaged aircraft as it spiralled out of control within feet of Jack's own. The pale, pain-stricken face of the rear gunner in his hospital bed and the empty space where the boy's legs used to be. The desolation of empty bunks after a particularly disastrous sortie. More recently, the starved faces of refugees waiting in their hundreds at the border posts.

He can cope with the nightmares – all his mates have them. It is the physical response of his body to quite ordinary, everyday reminders that he finds most difficult to manage: the sound of an aircraft overhead, the siren of an ambulance, an old lady shuffling into church with bowed shoulders and a scarf tied around her head. He finds himself breaking out into a cold sweat, his limbs seizing up and his chest so tight that he struggles for breath.

He expected, even hoped, that joining up would erase the emptiness of losing Rosa, but each time he returns home he discovers all over again that the house, the garden and the countryside around – hedges, ditches, fields, the river, the view of the valley – are deeply and irrevocably infused with the memory of her, like the aroma of whisky in the oak of a long-empty cask. They bring simultaneously the joy of remembering and the renewed agony of loss, like a dagger twisting in his wounded heart.

And it seems he cannot help punishing himself, grinding salt into his own emotional wounds: visiting the dell for a

cigarette, taking a canoe to paddle all the way to Bures and
buying a pint in the very same pub he took her to. At their
special place in the woodland the other side of the gravel workings, he finds himself weeping. He wonders whether he will
ever experience that intensity of feeling again.

She will never be free to love him, and he is realistic enough
to know that. But he will never be free of loving her, and he
cannot help wondering what has happened to her, what kind of
life she is living now. He longs to see her again, if only just from
a distance. In the pub, surrounded by inebriated friends, he
feels detached and lonely. He cannot share their optimism. Life
feels flat, empty and featureless.

Perhaps it would have been different had he not met her
mother that day, that extraordinary day, at the border crossing.
It feels like a dream now: that strangely familiar, ravaged face,
the moment she mentioned her daughter's name, the way she
explained to him, so innocently, how Rosa had escaped
Germany by marrying an engineer called Daniel. The way his
heart pounded so hard that it made him feel dizzy, and he'd had
to leave the room to have a cigarette and gather his emotions.

But he hasn't heard a word from Miriam Kauffman, not
since they parted at the border post. The passing of each day
leaves him more and more anxious for her safety. Surely she
would have written to him by now? Has she managed to reach
London, or did something happen to prevent her entering the
UK? Has she learned news of Rosa that she feels unable to tell
him? Or is she still waiting, hoping for something, anything, to
share with him?

In the dark hours of the night, he sometimes entertains the
notion that he was duped. Was she actually a Nazi, or a spy,
who had by some fiendishly clever means detected his connec-
tion to Rosa and Daniel and decided to milk it as a way of
gaining a visa? Is she, this 'Miriam Kauffman', even now selling
British secrets to the Nazi regime-in-hiding, or the Russians,

perhaps? Are perfectly innocent individuals being identified as spies, and marked for elimination? And when she is eventually detected and detained, will they discover Jack Preston's signature on the identity papers and her visa? He could be arrested, charged with treason and betraying the British nation, or some such.

'And what persuaded you, Captain Preston, to give this woman carte blanche to enter Britain?'

'I was in love with her daughter, sir.' He can almost hear the prison gates clanging shut behind him.

At last, one boiling hot Indian summer day in September, a letter arrives.

Dear Captain Preston,

Please forgive the long delay in writing to thank you for your help and great personal generosity. Each day I thank the fates for bringing us together at the border.

As you will see from the address above, I entered the UK with no problems, but soon after arriving I fell seriously ill with pneumonia. For several weeks I was not really conscious of my surroundings. Happily, thanks to the great care of the nursing sisters at this hospital, I am now on the road to recovery.

As a result, I have made no progress in locating Rosa. I feel a great urgency about this, since you told me that she and Daniel had planned to move to America, and the arrival of peace may have made this easier.

The doctors tell me I should be strong enough to leave hospital in a fortnight or so. I would dearly love it to be sooner, but this

*disease has weakened me so that I can still barely put one foot
in front of the other.*

I will write again when I have more positive news.

With best wishes, and once again my heartfelt thanks,

Miriam Kauffman

Jack grabs his coat and persuades his brother to run him to
the station – 'I'll buy the drinks for a whole week' – dashing
past the barrier and ignoring the shout of 'Oi, you, I need to see
your ticket.' He clambers on board, sweating and panting hard,
just as the guard blows his whistle. The train is already moving
as he slams the door behind him.

It is one of those carriages without a corridor, and the
compartment he has boarded – the one nearest the station
entrance – is already almost full. Ignoring the disapproving
looks from his fellow passengers, he squeezes himself into the
gap between a large elderly gentleman over-spilling his allotted
space in the corner, and a fraught-looking young woman
dandling a fretful baby on her knee.

Within a few seconds, he starts to notice an unpleasant
odour and realises that it is emanating from the infant. No one
is sufficiently impolite to remark on it or even to acknowledge it
with the wrinkle of a nose, and anyway, there is nothing to be
done. The mother cannot change the nappy here. The man next
to the window pulls on the leather strap to open it a few inches
and, as the train gathers speed, a welcome breeze whistles
through the compartment.

An hour and a half later, they pull into Liverpool Street and
Jack steps stiffly onto the platform with a sigh of relief.

The convent of Our Lady and All the Saints is within easy
walking distance of the station, and he is soon standing outside

an austere three-storey building of dark red brick, with Gothic windows and a steep slate roof. At the far end, a chapel spire towers above the surrounding office blocks. Six steps lead up to a front door flanked by pillars in a particularly ugly shade of red marble. Not short of a penny or two, these nuns, he thinks to himself as he waits for someone to answer the bell. He is about to give up when the door creaks open, just a crack, and an elderly face, wrinkled like a walnut and enclosed in a starched wimple, peers out.

'Hello. I have come to visit one of your patients,' he starts. 'Mrs Kauffman?'

'Visiting hour is six until seven.' The door closes.

Jack has three hours to wait. The pubs aren't open yet, and he wanders aimlessly, searching for a café or tea room, until he happens upon something better: a library. The smell of old books – slightly musty, earthy, even woody – transports him back to his school days, trying to commit chemical equations to memory. In the centre, between the stacks of books, is a large table where people are reading newspapers and periodicals.

He takes from a nearby rack a copy of *The Times* (Britain to sign United Nations Charter, and War Crimes Tribunal preparing to sit in Nuremberg) and *The Illustrated London News* (parades celebrating the fifth anniversary of the RAF victory on Battle of Britain Day). Before long, the silence and warmth and lull him into somnolence. He has not slept well since Miriam's letter arrived.

He gets up and meanders between the shelves of the reference section. What a lot of useless information there is here – or rather, useless until you need it, he thinks. And as though to prove that very point, the next title his eye alights on is *The London Trade Directory, 1940*. All at once he realises that this could provide precisely what he needs: a list of likely places for Daniel to have found work after leaving Preston's.

He soon discovers that there are literally dozens, perhaps

even more than a hundred companies in London that make fans and propellers for all manner of purposes: aeronautics, trains, cars, heating systems, refrigeration. He asks at reception for paper and a pencil and begins to note down the addresses of the most likely-sounding ones. He can come back another day if necessary. But this is a start.

As he rifles through the pages, he hears a voice: 'Closing at five thirty. Half an hour until closing time, ladies and gentlemen.'

After wandering around the streets for a further thirty minutes, he hears the bells of St Paul's Cathedral and a dozen other city churches chiming six o'clock.

The nuns direct Jack to Miriam's bed, halfway down a long and mostly empty ward. He barely recognises her at first. She is even more shrunken than before, her face shrivelled, the skin of her arms pale and almost translucent. She is dozing as he approaches, but seems to sense his presence and peels her eyes open; a crack at first, then widening with recognition.

'Captain Preston! What a wonderful surprise.'

'Thank you for your letter. I was wondering what had happened to you.'

'What a strange business it's been, losing all these weeks,' she says. He has forgotten how well she speaks English; the inflection is perfect. 'But I am getting better every day, they tell me. I can walk almost to the end of the ward and back without having to sit down. Tomorrow it's the stairs. It will feel like climbing a mountain, I expect.' She laughs, and her face becomes animated with pleasure, chasing away the pallor.

They chat for a while about her journey to England. 'Have you anywhere to stay when you get out of here?' he asks.

She shakes her head. 'That's a problem. Unfortunately when the landlady at the boarding house learned I was

German, she threw me out for fear of offending the other boarders, and that is when I found myself on the street in a rainstorm.'

Jack racks his brains. He has several former school friends who live in London, but it's been a while. 'Leave it with me,' he says. 'You won't be discharged for a week or so, I think you said? So not to worry, I am sure we can find you somewhere.'

She leans over and takes his hand. He looks into her face and sees there are tears in the corners of her eyes. 'Captain Preston ...' Her voice cracks, and she clears her throat enough to carry on. 'How can I thank you for your generosity? Had I not met you, I would probably be starving in a derelict German basement somewhere, trying to avoid the Russians. Now I am here in London, the same city as my daughter. Almost within touching distance. That is what I sometimes dream of.'

When he first encountered Miriam Kauffman in Germany, Jack saw something vaguely familiar in her face, but nothing that really reminded him of Rosa. Now he realises how blind he must have been. Was it the responsibility of his post, the formality of the interview room, the persona he was required to assume each time he put on the uniform? Here, as Miriam talks, he can't help seeing her daughter in every gesture: the lift of an eyebrow, the shape of her upper lip, the tone of her laugh, the twist of a hand as she gesticulates. Suddenly he senses with renewed urgency the need to help her with her search.

He squeezes her hand. 'We will do everything we can to find her,' he says. 'In fact, I've already made a start.' From his pocket he produces the piece of paper on which he has hastily scribbled the list of fan manufacturers. 'I'll write to them all,' he says. 'We'll leave no stone unturned.'

She smiles now. 'That's a new phrase for me. I shall store it for future reference. One day,' she says, with a faraway look, 'I hope to teach English once more.'

'Not a lot of call for it in these parts. We're all experts round

here,' he says, straight-faced, and it takes a moment for Miriam
to realise that he is teasing her.

'You're right,' she laughs. 'But seriously, I will need to earn a
living somehow.'

'What else can you do?'

'I'll do anything: cleaning, waitressing, serving in a shop.
But who would employ a German woman in a city we have
spent the past five years bombing?'

All too soon, it seems, a nun appears, ringing a small hand-
bell. 'Five minutes,' she calls. Visiting time is over.

On the train home – an almost empty compartment this time,
with no babies in sight, thankfully – Jack remembers Sam
Greene. He was one of his best friends at school, and was
Jewish. Not that you'd have otherwise known, but Jack recalls
that although Sam's family were not particularly religious, he
was allowed additional exeat days for the Jewish festivals –
Passover, Rosh Hashanah, Yom Kippur – and he never had to
do prep on Saturdays. At the time, Jack was envious and considered converting.

He hasn't seen Sam since they left school, but they've
exchanged a few letters. Although it was never spelled out, Jack
gathered that his friend's short-sightedness had kept him from
active service and his facility for maths had earned him a cushy
job in some secret part of the War Office. Sam was also the first
of their set to get married, to the good Jewish girl he'd been
sweet on for years. They were still living in London, and last
time he heard, there was a baby on the way.

Yes, Sam Greene would be the perfect person to help
Miriam. He might know of possible places for her to stay, and
even where she might apply for work. As soon as he gets home,
Jack writes to him.

24

In early December, Rosa and Daniel take Hans to Trafalgar Square to see the giant Christmas tree. Mrs Tanner says it's been donated by the Norwegians in thanks for British support during the war. 'There might even be carols,' she says. They are very excited, recalling those long-lost days when people gathered to sing 'Stille Nacht' around Christmas trees in the squares in Hamburg. It didn't matter what faith you held, or even if you held none, the tradition seemed to crystallise a renewed sense of hope.

In Trafalgar Square, there is indeed a choir singing carols – although few tunes that they recognise. The tree, adorned with glittering coloured lights, towers above the bronze lions, and street vendors are selling roasted sweet chestnuts, holly wreaths and sprigs of mistletoe. The square is thronged with families determined to enjoy their first peacetime Christmas in six years. The delight in Hans's eyes makes the long journey from the East End worthwhile.

At last he starts to grow weary, demanding to be carried, so they decide to head home. As they make their way through the crowds, they hear a voice from behind, speaking in German: 'Rosa Kauffman, can it really be you?'

Rosa turns to see a woman of her own age, with blonde hair and a small child much the same age as Hans, and instantly recognises the face. 'Marta? Marta Muller? Is it really you? Whatever ...?'

'I could ask the same of you,' Marta says. 'This is Freddie. We are Wilsons now. I married an Englishman, but he's still away serving. We hope to have him home by Christmas, don't we, Fred?'

'I'm Rosa Cooper now. This is my husband, Daniel, and my son, Hans. We came over in '39.'

They grin at each other, shocked into wordlessness as the crowds press around them.

'Listen, we must meet up,' Marta says at last. 'We live near Regent's Park, it's very easy to get to. Can you come for tea next Saturday? Three thirty?' She reaches into her handbag and brings out a small card. 'The boys can play and we can have a good catch-up. What a wonderful coincidence.'

The following Saturday, Rosa and Hans make their way to St George's Terrace, Regent's Park. It is one of those imposing crescents of Edwardian town houses with wide stone steps leading up to the front doors, sturdy pillars on either side supporting a balconied porch. The houses, once painted white, are stained and grey after years of wartime neglect, but that doesn't make Rosa any less nervous as they listen to the bell ringing hollowly inside, and wait for someone – will it be a uniformed servant? she wonders – to answer the door.

It is not a servant, but Marta and Freddie, accompanied by a bouncy terrier that jumps up and licks Hans's face, making him cry.

'Down, Jasper, down,' Marta orders sternly, pushing the dog

away and taking Hans's hand. 'Oh, I'm so sorry. Come in. We've got doughnuts. That'll soon dry your tears.'

They sit in the kitchen and tea is informal to the point of being mildly chaotic. Marta vainly tries to persuade the boys to eat fish paste sandwiches before allowing them doughnuts, but soon gives in, and before long both of them are covered in sugar and sticky jam.

Once they have been wiped down and have disappeared upstairs to play with Freddie's train set, Marta explains that she came to England through sponsorship from an aunt who lived in Norfolk. There, she met the son of some neighbours and fell in love. James spent most of the war abroad, leaving Marta with the in-laws in the depths of the countryside, which she hated. It is 'just bliss' to be here at the family's London house and away from her mother-in-law, who believes herself an expert in parenting.

'When the war ended, they didn't have any excuse for keeping me there, so here we are rattling around in this huge place. And of course when I was living with them in Norfolk, I was never able to speak a word of German. They even frowned if I dared to speak it to Freddie, and after a while I began to wonder whether I'd lose it altogether.'

'It's a joy to feel free to speak your own language without looking over your shoulder all the time,' Rosa agrees. 'Will the world ever forgive us, do you think?'

Marta shakes her head sadly. She explains, too, that she fears that both her mother and father died in the camps. 'And what about you? How did you get here?'

Rosa recounts how she married Daniel and came to England.

'What about your parents, and your little brother? Willi, wasn't it? What happened to them?'

'I've been writing ever since the end of the war, and asking anyone who might be able to help, but nothing yet,' Rosa explains. It is reassuring to talk to someone else who is trying to find out what has happened to their family, and to admit to feelings of hopelessness at the bleak news coming out of Germany.

Marta, making a second pot of tea, mutters to herself, 'I wonder whether Mrs Geller—'

'Mrs Geller? From the apartments in Hamburg? You're still in touch?'

She returns to the table with the pot, covering it with a pretty quilted tea cosy. 'Yes, we wrote to her immediately the war ended and someone must have forwarded it, because we heard back from her a couple of months ago. She moved to a village near the coast – perhaps you knew? Before the bombing, thank goodness. She and your mother were quite close, weren't they? She might have news. I'll get the address.'

Rosa writes immediately to Mrs Geller, and holds her breath. The reply comes just three weeks later, and she sits at the table with her heart racing, as though this rain-stained brown envelope with the German stamp on it holds everything she needs to know about her future.

'What is it?' Daniel says. 'You've gone as white as a sheet.'

'It's from Germany. Probably from Mrs Geller, but I can't bear to open it. What if it's bad news?'

She thrusts it into his hands, fidgeting impatiently as he goes to the drawer to find a knife and then slowly and deliberately slits the envelope, withdrawing the single flimsy piece of paper. At last she can stand it no longer, and with shaking hands she reaches out, takes the letter and begins to read:

My dear Rosa,

I am so pleased to hear that you are well and of course delighted to learn about little Hans. Congratulations to you both.

However, I am afraid I do not have any news about your parents.

By great good fortune they were not at home when the Gestapo came knocking, although that didn't stop the brutes smashing down the door and ransacking the place. Your family left just in time. Miriam wrote to me a few months later.

Perhaps you already know that they found accommodation and employment with a farmer, Herr Schmidt, near Bremerhaven. Their 'country retreat', as she jokingly called it. They seemed well and happy, although naturally very upset that they had missed the last Kindertransport for Willi and been unable to get visas to leave the country.

I moved out of Hamburg a few months later, and thank goodness for that, because the apartment and many of the buildings around us were flattened by bombs in 1943.

After the war, I wrote again to Miriam but received no reply. But it may be worth trying again. Herr Schmidt's address is at the bottom of this letter.

There is further difficult information I feel duty bound to share with you, my dear Rosa. I have suffered so much with guilt, knowing that it was I who introduced you to that monster Erich Steiner. You may have heard that he became high up in the local Nazi party and made it his business to rid Hamburg of Jews. His wife, my friend Alicia, was so distressed by this that she took her children and went to live in Switzerland, but before she left, she told me that Erich had become obsessed with finding you. What concerned me most was that your mother's letters to me appeared to have been tampered with, and it broke my heart to think that someone could be tracking her correspondence.

Dearest Rosa, you will I am sure by now know the terrible truth about what happened to so many Jewish people, so please write to reassure me if you find your parents. I was very fond of your mother and would dearly love to hear from you.

Mit freundlichem Gruss,

Helga Geller

Rosa slumps in her chair. Her head is spinning and she feels close to tears. Daniel takes the letter and reads it in silence. 'No news again. I'm sorry,' he says. 'Who is this Steiner fellow anyway?'

'The man I worked for, looking after his children, remember?'

'Why did he have it in for your family?'

'Because I left to come to England with you.'

'That's absurd. You had to get away. He'd have known that.'

'He's a Nazi, Daniel. He'd have needed to prove himself to the party. And he said I had betrayed him.'

How can she ever admit the truth? The guilt and anger writhe in painful waves, shaking her body like a fever. If only she had chosen to walk away from Steiner sooner, sought work elsewhere, or simply refused to succumb to his abuse.

When Mrs Tanner arrives home from school with Hans, he climbs onto Rosa's lap, cuddling his warmth into her. 'What's wrong, Mama?'

'Nothing, sweetheart,' she says, holding him tighter until he giggles and tries to wriggle out of her arms. 'How was your day?' She nestles her face into his hair, grateful for the distraction. He smells of school: pencil shavings, sweaty plimsolls and the artificial flavouring of the gobstopper in his pocket. It is usually the best smell in the world, full of her love, of their future in a world at peace. But that future is now indelibly stained by this new knowledge of the past. Frau Geller's letter has changed everything.

'Come, boy, let's get you some milk and a biscuit,' Daniel says.

Hans scrambles away, his warm body replaced by a chill emptiness and the turmoil of her emotions.

She hides the letter in the bedside drawer and goes to straighten her hair in the mirror. How strained and grey she looks, how much she has aged in the past few years. She takes a breath, lowering her shoulders and trying to smooth the frown lines from her forehead.

As she listens to Daniel and Hans in the kitchen, chattering about mundane things – school, the factory and what to eat for supper – she envies them fiercely their ignorance of the evil she has unknowingly unleashed. And in that moment, she makes a vow to herself. She will find out what has happened to her family and if she discovers that Steiner caused them any harm she will seek him out, and make his life hell.

25

When Miriam is able to climb the stairs without having to stop to recover her breath every three steps, she is deemed strong enough to leave the hospital. Outside, the sun feels warm on her back as she slowly makes her way to the address Jack has given her for Sam Greene and his wife, Sarah.

'They'll put you up for a while,' he told her. 'Don't worry, they come from the same background, and I've told them yours. They're happy for you to stay until you find somewhere else and ...' The words hang unspoken between them, but she knows he understands: she cannot envisage life beyond the search for Rosa. That is her sole focus.

She takes a taxi to the address south of the vast green space they call Hyde Park. 'You're going to stay in Knightsbridge, eh?' the kindly hospital almoner remarked, raising an eyebrow. 'You've landed on your feet, Mrs Kauffman.'

It is only when she finds herself looking up at the terrace of four-storey buildings with their grand porches and tall windows, a new coat of white paint gleaming in the sunshine, that she understands. There are no rows of doorbells beside each front door as there were on the apartment blocks in Germany. These people live in this entire enormous house.

As she presses the bell – heavy brass, with a high polish – she remembers Jack telling her that he was at school with Mr Greene. How could a young man have become so wealthy at such a young age?

Over cups of tea, Sarah Greene explains. She is petite and beautiful, with a thick mane of dark hair with auburn highlights that remind Miriam so powerfully of Rosa that at first it almost takes her breath away. She has two children under four, and has dark smudges around her eyes, as though she hasn't slept properly for months. Miriam feels a surge of maternal affection, an urge to gather this young woman into her arms and tell her that motherhood will get easier in time.

This was the house her husband grew up in, Sarah says. But her parents-in-law, Sam's mother and father, were both killed when the Underground station in which they were sheltering on the way home from a visit to the theatre received a direct hit. 'They found all the bodies almost untouched,' she says. 'But the bomb had sucked out all the oxygen. They'd suffocated.' Eighty-five people died. In a terrifying parallel to the cellar tragedies of the Hamburg firestorm, a place of safety became a giant tomb.

That evening, Miriam helps Sarah bathe the children and prepare the supper. Each small task feels both familiar and alien at the same time. It is six long years since she stood at a stove stirring a cooking pot or laid a table with plates and the full range of cutlery, not to mention glassware. And longer still since she bathed a child in a white porcelain bath or tucked them up warm and safe beneath the blankets. Everything she does in this house is a painful reminder of a family life that she will never know again.

Over supper, Sam probes her gently. 'Jack tells me you're looking for your daughter.'

Miriam explains that Rosa came to England with her

husband just before the war and is the only one of her family still alive. They nod gravely. They've read the newspapers. They're of the same kind as her. It is a relief that she doesn't need to go into detail.

Sam has been doing some research and comes up with a suggestion: the Red Cross has recently set up a tracing bureau, he says, retrieving from his study a map of central London and pointing to a street close to Trafalgar Square. 'It's somewhere here, I think. You just have to walk along and look for the sign on the door.'

That night, Miriam dreams of Rosa as a small child. She is weeping and tugging at her hem, crying to be picked up. 'Help me, Mama, help me.' Miriam tries to lift her, but her arms won't stretch far enough, even though Rosa's pleading hands are reaching up towards her. At last she manages to grip the little girl's shoulders, but she is too heavy and slips from her grasp. She wakes herself with a sob so loud that for some minutes she lies awake in the darkness, listening fearfully in case she has woken the children in the next room. At last she sleeps again, so deeply and dreamlessly that when she finally opens her eyes to the sunshine pouring between the curtains, it takes her a few seconds to remember where she is and how she got here.

Even though many of the streets she passes through have an air of neglect, battered and bruised by six long years of war, Trafalgar Square appears relatively undamaged. Miriam is impressed by the grandeur of the space and its surrounding buildings: the heavy pale stone, the balustrades and porticos and pillars and domes, like so many Roman temples, although some of the entrances are still barricaded with sandbags, their windows criss-crossed with white tape.

How Hitler must have longed to conquer this city, she thinks as she crosses the wide square with its fountains and imposing black lions resting on their plinths. He'd have replaced the statue of the man on top of that tall column with one of himself. And what a setting it would have made for one of his ghastly rallies.

But Hitler is dead. She stops, takes a deep breath and forces her face into a smile. The world is at peace again. Except that we are not, she thinks, at peace inside ourselves. She still crosses the road if she sees a dog, still jumps out of her skin when a car backfires, still mourns her beautiful Hans and Wilhelm, their life in Hamburg before the rise of the Third Reich. All that is gone. Hitler's evil lives on in the losses we suffered, she says to herself, and in our damaged lives.

She finds the street and begins walking down it, looking either side for a sign, or a red cross symbol. At last she finds both: *Red Cross International Committee Central Tracing Bureau. By appointment only.* It is a grey, anonymous building with most of its windows shuttered.

After what seems like an age, the door opens and a young, harassed-looking woman regards her with a surprised expression. 'Oh, we weren't expecting anyone today. Have you got an appointment?'

'No, I am afraid not.'

'Then I'm sorry, we can't help you.' She points to the sign. 'You'll have to write, or telephone.'

As she goes to close the door, Miriam blurts out: 'Please. I need your help. I have come from Germany, trying to find my daughter.'

The woman sighs, hesitates and then, with a shrug of her shoulders, says, 'Very well. Stay there. I will see if there's someone who can help you.'

She closes the door and Miriam sits on the dusty step, prepared to wait for as long as it takes. Office workers stream in and out of the buildings opposite: men in uniform, men in dark suits and bowler hats, young women who have done their best to look smart, although she can see, even from this distance, that their coats are threadbare, their shoes down at heel, and they have drawn seam lines on their bare white legs to look like stockings.

Could one of them be Rosa? she wonders. She cannot imagine that her daughter would ever be content staying at home, playing the dutiful housewife. A group of girls goes past, one of them with long auburn hair, the right height and build. Miriam catches her breath. But the girl turns and she is not Rosa. Of course she isn't.

The door behind her reopens and another, older woman appears, her lips tightened with impatience. 'Can I help?'

Miriam stands hurriedly, brushing herself down. 'Thank you so much. I have recently arrived from Germany, you see, and need to find my daughter. She is all the family I have.'

The woman's face softens. 'You are German?'

Miriam nods.

'I don't suppose you are getting the best of welcomes in this country.'

'Some people are kind,' Miriam says.

'Your English is excellent, if I may say so. You'd better come in then.'

The woman ushers her into a small room piled high with files that smells of mildew and old linoleum. 'Take a seat,' she says. 'I'm Mrs Blanchard, and you are?'

'Miriam Kauffman.'

'We don't normally take appointments on a Monday, you see,' the woman explains. 'It is our day for catching up. You say your daughter is the only family you have left?'

Miriam nods, avoiding the woman's concerned eyes. Kindness can easily reduce her to tears, especially when she is short of sleep.

'Forgive me for asking, but do I take it that you are Jewish?'

Miriam resists the urge to check behind her, to make sure

the door is closed, that they are the only people in the room. The persecution is over, she silently reminds herself. 'Yes,' she says at last. Even now it feels like confessing to a deadly sin.

'How did you avoid the camps, if you don't mind my asking?'

She rolls up her sleeve to reveal her inner arm, and hears a sharp intake of breath from Mrs Blanchard.

'You did well to survive, my dear,' the woman says matter-of-factly. She pulls out a file, writes *Miriam Kauffman* on the front of it, and opens it to a clean white sheet of paper. 'Now, tell me about this daughter of yours.'

Miriam explains about Rosa and Daniel, and where they were last seen. She tells her how Daniel left the fan-making company and that they might have been trying to make their way to America.

'Unlikely to have made it across the Atlantic that late in the day,' Mrs Blanchard says. 'But we can always run a check with the shipping companies. We need to try every avenue. There's also an organisation called the Central British Fund for Jewish Relief and Rehabilitation. They were involved in getting people out of Germany before the war. Children especially. Did you hear about the Kindertransport?'

Miriam nods. She cannot trust herself to speak. It is nearly seven years since that terrible night at the train station when Willi was refused his train ticket and visa.

'Well, we will do our best for you, Mrs Kauffman, but it may take a while, I'm afraid.' Mrs Blanchard gestures wearily to the piles of cardboard files stacked on the desk, a small city of untidy skyscrapers. 'This is a new service for the Red Cross and already we have many people on our books, as you see. However, be reassured that we will do our best. If your daughter is in this country, there's every chance that we will be able to find her.'

She stands, and Miriam follows suit. The interview is over.

'Now, where can we get hold of you?'

Miriam gives the Greenes' address. They have promised she can stay until she finds somewhere more permanent. Mrs Blanchard says that she will be in touch just as soon as she has any news.

Outside, Miriam stands on the steps and takes a deep breath. The reality of her good fortune is only now starting to sink in: thanks to Jack Preston, she has arrived in a country where the rule of law still applies; a country not ruled by a madman and his gangs of thugs; a country at peace, where she can actually admit her Jewishness without eliciting a frown or a scowl. Buildings may have been damaged, but trains and buses are running. There may still be rationing, but there is enough food to live on. There are kind people who want to help her. A great weight seems to be lifting from her shoulders. All she has to do now is find Rosa.

Two days later, once she has recovered her strength, she sets out once again, holding in her hand the address of the Central British Fund for Jewish Relief. She takes the bus to Oxford Street, as Sarah suggested, and then walks north into an area called Bloomsbury.

She finds the address and queues with three or four other individuals before being admitted. The building is shabby and, like the Red Cross office, smells of mildew and ancient paperwork. Inside, she is given a card bearing the number 32, and invited to take a seat in a waiting room.

Her companions are a mixed bunch: men and women, elderly, middle-aged and young, some well-dressed and some down at heel, some well fed and others with that haunted, starved look she has come to recognise in the mirror.

On the table is a pile of magazines, and she takes one, expecting to wait some time before she is seen. Under the magazine is a book, a paperback with a picture of a pig on the front. The title is *Animal Farm*, but it is clearly not about farming. She wonders what it is doing here in the waiting room, and assumes it must have been left by someone, so she puts it back on the table and starts to read the magazine instead.

She becomes so absorbed that at first she fails to hear the number being called. Her neighbour nudges her: 'Aren't you number thirty-two?' She starts and jumps up, spilling her book and the contents of her bag onto the floor. She scrabbles to pick them up, then an elderly woman with a strong European accent and heavy black spectacles leads her to an interview room.

'Take a seat,' she says kindly. 'How can I help you today?'

Miriam tells her story. It is becoming worn around the edges now, smoothed out like a pebble on a beach, but she tries to include every detail. When she comes to the end, the woman takes off her spectacles and wipes her eyes with a small handkerchief.

'My dear,' she says. 'You are only the second person I have met who has survived the camps. What can I say? You are remarkable, and deserve to live a long and happy life. We shall do our very best to find your daughter and her husband. So first of all, let me take down your name and address for my records.'

Miriam tells her.

'And the name of your daughter?'

'Rosa Levy.'

'Age?'

She has to count to remember. Rosa was born in June 1920. Germany was still in turmoil, with coups and strikes – she remembers wondering what kind of world she was bringing this child into. Hah! Little did they know then how much worse it would get.

'Twenty-five,' she says now.

The woman notes this down. 'And her husband?'

'I'm not sure precisely. Three or four years older. Perhaps twenty-nine?'

'And both Jewish?'

Miriam nods.

'Are we certain that they are in the UK?'

'That is the last news I have of them, although that was some years ago now.'

'You say they may have emigrated to the United States?'

'They hoped to go there one day.'

'They would have had to apply to the American embassy for a visa. Is it worth going there to ask? They may claim it's confidential information – those Yanks are terrors for officialdom – but if you explain your story as you have for me today, they might relent.'

Miriam nods. She is beginning to wish she had brought a notebook so she could write everything down. Searching for Rosa is going to be complicated, a major project. How will she ever manage it without any money coming in? she wonders. Perhaps her next task is to find some kind of job.

'However, if your daughter and son-in-law are still in the UK, I assume your son-in-law will be working somewhere, and it's rather a specific field. There can't be many fan manufacturers in the capital.'

'I have a friend who is checking all the engineering companies.'

'Excellent, excellent.' The woman writes more notes, then looks up again.

'Have you contacted any synagogues in London?'

Miriam shakes her head, feeling foolish. Of course, that would be an obvious place to start, but it hasn't even occurred to her that synagogues will still be open and operational.

'We're not very religious,' she says.

'Worth a try at least. Our Great Synagogue was tragically

destroyed in the Blitz, but I can give you a list of the other ones in central London.'

'Thank you.'

'Well, I think that covers it. We can cross-check your details against our records and will of course let you know if we get any leads. Please rest assured that we will do our very best for you, Mrs Kauffman. But you will have to be patient with us. We are just a small voluntary organisation, and as you see, we have many people to help. But we promise to contact you just as soon as we receive any news.'

She offers a hand. Miriam shakes it, wishing that she could hold on to it for ever, never letting go until they find Rosa.

26

On her way back to Knightsbridge, Miriam sees a woman with two large dogs on leads coming towards her. She steels herself. I need to beat this, she says to herself, refusing to cross the road even though she can feel the cold sweat breaking out on her neck. The dogs are of the same breed the guards tended to use in the camps. Those were mangy, vicious beasts, kept deliberately underfed. But these dogs are sleek and clearly well nourished. As they pass, they take no notice of her at all.

The owner smiles politely: 'Beautiful day,' she says.

Miriam smiles back. Perhaps it *is* a beautiful day when she can start to conquer her fears.

She finds a stationer's shop and spends her last few English shillings on a small notebook, a pad of Basildon Bond writing paper and some envelopes, two pencils and a fountain pen with a bottle of ink. When she returns to her room, she opens the notebook and writes:

Finding Rosa

Get a job and lodgings

Fan and engineering companies (Jack)

Write to synagogues

Visit American embassy

Her first letter is to Jack, thanking him again for his kindness in introducing her to the Greenes and reassuring him that she is settling in well. She also tells him about her visits to the Red Cross and the Jewish relief organisation, and how she plans to look for work so that she can become independent.

Over supper that evening, after the children are in bed, Sam and Sarah invite her to join them in the living room. She perches awkwardly, anxiously on the edge of the chair. 'We've been wondering,' Sam starts, 'what your plans are for the next few months.'

Miriam responds hastily: 'Of course, my priority is to find work and a place to live, so I do not trespass on your kind hospitality any longer than necessary.'

She sees the couple exchanging smiles, and Sam continues: 'The thing is, Miriam, Sarah's been telling me how helpful it's been having you here these past few days. The children like you and trust you, and you are so handy around the house ...'

Sarah joins in: 'Honestly, having you around has been like a breath of fresh air. You have fitted in so easily, and it's been wonderful to have an extra pair of hands and eyes to help with the children, not to mention in the kitchen.'

Miriam is holding her breath, expecting to hear the word 'but' at any moment: but we really need our spare room back ... but our plans have changed ... but we are moving house.

'So we were wondering,' Sam continues, 'whether you would consider making the arrangement a bit more formal. If you are agreeable, we would like to offer you a position as our nanny and housekeeper, in return for board and lodging and a weekly allowance.'

Board and lodging in this beautiful house, right in the centre of London? A weekly allowance? Miriam cannot quite believe what she is hearing, and discovers she has no words. A small gasp issues from her mouth.

'I'm sorry, we didn't mean to insult you. Or upset you.' Sarah leans forwards, a frown of concern on her beautiful young face.

'No, you haven't upset me. The very opposite, in fact. It's just that such kindness is ... is ...' Miriam takes a breath. 'I am not used to it.'

'But what do you think of our suggestion?' Sam urges after a moment.

'I can think of nothing I would like better,' she says.

A few days later, Jack arrives. He and Sam have not seen each other since they left school, and their lives have taken very different paths, but it is obvious why they became friends in the first place: they share the same sense of humour, the same interest in politics, the same passion for creating a better society. After a very congenial supper during which two bottles of wine are consumed, they all retire to the living room and the men start on the brandy.

'So I've told you about my exciting life in the world of fan-making,' Jack says. 'It's your turn, Sam. What do you do for a living that allows you to keep your lovely wife in this beautiful house?'

'I can't say, old boy. You know how it is.'

'Top secret, is it?'

'That sort of thing,' Sam says. 'Tell me about your war. I'm sure it was a lot more interesting than mine.'

And they are off. After a while, Sarah yawns discreetly and

excuses herself. Miriam follows. She needs to conserve her strength for the following day.

The plan is that Miriam and Jack will go to the American embassy in Grosvenor Square, which is just a short step from Knightsbridge, but Jack is slow to rise, and by the time they get there, it has started to rain and the queue is long. They join it anyway, but after an hour, they have barely moved.

'Let's come back later, see if it's moving better then,' Jack suggests. 'Tell you what, we can to Fortnum's.' It's a real London institution, he says, and just around the corner. 'They're famous for their cakes. Or you could have an ice cream sundae.' He has to explain to Miriam that a sundae is not the same as Sunday, and tells her he has never forgotten being taken to the café by an uncle when he was a boy. She tells him about their favourite place in Hamburg, with delicious apple strudels and cinnamon rolls, and then goes silent as she remembers that what she is describing is now probably flattened into a pile of rubble.

Fortnum and Mason's tea room is light and bright, with pastel panelling and walls painted with flowers and trellises designed to make you feel as though you are in an English country garden. How different from the comfortingly sombre interiors of the cafés at home, Miriam thinks, with their dark wood and low lamps over each table creating pools of intimacy. Nevertheless, rationing doesn't seem to have affected the quality of the cakes and the coffee here. Both are delicious.

'You are looking so much better than when I last saw you,' Jack says. 'You actually have some colour to your cheeks.'

'Sam and Sarah are very kind to me. Did they tell you they've asked me to stay and be their housekeeper?'

'Sam mentioned it.'

Miriam knows what she wants to say but finds it hard to

start. A few awkward moments pass as they sip their tea. 'Look, I ...' Jack says, at the same moment as she says, 'You know ...' They laugh and he says, 'Go on. Ladies first.'

'I just don't know how to say it,' she blurts out, in a rush. 'Through all the hardships of the past few years, the one thought that has kept me alive is to find Rosa. Now I am here, in the city where we believe she is too. I keep imagining that I will simply bump into her. My heart stops every time I see a young woman with auburn hair. I cannot believe my good fortune. And it's all thanks to you. How can I ever repay you?'

'You don't have to thank me. I want to find her as much as you ...' He stops, and she watches the deep flush that rises up his neck and into his cheeks.

She smiles at him gently. 'You see her too, don't you?'

He nods, his eyes lowered and unable to meet her gaze. She knows that her instincts are right: Jack Preston is in love with her daughter. But to acknowledge that would make him feel uncomfortable, and she is too sensitive to do that for fear of putting him on the defensive.

'So,' she says, 'all we have to do now is to find her. Have you heard from any of the engineering companies about Daniel?'

'Not yet. It's early days, though. I'm still optimistic.' His smile shows relief at the change of subject.

'We just have to keep trying,' she says. 'I don't know why, but I know deep down that Rosa is in this city somewhere, and all I have to do is to try every avenue and one day I will find her. Unless, of course, she is in America.'

It has stopped raining, and back at the embassy, the queue has reduced. Half an hour later, they are inside the building. It is a vast echoing hall like a palace, with a black and white chequered tiled floor and grey marble pillars rising either side of a wide stairway. On the walls are larger than life-size portraits of grand old gentlemen, probably American presidents.

'How may I help you?' says the man at the desk. He is

young, clean-shaven and eager, wearing uniform, his hair close-cut in US military style. His smile displays two rows of perfect white teeth.

Miriam explains and he writes down their names on an already long list.

'Thank you, ma'am. Now, if y'all would care to take a seat over there,' he gestures to a row of chairs against the wall, 'I will enquire whether we are able to help you.'

An hour passes and they watch as the young man greets a continuous stream of new arrivals, answering queries, directing them this way and that. 'You'd think they would give him some help,' Jack whispers, his leg twitching with impatience. 'He's never going to get time to deal with the backlog.'

At last there is a lull and the man picks up the phone. He speaks into it, then nods as he listens. 'Yes, sir. Will do, sir. Thank you, sir.'

He looks up and beckons towards the chairs. Ten people stand up. 'No, just you and you.' He points to a couple of people at the other end of the line. Jack and Miriam sit down again. The pattern is repeated several times: more people are greeted, more people join them on the chairs, more phone calls, more people leave or are issued with paper passes, and some of the chosen ones are directed to climb the stairs.

'He certainly earns his living, that young man,' Miriam remarks.

At last it is their turn to be beckoned forward. 'Thank you for your patience,' he says. 'It gets a little busy around here. Now, you have a question about visas?'

'Yes, we would like to know if you can tell us whether the embassy has issued a visa for my daughter and son-in-law, Daniel and Rosa Levy,' Miriam says.

He picks up the phone: 'Ah, hello, sir. Lady here wants to know whether we can tell her if we have issued a visa to her daughter and son-in-law. Sir.'

A frown furrows his forehead as he listens to the few brief words of response, then he puts down the receiver. 'I am so sorry, ma'am, but my boss says we cannot divulge such information. It is confidential.'

'They are my sole remaining relatives, young man,' she says. 'We are desperate to find them.'

'I am sorry, ma'am. The regulations ...'

She is about to tell him again how far she has come to find Rosa, how important it is to her, but she feels a tug on her arm and hears Jack whispering, 'It's no good, Miriam. If it's the rules, they won't budge. We'll just have to try another way.' Meekly she follows him out of the echoing hallway.

Autumn has arrived and Miriam finds herself falling in love with their part of London: the grand shops and little boutiques, the way the leaves turn yellow and then red, the berries that appear on the shrubs that border the small gardens in residential squares. These were once enclosed by metal railings, Sarah tells her, until they were taken to help build aeroplanes. Either way they make ideal playgrounds for the children. She loves the parks with their ponds: especially the one in St James's Park with its exotic pelicans and regal swans. She even enjoys shopping. There are still queues sometimes, but the English are very disciplined at queuing. Not like the crazy, desperate fights people would start trying to buy bread in Hamburg.

She is getting better at managing her anxieties: doesn't cross the road to avoid dogs, at least the ones on leads, and doesn't jump out of her skin when a car backfires. London is helping me to recover, she tells herself. And my recovery will be complete when I find Rosa.

She takes the children to the newly reopened Natural History Museum and the Science Museum, and the family make a weekend visit to Kew Gardens, which Miriam loves. She remembers the historic botanical gardens in Hamburg, where the children loved to play by the lake in summer and enjoyed the warmth of the greenhouses in winter, and wonders whether it survived. She has always longed for a garden of her own.

The only thing about London that she really dislikes is the rain, which seems to fall almost every day. Now she understands why the coat stand in the hallway has a basket around its base filled with umbrellas. The Greenes say it is the worst September weather they have seen for years, and newspapers carry warnings from farmers that the rain is ruining the harvest, so bread rationing won't ease any time soon.

Miriam receives replies from some of the synagogues, but as she feared, none know of Daniel and Rosa. Jack writes to say he has had little luck with any of the fan-making companies. *I'm planning to contact general engineering firms next,* he tells her, *but it'll take some time. There are more than two hundred of them. It's a bit like looking for a needle in a haystack.* Miriam adds this curiosity to her list of English idiomatic phrases.

She resists revisiting the Jewish Relief Centre for as long as her impatience will allow, but by October it gets the better of her.

'Miriam Kauffman, you say?' The lady with the thick-rimmed glasses regards her carefully. 'Ah yes, I remember. The camp survivor. You are looking very well, my dear. Much better than when we first met you. I barely recognise you. So, let me double-check whether we have heard anything. Remind me who you are looking for.'

'Rosa and Daniel Levy.'

Minutes pass as the woman flicks through several boxes of card indexes, their paper tabs fraying with use. 'No, sorry, nothing here. Is there any other name they might have decided to use? Some of those who lived here through the war anglicised their names, you know.'

Miriam racks her brains and can think of nothing.

The lady is well accustomed to managing people's disappointment. 'Never mind, my dear. If they are still in London, I am sure they will be searching for you too,' she says smoothly. 'We just have to be patient.'

Weeks pass, and Miriam is growing accustomed to this new way of life. She loves the way they make her feel part of the family, and is pleased when they seem to appreciate her cooking. Sarah is much more relaxed now that the baby is sleeping through the night. The dark bruises around her eyes have disappeared, she rarely snaps at the children these days, and Miriam sometimes overhears her humming a popular melody. Everyone loves it when Miriam saves up the rations and bakes her favourites: cherry pie, strudel and almond biscuits.

The best times are when Sam and Sarah go out and she is left to put the children to bed. Snuggled up with a child on each side, she reads *Peter Pan, The Wind in the Willows* and *Winnie-the-Pooh*. She finds the stories fascinating, providing insights into British society that she would never learn from a history book.

Most of all, these quiet, intimate moments remind her of when her own children were young: that feeling of peace and security, the bustle of the day behind them. That was when she felt closest to them, when secrets could be whispered or worries admitted to. Rosa learned to read early, but enjoyed being read to right up until her teens. Willi was a slowcoach in everything academic, and found it hard to sit without wriggling for more than a few moments at a time. But when a story captured his imagination, he would listen enraptured for hours, sometimes imploring her to read on because he wanted to know what happened next. Poor, sweet Willi, are you up there looking down at us, envying these warm, living children snuggling up to me in your place?

And Rosa? She is an adult now, and perhaps even has children of her own. Miriam's heart thrills at the possibility. Could she be a grandmother and not even know it?

Little Josh digs her in the ribs. 'C'mon, Mrs K. It isn't even the end of the chapter. What happens next?'

Autumn turns to winter, and as Hanukkah approaches, Sarah digs out from a box in the attic a slightly battered menorah, which she places in the window of the living room. Candles are difficult to get hold of these days, but in the box there are a few short pieces and a longer one they cut into three, to make eight small stubs. Miriam can remember so clearly the last time the family dared to light their own menorah in Hamburg, and the golden glow that enfolded them like a blessing. She hopes that Hans and Willi are looking down from heaven, watching as the Greenes gather to light the first flame.

'We didn't usually bother before the war, but it's a way of saying thank you for peace, and we thought it would be nice for you, Miriam,' Sam says. 'And what a sign of hope it is, remembering how the Jews defeated the enemy and got back their lands.'

Miriam can feel the tears already streaming down her face, and Sarah gives her a hug. 'You will find your Rosa soon, I am sure of it,' she says.

Christmas is only a few weeks away, and London seems determined to celebrate for the first time in six years. Coloured bulbs light up houses that previously seemed dark and uninhabited, and shops create red and gold window displays with nativity scenes or images of Father Christmas, using cotton wool to represent the snow that has failed to arrive in real life.

Miriam shows the children how to cut out giant snowflakes from folded newspaper, and they show her how to make paper chains, which they paint in primary colours. The effect is gaudy and messy, but no one seems to care.

In early December, Sam returns home from work with the news that an enormous Christmas tree is being raised in Trafalgar Square. 'They're turning on the lights this weekend,' he says. 'We should take the children.'

When they get there, the square is packed with families. The tree – apparently donated by a grateful Norwegian government for Allied help in their liberation – is certainly impressive, adorned with glittering coloured lights. A choir sings carols, most of which Miriam does not recognise, but the Greenes join in gleefully with the choruses: *Gloo-oo-oo-oo-oo-ria, in excelsis Deo.*

Miriam wonders whether Miriam and Daniel could possibly be among the throng. She sees several faces that give her momentary cause for a second look, but they turn out to be other couples of similar height and build. It is difficult to tell, when everyone is so well wrapped up in hats and scarves. Each time she tells herself not to be so silly, that there are a few thousand people here in a city of millions, but her eyes won't obey and they begin to scan again.

The children start to whine and Sam decides it is time to find a cab home. As they make their way through the crowds to the edge of the square, Miriam sees a face she almost recognises, although she cannot place it. Probably someone who just looks like someone I once knew, she tells herself as they pile into the cab, grateful for its warmth.

That night, as she prepares for sleep, she lies in bed thinking of those good times with her own family. It is a sign of her gradual recovery, she feels, that she can allow herself a few memories: lighting candles for Hanukkah, singing 'Stille Nacht' around the Christmas tree. For years she has shut them firmly from her mind because she fears the way that grief can send you mad. She has seen it happen.

Slowly and tentatively she tests herself, choosing the memories carefully: Rosa at five, dancing to a tune on the radio; Willi with a toy car or lorry always clasped in his hand, even at mealtimes. Resting her head on her husband's chest, hearing his deep, reassuring voice rumbling into her ear ... No, that one is too painful, and she moves on quickly.

She recalls their apartment, how bright and airy it was, with its southerly views over the park. Then she remembers how they were forced to move into a smaller place: those dark, cramped rooms where the sunlight never seemed to reach, the dirty stairway and passageways that always smelled of stale cooking fat and worse.

And there is Mrs Geller standing in her doorway. The memory propels Miriam to sit up in bed, eyes wide, reaching for the bedside light switch. Dear God, Mrs Geller! Of course. Why has she not thought of contacting her before now?

How blind she has been. Rosa will have been searching too, but she has no idea that Miriam is in London, so she won't have been looking here. Instead, she will have been writing to anyone they used to know in Germany, and Mrs Geller would be an obvious starting point. The apartment building may not have survived the bombing, but surely it is worth a try. The post office used to provide a forwarding service. Will it be operating again now, nearly seven months after the end of the war?

And then, just as though a light has been switched on or a candle lit, she sees again that face from Trafalgar Square. Surely, she thinks, it was Marta Muller, the girl who lived on the other side of the landing in Hamburg, who was friendly with Rosa for a while. Great heavens, Marta Muller also in London? With a little boy in tow, too. The two friends, both in the same city – is it possible that she and Rosa know each other here?

After this, Miriam cannot sleep a wink. She goes to the small dressing table she has adapted as a desk by folding up the wings of the triple mirror – she prefers not to look at herself and certainly has no need for make-up or fancy hairstyles. She takes a sheet of writing paper and begins:

Liebe *Frau Geller,*

Greetings. I am sure that life has been very difficult for you over the past few years and that the Allied bombing may have affected our old building, but I pray this letter reaches you somehow, and finds you and your family well.

You might be surprised to learn that I am in London, having managed to obtain a visa to come here in search of my daughter, Rosa. Sadly the rest of my family perished in the camp, but I was fortunate enough to survive.

My purpose in writing is to ask whether you have received any news from Rosa. I wondered, too, whether the Muller family still live in the building, and if so, whether Marta may have heard from my daughter. The girls were such good friends. Would you be able to make discreet enquiries, perhaps?

The world is no longer the place we once knew, but I hope that one day we may meet again, in happier times.

Mit freundlichem Gruss,

Miriam Kauffman

This is the version she ends up with after several false starts, wasting precious sheets of writing paper. Next day she mails it, whispering, 'God speed, little letter' as it disappears into the depths of the tall red postbox on the corner of the street.

27

When Hans turned five, old enough to need his own bedroom, Rosa and Daniel moved into a new house, just down the road from Mrs Tanner. It is a terraced back-to-back, with just two rooms downstairs and two bedrooms up a steep flight of stairs, but it feels like a palace. It has no bathroom, but there is a proper water-flush toilet in a lean-to shed at the back of the house, and even a little yard where Hans can kick a ball about.

To celebrate their first Christmas in their new home, Rosa bought a small fir tree from a trader in Bethnal Green market. They set it up in the bay window of the front room and decorated it with coloured paper, topping it with a painted plaster angel given to them by Mrs Tanner. She would have liked to light a menorah at Hanukkah, but doing something so overtly Jewish still felt dangerous, even here in England, even now Hitler was dead and the war was over.

She and Daniel have learned to live alongside each other, so long as she succumbs to his nightly attentions. He never tells her that he loves her, and she feels nothing for him, but her work is fulfilling and little Hans is a constant source of joy. Following the passions of his English school friends, he has become an ardent supporter of West Ham football club, and they go to the park after school every day and each weekend so that he can play football with his friends.

These small delights of everyday life help to keep Rosa's mind from straying into the dark depths of fear about what fate has befallen her family. Weeks have passed since she wrote to her parents at the farmer's address, and there is still no news. Neither has there been any contact from the Jewish relief organisation.

Some days she finds herself actually content, and then feels guilty about it. How can she be truly happy when her family are missing, most likely murdered? The grief is how she imagines it might feel to lose a limb: painful all the time, but somehow you get used to coping.

And then, quite out of the blue, a letter with a German stamp arrives. The handwriting is unfamiliar – not Mrs Geller's. She opens the envelope and her eyes flick to the signature, not recognising it. Only as she reads the letter does she begin to understand.

Dear Mrs Cooper,

I am sorry it has taken me so long to reply to you. Unfortunately my father died recently and I discovered your letter when we were sorting out his possessions before selling the farm. Sadly, he never really recovered from the torture he received at the hands of the Gestapo during the war.

Before he died, he told me about your parents, and how fond he had become of them when they stayed on the farm to help him in the early part of the war. He especially doted on your little brother, Willi, and I know he was devastated about what happened to them.

Rosa finds that she has closed her eyes, too terrified to read on. She feels as though she is standing on the edge of a cliff, about to jump into the unknown. Can she bear to know what this unknown woman is about to tell her?

She is on a day off and Hans is due home from school any minute. She looks out of the window, up and down the street, but sees no sign of children in school uniform. She takes a breath and turns the page.

When my father learned that the police had become suspicious, he tried to arrange for your family to escape to Sweden with a local fisherman. But there must have been a network of agents working in the town, for they were betrayed.

Your parents and Willi were arrested near the quayside and taken away by the police, along with the fisherman. My father was also imprisoned but released after two months as they could not prove his involvement. Your family must have been very brave, for it seems they never gave my father away. For that we are eternally grateful.

I regret that I do not have any further knowledge of what happened to your family. If I can be of any help, though, please do not hesitate to let me know.

How vividly she can picture the scene: the three of them waiting for their contact at that little North Sea port, huddled together against the fierce winds that blow direct from the Arctic onto that bleak coastline for most of the year. Sensing his parents' anxiety, Willi would have been holding their hands, an intimacy he would normally have avoided at all costs. She can see her father's shoulders, sturdy as an oak, as he tried to be strong for his family. Having already experienced the brutality of the regime, he would have known only too well that there would be little mercy if they were caught.

Her imagination quails at what must have happened next. The sound of boots, the arrival of black-clad police or Gestapo – whatever they were called by then – the harsh voices, the heavy hands, the brandished guns. Her father would have gone quietly, knowing the fruitlessness of resistance. But Mama might have fought like a mother tiger, scrapping with whatever strength she had to protect her boy. To no avail, of course.

Later that evening, after Hans is in bed, she shows the letter to Daniel.

'Who's this from?'

'The daughter of the farmer my family stayed with.'

He reads it and puts it down with a sigh. 'At least now you know what happened, my dear. They were betrayed by local agents.'

'No. I think it was Steiner who betrayed them. Remember what Mrs Geller wrote? She thought he might be tracking my parents' correspondence – he must have discovered their address that way.'

'Everyone was betraying everyone else, Rosa. Surely his tentacles could not have reached that far?'

She will never be able to prove anything, of course, but she knows deep in her heart that Steiner tracked her family down and organised their arrest. It was an act of pure vindictiveness, for which she will never forgive him.

It is a small newspaper report – just a photo caption really – that changes everything. How she wishes that she had never seen it.

'What's your lunch shift?' Paula asks that day.

'Twelve to one. Yours?'

'The same. It's stopped raining for once. Shall we go to the Embankment? If we're quick off the mark, we'll get a bench.'

They are required to read the newspapers every day to keep up to date with current affairs – or, as Mrs Sidebottom calls it, 'gaining vital context for your work'. She sometimes tests them: 'What did the Prime Minister announce yesterday, girls?' or 'What is the latest situation in Romania?' Now, on their lunch break, they stop at a newsstand and purchase a copy of *The Times*, which they usually split into inner and outer pages, halving the task.

Today it is Rosa's turn to get the inside pages, which include the entertainment news. She tends to skate over this. It is unlikely to contain any 'vital context' for Mrs Sidebottom, and she isn't the slightest bit interested in the silly antics of film stars. She skims the headlines and is about to turn the page when her eye is caught by a photograph captioned *VERONICA MARSHALL MARRIES AGAIN*.

She has no idea who Veronica Marshall is and feels certain she has never seen any of her movies. Pretty young thing, she thinks, glancing briefly at the picture. But when her gaze strays to Veronica's beaming groom, her stomach flips. Surely not? It couldn't be him.

The caption continues: *Starlet Veronica Marshall weds up-and-coming director Eric Stewart, who is co-directing her new movie,* The Spanish Princess, *set in colonial Argentina. They will be filming at the Lumiton studios, Buenos Aires. Miss Marshall says, 'We are so looking forward to enjoying this new adventure together, as man and wife'.*

No, she must be imagining things. The photo is black and white, of course, and grainy, but the man looks so like Steiner. She peers at it again, more closely. He is wearing sunglasses and his hair is much darker than before, but how could she forget that thin face, the cleft chin, the smile that never looked genuine? Unless he has a twin brother, this is definitely Steiner.

Rosa has followed reports of the Nuremberg trials with reluctant fascination, appalled at the evidence emerging from witnesses and astounded by the photographs of the defendants. It is a source of constant astonishment that such evil men can look so very ordinary, like bank managers, or estate agents. The sheer mundanity of their accounts makes their crimes, the torture and mass killings of tens of thousands of Jews, gypsies and homosexuals, all the more shocking.

She assumed that Steiner would have been arrested and imprisoned – or at the very least would be living in secrecy. But here he is, fit and healthy, apparently unconcerned about arrest and even courting publicity with a beautiful new wife on his arm. How did he escape from Germany after the war, when the occupying forces had secured the borders so tightly? He has obviously anglicised his name, but how can he be so brazenly confident of immunity from the law? And whatever has happened to Alicia and their three children?

'What's up? You've gone very quiet,' Paula says. 'Something fascinating in the movie news, is it?'

Rosa passes the paper over. 'Look at this photo. This man is a Nazi criminal and he's free, living the life of Riley in South America.'

'How do you know he's a Nazi?'

'I met him in Hamburg.' Rosa feels light-headed even talking about him. 'How does he get away with it? Living so openly?'

Paula peers at the caption. 'Ah, that'll be why. He's in Argentina. The military dictatorship there is pro-Nazi and they've given plenty of them refuge. It's a safe haven, apparently.'

Rosa is silent, consumed with outrage. Steiner, the lawyer, the Nazi, now a film director? Her sandwich curdles in her stomach as she remembers him describing movie-making as his passion, the equipment set up in the marital bedroom, the whirr and click of the reels becoming the soundtrack to whatever new outrage he had chosen for that day's abuse. She had by then learned how to think of other things, to absent her mind from the scene so that the pain and indignity seemed to be happening to someone else. But the sound of the camera always brought her back into the room.

Paula nudges her. 'You haven't finished your lunch.'

'I'm not hungry,' Rosa says, gathering up the brown paper bag. 'C'mon, let's go.' She tears out the cutting and pockets it, then throws her sandwich and the rest of the entertainment news into a rubbish bin.

'What is it about that man in the photograph?' Paula asks as they reach the office. 'You went as white as a sheet.'

'I believe he betrayed my family. But I can't talk about it now, I'm sorry.'

'What a monster. You poor thing. But look,' Paula pauses outside the door, 'if you change your mind and do want to talk about it, I'm here.'

After that, Rosa finds it harder and harder to keep the memories at bay. At any time of the day or night, Steiner ambushes her thoughts, side-tracking her concentration and interrupting her conversations. Her work begins to suffer, and before long, Mrs Sidebottom invites her into the private office for 'a little chat'.

'Are you all right, Mrs Cooper?' she asks in the kindly manner that Rosa knows all too well conceals a tough-minded obduracy. 'You seem to be making a lot of silly mistakes at the moment. Quite unlike you, my dear.'

'Time of the month,' Rosa mutters.

'Then it's been that time for several weeks, Mrs Cooper. Do

you think you should see a doctor? We can arrange it for you, if you wish.'

'No, no. I've been feeling quite better these past few days, thank you. I promise my work will be perfect from now on.'

Mrs Tanner also senses something is wrong. '*Libinke*, sweet girl, you have dark rings under your eyes. Are you not sleeping?'

Rosa can fall asleep all right – she is exhausted – but always finds herself wide awake in the early hours. She tries getting up and making cocoa, reading a book, doing deep breathing. Nothing seems to work. For more than a week now, she's had no more than three hours' sleep each night, and Mrs Tanner's sympathy proves to be the last straw.

'Oh my dear,' the older woman says, offering a handkerchief. 'I'm so sorry. Was it something I said? Here, let me put the kettle on. Sit, sit, *meine kinder*, and tell me all about it.'

Slowly, haltingly, Rosa starts to tell the story. Not about the abuse, of course, but about Steiner's fury when she left his employment to get married, and what she feared may have happened to her family as a result of his betrayal. How she tried to put it from her mind and get on with her life, until the discovery of the newspaper photograph undermined her determination and now she can hardly go an hour without thinking about him.

'I am so angry that he's enjoying peace and prosperity after all the evil he's done. The leaders are being punished, but middling Nazis like him are just getting away with it. The anger is just eating me up and I don't know what to do about it.'

A few weeks later she arrives home to find an envelope on the kitchen table. It is stamped with the logo of the Central British Fund for Jewish Relief and Rehabilitation. Mrs Tanner – sitting with Hans as he eats his tea – gestures to it with a tilt of her head.

'Get yourself a cuppa, dear. The kettle's just boiled. You can take that and open it in your room if you wish. I've got time to stay another half an hour.'

The letter reads:

Dear Mrs Cooper,

I regret to tell you that I write with sad news. Records recently forwarded from Berlin confirm that a Mr and Mrs Kauffman of Hamburg and their son, Wilhelm Kauffman, were admitted to Auschwitz concentration camp on 4 April 1942. I am afraid we have no word, as yet, about survivors.

28

Now she knows for certain. She has read enough about the concentration camps, the gas chambers, the starvation, the typhoid and the death marches to know that hoping for any of her family to have survived is fruitless. But somehow she finds it impossible to cry. To cry is to accept that they are dead.

Instead she finds herself consumed with rage. It burns inside her like a volcano ready to erupt at any moment. It seems to bend her mind, and she wonders sometimes if she really is becoming slightly unhinged by it. She does irrational things like putting her coat in the larder, and sometimes buys the same item twice, forgetting that they already have plenty of, say, porridge oats. She finds it impossible to hold a reasonable conversation with anyone, and argues with Daniel over the tiniest thing. He grumbles that he can do nothing right, and she realises that his complaint is fully justified.

'You have to stop being like this,' he pleads, helplessly. 'I know it's tragic. But you have to remember that life goes on, and at the moment you are making that life a misery for everyone around you.'

Hans drops his toast on the floor, and Rosa shouts at him for wasting precious food.

'Sorry, Mama,' he mumbles into his chest, unable to meet her furious gaze.

She snaps at Mrs Tanner, who responds with typical bluntness. 'You're lucky I've turned up today. You was so rude to me yesterday, I was on the brink of handing in me notice.'

Rosa is shocked. She can't remember being rude until she recalls how Hans pushed his overcooked boiled egg away and she snapped at Mrs Tanner: 'Why do you never use the timer? You know he hates it like that.'

'I'm sorry, Mrs T,' she pleads now. 'I was out of order. Please don't go. We need you.'

One night she has the most graphic, realistic nightmare she has ever experienced: Steiner is pinning her down, leering over her, yet somehow she has a kitchen knife in her hand, and she plunges it into his neck from behind, again and again and again. The blood starts to drip from his face into hers, and the drip turns into a flood. Her mouth is full of his blood and it is choking her and she gasps, 'No no no no!'

It is only Daniel's hand on her shoulder, shaking her, calling her name, that rouses her from sleep. She falls into his arms with gratitude, slowly coming to understand that it was all just a terrible dream.

'What on earth was that all about?' he asks.

'I dreamed about killing Steiner.'

'Good plan.' He turns to look at the alarm clock on the bedside table. 'For goodness' sake, it is three in the morning. Go back to sleep.'

She doesn't, of course. She lies awake plotting revenge, and wondering whether the combination of loss and anger is actually causing her to lose her mind.

It isn't any easier in the office. She rushes through her work impatiently, caring little for accuracy and entirely unable to concentrate. Mrs Sidebottom invites her into the inner sanctum once more and shows her a manuscript covered in red ink corrections. 'This is your final warning. Pull your socks up sharpish, Mrs Cooper, or I'll have to let you go.'

Even Paula gets the rough end of Rosa's tongue. 'Don't bite my head off. I was only trying to help,' she says.

'I know, I'm sorry. I'm just so angry with that man. He betrayed my family, Paula. Had them sent to an extermination camp. The anger is just eating me up. It's so unfair. I resent anyone who hasn't suffered like this.'

At last Paula's patience snaps: 'Look, Rosa. There's been a war. Lots of people have died. I cannot imagine what you must be feeling, losing both of your parents and your brother. You've had a terrible shock and heaven knows I'm not sure how I'd be reacting, in your circumstances. But being so angry all the time isn't helping. You have to do something about it.'

'But what? What *can* I do about it?'

'Okay, let's consider the choices. You could forget about it.'

'Tried, doesn't work.'

'You could write to the prosecutors at Nuremberg with evidence of what he did to your family, and where he is now.'

'They're only dealing with the really senior people at the moment.'

'Go and see a psychiatrist, then.'

'I'm not a nutter, for goodness' sake,' Rosa snaps. 'Anyway, who can afford that?'

'Sorry, sorry, just a suggestion. Have you got any better ones?'

'I want to confront him and tell him to his face that he's a murderer.'

'Pah,' Paula scoffs. 'And what would that achieve?'

'The satisfaction of ruining his life by letting everyone know what he's done. Maybe getting him arrested.'

'Be realistic, Rosa. It's not going to happen, is it? How are you going to get to South America? The sea passage must take weeks and weeks, not to mention the cost.'

Rosa knows it is a ridiculous idea, but somehow talking about it seems to make it feel more possible. If he ever thought of her at all, Steiner would probably assume she was dead. What a shock it would be for him to discover that she is not only alive, but so much stronger now. The last time she saw him, she was a cowering wreck, apologising for leaving him. Apologising! When he'd been abusing her for months. How she wishes she could meet him face to face, to show him how she has survived. She would tell him that she had clear evidence of how he had hounded her family in the full knowledge that it would lead to their deaths. She would expose him for what he is, a murderer and an abuser.

But there is no point in wishing. Paula is right. Buenos Aires is the other side of the world. It would cost a fortune to get there. It's a ridiculous idea.

And then, on her way home that very day, fate seems to intervene. Walking along Piccadilly, she passes an airline office displaying a large poster featuring a colourfully costumed couple dancing the tango: *British South American Airways is delighted to announce its new route, London to Buenos Aires, launching September 1946.* People will actually be able to *fly* there? Improbable though it seems, here is the evidence before her very eyes, in large letters and bright primary colours.

She walks on, telling herself not to be so ridiculous. To go all that way and spend all that money – the fare is sure to be much more than she could afford – just to confront Steiner? Besides, how could she possibly leave Hans and Daniel, not to mention her job? She doesn't even have a proper passport, just identity papers. No, she must put the whole idea to the back of her mind and get on with her life.

Even so, at lunchtime in the park the next day, she finds herself telling Paula about the advert. 'D'you know, you will actually be able to fly to Buenos Aires from September?'

Paula raises an eyebrow. 'And may I ask why this is of interest? You're not still thinking of going there, are you?'

Rosa shakes her head. 'Oh, forget it.'

'And that is what I suggest *you* do, too,' Paula says firmly. 'You really do have to forget your obsession with this man. It is not for us to bring these individuals to justice.'

Rosa takes a bite of her sandwich and chews for a while, thinking. Is this really an obsession? How unreasonable is it to seek some kind of justice for her family? If they'd died of natural causes, or an accident, it would be so much easier to accept. But the fact that all the people she held most dear were wiped out by one man, probably at the stroke of a single signature, is impossible to forgive.

'Oh, I don't know, Paula. I can't stop being so angry about the fact that he's getting away with it, living his happy life with his pretty little wife when he effectively killed my family and brought such evil to so many. It's eating me up.'

Paula leans across and takes her hand. 'I'm so sorry, Rosa. I'm out of my depth here and don't know how to help you. I suppose you just have to get on with life, like everyone else.'

Soon afterwards, Rosa finds herself walking past the airline office again. No harm in discovering how much it would cost, she says to herself, taking a deep breath and stepping inside.

The sum they mention for the return ticket takes her breath away – it is more than four months' salary. Next day, she checks her bank account. She has been setting aside a small amount each week for eventualities such as Hans's education, or fares back to Germany when restrictions are eased. But four years of saving only amounts to a third of the fare. So that is that, then. She definitely isn't going. It was a crazy, stupid idea anyway.

She finds herself confiding in Marta the following weekend. They've become good friends again since the night in Trafalgar Square. They meet regularly and the two boys play happily together, leaving them plenty of time to reminisce about the old days and eat the delicious cakes that Rosa brings from a Swiss bakery near her office.

She explains about the newspaper cutting, and how she has even entertained the notion of flying to Argentina.

'Buenos Aires? You're crazy. It's the other side of the world,' Marta says.

'It's just that ... Oh, it's hard to explain. I'm so angry about how he betrayed my family. Guilty, too. If only I'd never gone to work for him. It's been eating me up. And if I could just tell him, threaten to expose him ... I don't know. It would let me get on with my life.'

'Why can't you just write to the Argentinian authorities?'

'They've been pro-Hitler since the thirties. Dozens of former Nazis have been given refuge there. It's well known, apparently.'

'I didn't know.'

'Nor I, but I'm told there's no point in trying to get them to do anything.'

'So that's that?'

'I'm afraid so. But it doesn't stop me lying awake at night imagining what I would say if I was ever ...' Rosa's voice cracks, tears pooling in her eyes.

'Oh, my dearest Rosa.' Marta is by her side with an arm around her shoulder, offering a handkerchief. Rosa takes it, wiping her face and saying sorry, so sorry for being such an idiot.

'Not an idiot. It's perfectly understandable. That man is a murderer, and he needs to be in prison, but there really is nothing you can do about it,' Marta says. 'You have darling Hans, a brilliant job and a good husband. We live in a country free from persecution and fear, where the rule of law is clear and fair. We have much to be thankful for.'

Rosa takes a breath, tries a weak smile. 'You are right, dear Marta, as ever. I need to look forward, not backwards all the time.'

'Here's to that.' Marta raises her teacup.

'Here's to that.'

Even though Rosa has tucked the newspaper cutting away in the back of a drawer, determined to forget it, the image of Steiner's self-satisfied face haunts her thoughts. 'I've got away with it,' it seems to say. 'Not only that, but I'm a film director and have married a beautiful starlet. Look at me, living a wonderful life.'

A few weeks later, she finds herself talking about it with Marta all over again.

'I can't get him out of my head,' she says.

Marta is about to say something, then stops.

'What is it?'

'I've been thinking, but ...'

'But?'

'I don't want to upset you again.'

'If I promise not to cry, will you tell me what you have been thinking?'

She takes a breath. 'What you really want to do is expose him, isn't it? To tell the rest of the world what he did in the war, and how he's got away with it.'

Rosa nods.

'I was talking to James about it the other day, and he suggested you might get in touch with our friend Frank Parker. He's a journalist.'

Rosa frowns. She's never had any dealings with newspapers and generally considers journalists to be an untrustworthy lot. 'What could an English journalist do about a man in Argentina?'

'He could contact the embassy there, for a start. Find out if the Argentinian government really are protecting ex-Nazis. The newspaper might have a foreign correspondent who works there. It could make quite a good story for them: "Film director revealed as Nazi murderer". Something like that.'

'How on earth do you know about such things, Marta?'

'Frank's an old school buddy of James's and he now works for *The Times*. I'm sure he'd do what he can.'

'But can you trust a newspaper?'

'I'd trust Frank. And I think he values his friendship with James sufficiently not to let you down. Give it a go.'

Rosa leaves Regent's Park with a card inscribed: *Frank Parker, The Times, 22 Fleet Street, London.* She puts it into her pocket and tries to forget the whole idea. The prospect of sharing her personal information with the rest of the world is just too daunting, even distasteful. But the journalist's name keeps appearing in the newspapers she and Paula are required to monitor. A busy man, this Frank Parker, she thinks. He reports on a wide range of topics, and seems to have a particular interest in politics.

Her journey home from work normally involves changing buses at Liverpool Street, but one day later that week, there are roadworks – something to do with removing rubble from bomb-damaged houses – and the bus stops at Threadneedle Street instead. She will have to walk to Liverpool Street to catch the next one home. Then she sees the sign: *Fleet Street*, and on the building in front of her, in enormous letters: *THE TIMES NEWSPAPERS.*

As she hesitates, a uniformed doorman appears at the top of the steps.

'Can I help you, madam?' he enquires politely.

'Erm, I don't think so, thank you,' she mutters.

'Was there someone you were waiting to see?'

The words are out of her mouth before she can stop them. 'Frank Parker.'

'If you would like to step this way, madam, I will enquire whether Mr Parker is available.' He holds the doors open and she walks through, feeling as though she is in a dream.

Rosa warms to Frank Parker from the very first moment she sees him bounding enthusiastically down the stairs to the foyer where she is waiting. He reminds her so much of Jack Preston – that easy laugh, the crinkly smile, freckled nose and curly hair – only Frank is older, in his thirties, she guesses. His suit jacket has clearly been thrown on so hastily that the collar is still turned in, his tie askew and his shirt crumpled.

She explains that she is a friend of James and Marta Wilson and wants to ask his advice about an escaped Nazi.

'Two excellent reasons for coming to see me,' he says, smiling even more broadly. 'Do you want to talk now?'

He leads her up the wide staircase and through an enormous, chaotically busy room that appears to occupy the whole first floor of the building. It reminds her of a warehouse, with electric lamps hanging from bare metal beams in the ceiling, and rows of paper-strewn desks at which men in shirtsleeves are typing or writing in longhand, cigarettes hanging from their lips. The air is blue with smoke, the noise tremendous: the clattering of typewriter keys, the crashing of their carriages and loud shouts across the desks. Coming from somewhere else in the building is a low rumble of heavy machinery that seems to shake the very floor they are standing on.

'Let's go in here, it's a bit quieter,' Frank says, ushering her into a small, cluttered office to the side of the newsroom and closing the door.

'Have a seat.' He clears two chairs of accumulated newspapers, books and magazines. 'Now, tell me about this Nazi.'

Rosa sits, feeling overwhelmed, uncertain: 'I'm not sure ...' she stutters.

'You can trust me.' He leans forward, holding her gaze. 'Let's say everything is off the record for the moment. The last thing I'd want to do is to cause a friend of James and Marta's any pain or embarrassment. It might be how some journos work, but it's not the way I operate. We won't publish anything until you are happy with it.'

After the first, faltering moments, the story pours out: how she went to work for Steiner, how angry he was when she resigned, swearing to take revenge on her family; her escape to England, how she learned of Steiner's rise to power within the party, the information she gathered from Mrs Geller and Mr Schmidt's daughter.

Frank studies her face with those hazel eyes. 'Is there something you're not telling me about this man, Mrs Cooper? Exactly why would he be so furious that you were leaving his employment? You were getting married, weren't you? Surely that's a perfectly legitimate excuse.'

The room feels suddenly hot and stuffy. 'I prefer not to say, Mr Parker.'

He nods. 'Fair enough. But it's quite a story, all the same. Do you know where this man is now?'

She tells him about the newspaper cutting and the photo of Steiner with his new wife filming at the Lumiton studios in Buenos Aires.

'Phuh. What these monsters get away with. It's outrageous. So now the real question is, what do you want from me?'

'I want to expose the fact that he has escaped from

Germany, and to confront him and tell him about the misery he has caused. And then I want him to be arrested for war crimes.'

He smiles. 'That's quite a tall order, Mrs Cooper. Especially when he's in Argentina.' He explains what she already knows: that because the Argentine authorities were sympathetic to the Nazi cause, Steiner will be virtually untouchable, while the Argentinian newspapers are afraid to run stories about fugitive war criminals.

'That wouldn't stop us telling the story in the British news-papers,' he says. 'Which might embarrass him, but it won't get him arrested. Can you leave it with me for a day or so? I have a colleague who spent some time in Buenos Aires. He may have people there we can ask. Where can I contact you?'

She is about to give her home address, and then realises that she can't risk it. Daniel would be instantly suspicious of a letter in an unknown hand, and furious – incandescent, even, she could imagine it right now – if she told him she'd been talking to a journalist. So she gives her work address.

'You work *there*, eh? I'm impressed,' Frank says, raising an eyebrow.

'I'm only a translator.'

'Even so,' he says with a knowing smile. 'Interesting place to work, I'm sure.'

A week passes, and Rosa begins to wonder whether she has simply imagined her visit to the *Times* newsroom and the meeting with Frank Parker. Was it all just a dream? She says nothing to anyone: not Paula, or Mrs T, and definitely not to Daniel.

The anger still smoulders: Steiner is not only alive, when her family and heaven knows how many other thousands are dead, but he is apparently enjoying a charmed life with a beau-tiful new wife and a sparkling new career. Where is the justice in that? The word echoes in her head, keeping her awake at night, distracting her by day. *Justice, justice, justice.* Even when she is thinking about something else, it is always there in the back of her mind.

But what hope has she got of confronting him when he is thousands of miles away?

29

She has almost given up hope of hearing from Frank Parker when Mrs Sidebottom appears at her desk with a letter in her hand.

'I sincerely hope that this is not *personal* correspondence, Mrs Cooper,' she says. 'You know that giving this address to anyone outside of work is absolutely forbidden?'

Rosa struggles for a credible response, but finding no inspiration, she decides to tell the truth. She must once have known about that rule but had momentarily forgotten, she explains carefully. She is very sorry. 'There won't be a next time, I promise.'

The letter burns a hole in her pocket until lunchtime. She is alone on their bench, since Paula is not at work that day. She opens it with trembling hands.

Dear Mrs Cooper,

I have checked out your story and Erich Steiner was indeed the Ortsgruppenleiter – *local group leader – for the Hamburg area. As such, he would have had oversight of all the Nazi*

*activities there, including rounding up Jews. He would most
certainly now be classified as a war criminal.*

*Our entertainment editor tells me that the London premiere of
a movie starring Veronica Marshall will be held at the Empire
cinema in Leicester Square within the next couple of weeks. It
is possible that Stewart might feel so confident of his new identity that he will accompany his wife. From what you told me,
he's probably arrogant enough to believe that he is immune
from prosecution. We shall have to wait and see. I will be in
touch when I find out more.*

Steiner coming to London? Rosa's heart starts to hammer as
she imagines him walking these streets, through this very park.
What would she do if she saw him coming towards her? Would
she have the courage to confront him?

'Hello, Erich. Remember me?' she imagines herself saying.
'It's Rosa, your dirty little Jewess. Remember that's what you
used to call me as you raped me? Remember the movies you
took, how you used to show them to your friends? How would
your pretty little new wife like to know about those, eh?'

She would show him the precious photograph of her family,
the one that she's carried with her for the past seven years. 'You
betrayed them, didn't you, sent them to their deaths? Well, I'm
still here, and I will bear witness in court when the authorities
track you down. You will pay for what you did.'

That is all she wants to achieve. From then on, Steiner
would have to live with fear, knowing that the police could
come knocking at any time. No more happy little life with his
starlet wife, his reputation in the film industry destroyed. He
would try to run, but the English police would be on the look-
out. He would be a fugitive once more. Even so, she would be
letting him off lightly.

Before leaving work that day, she pens a short reply to

Frank Parker, thanking him and asking him not to deliver any more notes to her work address: *Sorry, but they're not keen on personal letters arriving there. I will call at your office next week.* She gets off the bus at Fleet Street and leaves the note at the *Times* building.

She doesn't have to wait long. Three days later, she receives a letter from Marta: *Please get in touch with Frank Parker. He has urgent news and says you've asked him not to write to you. Sounds exciting. Very cloak-and-dagger. Keep me posted.*

Frank is in a more thoughtful mood when she calls in to see him the following day. Once again he ushers her into the tiny, untidy office. This time he takes out a crumpled pack of cigarettes. 'Smoke?' he asks.

She shakes her head. 'Marta said you had news.'

'It's confirmed. Veronica Marshall will be in London in a few days' time.' he says.

'Crikey.' She wishes she'd accepted that cigarette now. 'Is he coming too?'

'That's the thing,' he says. 'We have absolutely no idea. But it's a prestigious event, and they're newly married ...'

'He might decide to risk it.'

'Absolutely. But if he does decide to come, it's very unlikely that he will advertise it.'

'So how can we find out?'

'Only by going to Leicester Square that night.' He looks up at her for almost the first time.

'And if he's there?'

'You can confront him. Isn't that what you want? But there's a catch.'

'Which is?'

'We also need to make sure that he doesn't do a runner.'

'Where would he run to?'

'These people have friends, places of refuge, I suspect. So we should also inform the police, so that they can arrest him as a war criminal.'

'That's what I want. For him to go to trial at Nuremberg,' she says.

'That could take years. You wouldn't get the chance to confront him, and I wouldn't get my story, because once he's under arrest, all your testimony would be *sub judice*.'

'*Sub judice?*'

'It means that once legal proceedings have started, we can't report any of the details of the case publicly until after the trial.'

Suddenly everything seems to have become very complicated. 'So what is the alternative?'

'We do two things, separately and simultaneously,' he says, stubbing out his cigarette. 'We go to the cinema, and if he's there, you can confront him and I get the chance to take a photograph, which I can run with my story in the next morning's newspaper. I will also tell the police so they can arrest him before he scarpers back to Argentina.'

She's seen enough photographs of crowds outside movie premieres, the stars in their beautiful dresses smiling distractedly on the red carpet. 'But what if he just walks inside and ignores me?'

Frank reaches into his inside jacket pocket and pulls out a thick card. On it, in heavy black capital letters, is printed the word *PRESS*. 'The magic word,' he says, smiling now. 'It gets you close to the action.' He stands and goes to a tall metal filing cabinet, opening the top drawer and taking out a brown leather case the size of a hat box with long straps. 'You will be a photographer.'

The box is heavier than she imagined. She flicks open the catches and peers inside at the strange metal contraption nestled in soft fabric. 'But I've never used one of these in my life.'

'There's nothing to it with these modern machines,' he says cheerfully, and proceeds to give her a short training course on how to operate the heavy camera, how to focus the lens, how to click the metal lever to take the photograph. The camera has a strap that goes around her neck and means she can hold it steady without the need for a tripod. In the side pocket of the leather case is a zipped pouch containing rigid photo plates that must be changed between each image.

'You probably won't need to use it,' Frank says cheerfully. 'If we see Steiner, I'll take the camera and try to snap you talking to him.'

'A photo of me? Do you have to?' she asks, alarmed. 'Can't you just photograph him?'

He laughs. 'There has to be something in this for me, Mrs Cooper. You're getting to confront the man who murdered your family. I get a stonking good story for my newspaper, and the respect of my peers. But I need a photograph to illustrate it. "A picture is worth a thousand words." It's the mantra in the newspaper trade.'

He chuckles to himself, his mood seeming to lighten. 'My entertainment editor was more than a little surprised that I wanted to go to a film premiere. I'm a political journalist and haven't shown the slightest interest in show business before – in fact, I tease him about it being so frivolous – but I told him I had a crush on Veronica Marshall and he agreed to let me go.'

'And when is all this happening?'

'Thursday.'

Rosa's heart leaps in her chest. So soon?

'Meet me at Leicester Square Tube station, six o'clock sharp.'

30

Frank is already there, leaning against the tiled wall of the entrance to the station, lighting a cigarette. For a second time, she is struck by how much he reminds her of Jack. Something in his gestures, the way he holds the lighter, perhaps?

'Evening,' he says, so casually. 'Smoke?'

'No thanks.' She is about to have the most important and terrifying encounter of her life; her insides are coiled in knots and she's anxious to get on with it.

When she'd told Daniel where she was going this evening he'd gone crazy.

'What on earth . . .' he'd spluttered. 'You think you're righting the wrongs of the world by getting some stupid newspaper involved.'

'Without their help I wouldn't even have known he was coming to London.'

'It would have been far better if you didn't. You'll probably end up getting arrested yourself, you stupid woman.'

'Well, I'm going anyway. It's my only chance.'

'Then don't bother coming back,' he'd shouted, slamming the door behind her.

.   .   .

'Okay then,' Frank says now. 'Let's get going.' He hands over the camera case and pulls out the press badge on its long tape, slinging it around her neck.

Crowds are already gathering behind thick ropes in the street in front of the cinema, guarded by uniformed men with stern faces and plenty of braid. In the brilliant glare of the floodlights, the carpet covering the cinema foyer and the area of pavement in front of the doors is dazzlingly red. In the grainy monochrome press photographs it is always grey, and somehow Rosa imagined that 'red carpet' was just a turn of phrase used by show-business writers.

Frank beckons to one of the guards and shows his pass. 'Frank Parker, *The Times*. And my photographer, Mrs Cooper.' She marvels at his casual air.

'Over there.' The man lifts the rope to allow them to pass to an area where reporters and photographers are assembled among a thicket of tripods and film cameras, like a gathering of malign insects.

Several of them hail Frank like old friends.

'Whatcha doing here, Frank Parker? Bit lowbrow for you, isn't it, mate?'

'Slumming with the stars this evening, are ya? Prime ministers more your line, I'd have thought.'

'And who's this pretty young thing, you old devil?'

'New recruit to the snappers,' Frank says as he takes her elbow and leads her to a corner close to the doors.

'Take out the camera and fiddle with it as though you're getting it ready,' he whispers.

'And what do we do then?'

'We wait, watch the cars arriving and just hope he's come with her.'

After another moment, he nudges her again. 'The plain-clothes cops have arrived.'

She can only see the cinema security guards and a couple of police in uniform. 'Where?'

Frank tips his chin towards the opposite corner, where three well-built men in matching crumpled grey suits and fedora hats are lurking, trying to look inconspicuous in the crowd. Rosa allows herself a smile: what a cliché those hats are. But it is their alert expressions and darting eyes that really give them away.

The knots in her stomach tighten painfully as she watches them. She cannot quite believe that after all this time, she might soon come face to face with the man on whom she last set eyes when he spat at her as she left his apartment in Hamburg. She can feel the sting of his hand on her cheek even now. And those men are ready, waiting to arrest him on her say-so.

Frank has made some kind of gesture that gets their attention, and the tallest one lifts an eyebrow in acknowledgement, the slightest glimmer of a smile curling his lips.

'They're ready for him,' Frank whispers. 'As soon as you see Steiner, I'll call him over, but if he refuses to come, you'll have to approach him so I can get my photograph before the police move in.'

Time seems to slow down, and after what feels like an interminable wait, the first of the limousines arrives. Soon there is a parade of shiny black cars lining up to disgorge their cargoes of beautiful women in furs and ball gowns, smiles pasted on and jewels glittering in the floodlights, accompanied by men in dinner jackets. The photographers and pressmen burst into action, shouting a cacophony of questions. Rosa is astonished that they can recognise so many of the stars, especially the men, who all seem to look much the same.

'Over here, Miss Aldiss, if you please.'

'This way, Mr Drew. A quick word?'

'What do you make of our great London welcome, Miss Wilding? Having a good time?'

Some of the stars oblige, coming over to answer questions and signing the occasional autograph. Rosa is beginning to wonder whether Veronica Marshall has pulled out at the last minute, but at last the whisper goes round: 'Miss Marshall is on her way.'

And now it is happening. Out of the car emerges a strikingly beautiful young woman in a slinky blue silk gown that seems to cling to every curve. As she totters on improbably high heels towards the doors, the reporters call out again.

'Miss Marshall, over here, please.'

She turns towards them, blinking in the flash of a dozen cameras, smiling sweetly.

'How can I help y'all, fellas?' she drawls in an accent Rosa recognises from *Gone with the Wind*.

'How do you like London, Miss Marshall?' one asks.

'I like it just fine, guys.' She beams towards the waiting crowd. 'Y'all pulled through some tough times here, but at last we got peace, and there's a bright future for this city, I can tell.'

This woman is a goddess, tall, elegant and beautiful, her blonde hair perfectly coiffed, her teeth the whitest in the world. It is hard to believe that she is made of real flesh and blood, yet she is talking quite informally, as though chatting to friends. The crowd roars in approval: Rosa knows that the British are so grateful for US intervention in the war that anything American is the best thing since sliced bread.

She is so dazzled that she momentarily forgets to check the retinue of men following Veronica Marshall. Frank digs her in the ribs. 'Any of those fellas him?'

She scans the faces carefully, but none of them is Steiner. 'He's not here,' she whispers, feeling simultaneously relieved and deeply disappointed. She felt sure, somehow, that he would not be able to resist the reflected glory of walking the red carpet on the arm of his beautiful new wife. Perhaps he decided that the risk of being recognised was too great.

Suddenly a tall man appears in the crowd and shows a pass to one of the guards, who allows him to slip under the rope onto the carpet. Rosa stares at him intently. Could this be Steiner? If so, the disguise is remarkably effective: he is wearing glasses, his hair dyed brown, and is sporting a dark moustache, obviously also dyed. There is nothing left of the angular blonde man with the piercing blue eyes she grew to fear so much.

Then she sees Veronica Marshall discreetly blowing him a kiss. He returns the gesture, holding his fingers to his lips. Those hands, those long, elegant fingers, those perfectly manicured almond-shaped nails; Rosa will never forget them. All at once she knows that it is him: this man has the same upright bearing, the lift of his chin, the stride that claims the world as his own. The terror of those months in Hamburg floods back. How she suffered at those hands. The air around her seems to grow thick, making it hard to breathe.

'Over there,' she manages to whisper.

'Steiner? Sure?'

She nods.

Frank calls out, loud and bold: 'Mr Stewart? *Times* of London newspaper. Congratulations on your recent marriage to Miss Marshall. May we have a word?'

Steiner hesitates, but he is clearly flattered and there is a slight smile playing on his lips. Rosa can see that his figure is fuller, his face bronzed from the South American sunshine. 'She really is the most remarkable woman, such a talented actress,' he says in perfect American-accented English. But that voice, sharp as a knife, seems to slice into her heart.

He is just a few yards away, but even this close up, he clearly does not recognise her. How could she have forgotten how tall he is, how overbearing? Nearly two metres, he used to boast. Perfect for a man born to command.

She feels Frank nudging her. 'Now, Rosa, now!' he hisses. 'This is your chance.'

She takes a few steps towards him, forcing her lips into a smile. 'Erich Steiner?'

He frowns, appearing genuinely confused.

'Do you not remember me, Herr Steiner?' she says, in German.

'I do not understand you,' he answers in English.

She laughs out loud at the shameless effrontery. It was always his hallmark. 'I know it is you,' she says.

'Not me,' he replies, betraying himself by understanding her. 'Who is this Steiner you speak of? I am Eric Stewart, as you well know. And you can stop that snapping,' he shouts, clearly rattled now, flicking his hand towards the clicking cameramen.

'Stop pretending you don't remember me, Herr Steiner,' she says. 'I am Rosa Kauffman.'

He shrugs again, but his pretence is wavering. For a fleeting moment, she sees a flash of fear in his eyes, and a surge of power propels her to continue. Out of the corner of her eye she can see the uniformed guards moving towards them, ready to eject her, but the script she has rehearsed over and over comes easily to her lips.

'That's right, Rosa Kauffman, your dirty little Jewess. That's what you used to call me. Remember the movies you took as you raped me, how you used to show them to your friends? How would your pretty new wife like to know about those, eh?'

'I haven't a clue what you are talking about.'

'Ah, but you do, Erich Steiner. And you understand every word of what I am saying.'

He glares at her, his jaw working, fists twitching at his side. '*Scheisse*,' he hisses under his breath. '*Verpiss dich, du dumme Judenschlampe.*'

She pulls the photograph of her family from her pocket and holds it up with trembling fingers. 'Remember these people,

Erich? This is the family you betrayed, who you sent to the concentration camps to be murdered.'

The punch comes out of the blue. She didn't even see it coming, but the pain in her cheek is sharp and instant and the force of it knocks her from her feet. She stumbles, slamming her head on the side of a pillar before slumping to the ground.

After that, everything is a blur. She hears the shocked gasps of several hundred people in the crowd, and sees the dark-clad legs of the plain-clothes men rushing past her. 'Mr Stewart? Come with us. You are under arrest.'

She hears Frank swearing. 'Call an ambulance,' he shouts. 'Hurry.'

He is crouching by her side, cradling her head and whispering, 'Help is coming, Rosa. You'll be fine.' And that is the last thing she remembers.

31

Miriam is always first downstairs in the morning and the post arrives early, so she usually sorts it and leaves it in two piles on the hall table. There is rarely anything addressed to her, apart from the occasional letter from Jack, but this time it is impossible to miss the envelope with her name written in that distinctive German handwriting, bearing a German stamp. She tears it open with trembling fingers. It is more than three months since she wrote to Frau Geller, and she had almost given up, assuming she must have moved away and left no new address.

Liebe *Miriam,*

It is truly the greatest joy to learn that you are still alive, although I am so sorry to learn about Hans and Willi.

I am sorry it has taken so long to reply. Your letter was forwarded by the Hamburg post office, as our apartment block was destroyed in 1943. Happily by then I had already moved to the village of Hochenkirke, just thirty kilometres north, where my old mother lived, although she is sadly no longer with us.

Rosa wrote to me just a few months ago seeking news of you and her family, but unfortunately I was unable to help. She and Daniel have changed their surname to Cooper. Her address is 33 Blenheim Street, Bethnal Green, London.

I wish you every good fortune in finding your daughter.

Mit freundlichem Gruss,

Helga Geller

Miriam lets out a yelp of delight and sits on the lower step of the staircase, reading and rereading the letter. Rosa is here, in London. Her heart floods with gratitude. If she believed in a God, she would have thanked Him, but instead she just thanks the fates that have somehow delivered them to each other.

And now she understands why her search was so fruitless, why no one was able to help. Rosa and Daniel have changed their names.

'*Rosa, oh mein schatz Rosa. Ich bin auf dem Weg,*' she whispers. I am coming to you.

On her way to the bus stop, she sends a telegram to Jack: *HAVE FOUND ROSA STOP LIVING LONDON STOP VISITING TODAY WILL UPDATE SOON STOP MIRIAM.*

Sitting on the bus as it sweeps along the Embankment, with the Thames glittering to her right and the grand white buildings to her left, she hugs herself, imagining his delight, remembering the way his eyes lit up when they talked about Rosa across the table in Fortnum and Mason's tearoom, his silent acknowledgement when she asked whether he felt her presence in the way she did. She feels sure that he will come just as soon as he can.

She has to catch three buses to the East End, and the journey takes nearly an hour and a half because the route is constantly disrupted by falls of masonry and workmen mending pipes. Even now, nearly a year after the end of the war, evidence of the Blitz is everywhere, and in some places the process of reconstruction appears barely to have started.

She alights and walks around the corner: *Blenheim Street*, announces the sign. On the corner is a small shop, a newsagent and general store, with a billboard outside: *WOMAN CRITICAL AFTER INCIDENT AT FILM PREMIERE.* She takes little notice; she couldn't care less about film premieres. They are a world away from what is about to happen, an event that will change her life: seeing her daughter again for the first time in seven years.

The houses are narrow and piled up against each other like dominoes, front doors opening directly onto the street. At least they are largely intact; there are no snag-tooth gaps left by the bombing as in so many other streets. But the buildings are down at heel, with peeling paintwork and broken windows mended with tape. Some even have shrubs growing out of the guttering. As she walks along, counting the numbers, motherly concern rises in her chest: poor Rosa, living in such a run-down area.

Coming down the street towards her is an older lady, a grandmotherly type, with a young boy of, she guesses, about six years old. He has a mop of dark hair, a little like Willi at that age.

'Afternoon,' the woman says as they approach. 'Rain's holding off, at least.'

'Good afternoon,' Miriam replies, surprised. They don't greet strangers in the street in Knightsbridge. She feels a tinge of envy as they pass, the boy skipping along, holding the woman's hand. They are chatting about what she will cook for his tea, and both are laughing. Perhaps one day that will be me with my grandchild, Miriam thinks, as the pair slip out of sight.

A few moments later, she is standing outside number 33, waiting for a response to her knock, her heart pounding so hard she can scarcely catch her breath. She waits and waits, knocks again and waits some more. She cannot believe that she is actually here on her daughter's doorstep, and that any moment now, Rosa will open the door and fall into her arms. How vividly she has imagined their meeting, their embrace, the tears.

She steps back and looks up at the house. Unlike the rest of the street, the paintwork looks fresh and new, the brass knocker polished. There are flowers in the window box. Her heart lifts. Rosa was always so house-proud, her room always pin-neat. She recalls the compliments relayed from her employer to Mrs Geller, his wife's friend: 'She's a great little housekeeper, your daughter. Nothing is ever too much.'

She takes a step forward to peer into the front window, trying to see through the lace curtains, and then retreats sharply when a neighbour appears at her own front door, just a few feet away.

'Can I help?' the woman asks with a suspicious glance.

'I believe my daughter lives here,' Miriam says. 'Rosa Lev ... er, no, Cooper. Rosa Cooper.' Why have they chosen Cooper? she wonders. Such an ordinary, unpoetic name.

The woman looks sceptical. 'They're all out,' she says curtly.

'Do you know when they will return?' Miriam asks.

'Not till late afternoon usually.'

Miriam thanks her, and she disappears.

What to do now? After all the excitement of receiving Mrs Geller's letter, the anticipation of this longed-for meeting and the very real prospect of actually being able to hold her daughter at last, she feels like a deflated balloon.

She takes a seat on a low wall and waits, grateful that the rain is indeed holding off and wishing she'd asked more questions of the neighbour. She considers knocking again, but decides not to be a nuisance. The woman said they were 'all' out, which sounds like more than just a couple. Perhaps they have a lodger. That's probably it. So where are they? She assumes that both Daniel and Rosa are at work. What kind of jobs do they have? As far as she knows, Rosa has no skills beyond domestic ones, although she does speak good English, at least.

Time drags by. A bell chimes somewhere in the distance. At least one church tower has survived the German bombs. So many in central London were destroyed. Half past three, four o'clock, then half past. She walks around to stretch her legs but always keeping number 33 in sight. People go about their everyday occupations: sweeping doorsteps, cleaning windows, pushing prams and returning with loads of shopping, and she wonders what life in London has been like for her daughter. Has she made friends? Dare she hope that Rosa and Daniel have produced a grandchild for her? Or grandchildren – there's been time enough. Above all, has she been happy?

At first she barely recognises the man coming down the street towards her, carrying a bag. Daniel, the once smart, stiffly formal young man she waved off from the station that day in 1939, looks exhausted and careworn. His scuffed cord trousers and tweed jacket have definitely seen better days. His hair is tousled, grown longer than his mother would ever have allowed back in Germany, and his cheeks are dark with stubble. He is also taller than she remembers – or has she shrunk?

She leaps to her feet. 'Daniel? It's me, Miriam Kauffman. Rosa's mother.' The German feels strange and lumpy in her mouth. She hasn't spoken it for many months.

He stops in his tracks, gaping at her, and puts down the bag he is carrying. It clinks, sounding like bottles. 'Great God. Is it really you? Miriam Kauffman?'

'Is Rosa with you?' Miriam says, brisk with impatience.

Surely any moment now her daughter will appear. She can hardly breathe for the anticipation.

'Rosa? Oh, um, no. She isn't here, I'm afraid. Not right now.' Daniel seems confused, stumbling over his words.

'May I come in?' Miriam asks.

Again he falters. 'Um ... Yes. Of course. We're in a bit of a muddle, I'm afraid,' he says, putting his key into the lock and ushering her inside.

The front door leads directly into a living room, modestly furnished, with two chintz-covered armchairs and some cheap pictures on the wall – one of the Alps, she notices. The place is in a mess. Precarious piles of dirty plates, glasses and bottles cover a low table to one side, and the air is pungent with the smell of cigarettes and stale beer. Rosa would never leave her house in such a state.

'Where is she, Daniel? Is she still at work?'

He shakes his head before slumping into a chair and lighting a cigarette. 'I told her not to, but she would do it. Chasing after that bloody man.'

'Do what, Daniel?' He's speaking in riddles and she feels like shaking him.

'She was talking some rubbish about going to find Steiner. The man she worked for in Hamburg.' Reaching into the bag, he takes out a bottle, flicks off the top and gulps from it.

Miriam frowns, trying to make sense of what he's saying. Whatever is Rosa doing going after Erich Steiner? And what on earth is the man doing in England? She racks her brains, trying to recall something, anything that Rosa might have hinted at. It is all so long ago now, so far away. She has lived many lifetimes since then. Suddenly she remembers: didn't Rosa warn them that Steiner was a member of the Nazi party? So why would she run away with such a man? Nothing makes sense.

'Do you know where she is now?' she finally manages to ask.

'At the hospital.'

Another riddle. 'Hospital? Is she a nurse? Does she work there?'

He shakes his head.

'What? Is she hurt?' Icy fear runs through Miriam's veins.

'It's not good.' His voice cracks and his chest heaves.

'What do you mean, not good?'

He puts down the bottle and rests his head in his hands, as though it is too heavy for his neck. She feels like shaking him.

'Tell me, Daniel. What has happened? Was it an accident? Where is she? Can we go at once?'

'St Thomas's Hospital,' he mumbles.

'Where's that?'

'Just south of the river at Westminster Bridge.'

'Then we'd better get going. Let's go together.' She is already turning for the door.

'Just give me a few minutes,' he says, picking up his beer bottle again. 'Visiting time doesn't start till seven.' He remains stolidly in his chair, and she is losing patience. Any minute now she will storm out and go without him.

'What happened, Daniel?' she asks again.

'Bloody man pushed her. Fractured skull, apparently. She's still unconscious.'

Heavens, could the news get any worse? 'Which man?'

'I only know what it says in the newspaper. That it was Steiner. Or Stewart, as he calls himself these days.'

'Where did this happen?'

'Leicester Square. At the cinema.'

'Whatever was she doing there?'

'She was with a journalist, apparently.'

'Have you got the newspaper?'

He reaches into his bag and pulls it out, handing it to her. It is folded open at the headline: *WOMAN CRITICAL AFTER INCIDENT AT FILM PREMIERE, by Frank Parker.*

Miriam gasps: the same story that she noticed on the billboard. Her daughter is headline news.

A grainy photograph shows a tall, thin-faced man with a dark moustache and glasses. Also in the photograph, with her back half turned to the camera is a woman. Miriam realises with a sick jolt that this is Rosa. The words blur as her eyes rush down the column, struggling to take it in.

> *Eric Stewart, film director husband of American starlet Veronica Marshall, was arrested following an incident at the Empire cinema, Leicester Square, last night. They were attending the premiere of the movie* One Day in Paris, *in which his wife stars.*

> *Mrs Rosa Cooper, 26, was in conversation with Mr Stewart when she was punched to the ground. She was taken to St Thomas's Hospital, where she is said to have a fracture of the skull and is gravely ill.*

> *A source close to Mrs Cooper has suggested that Mr Stewart is in fact a former Nazi commander, Erich Steiner. Mrs Cooper was formerly resident in Hamburg, Germany.*

'Gravely ill. Whatever does that mean?' Miriam gasps. Of the grave?

'She may recover, because she's young and strong, they said.'

'*May* recover? Does that mean there's a possibility she might not?'

'That's what they said. It's difficult with head injuries.'

'She might die?'

He nods, face lowered. 'Suppose so.'

The ground has shifted beneath Miriam's feet. She has begun to take for granted the feeling of safety, of protection, that

England has offered her, but now the fear of random, unpredictable violence that they lived with every day, every hour, in Hamburg, has come to London. And Rosa, her beloved daughter, is in mortal danger once more.

'Look, I don't care about visiting hours. I'm going to the hospital *now*. Are you coming with me?'

He shrugs, takes another swig of beer.

'Then I'll go on my own.' She turns and makes for the door. 'See you soon, Daniel.'

As she strides back down Blenheim Street, she hears his footsteps behind her. 'Okay, okay, I'm coming too,' he pants as he draws up alongside beside her. 'Look, please don't blame me, Mrs Kauffman. I tried to dissuade her.'

'Why would I blame *you*? She's always been hot-headed, as you well know. But how on earth did she discover Steiner was in England?'

They reach the bus stop, and as she turns to look at him, she sees how gaunt his face has become. Time has not treated Daniel kindly, she thinks to herself.

'It was that wretched newspaper,' he says, taking out a packet of cigarettes and offering it to her.

'No, thank you.'

His hand trembles as he holds the match, and she wonders how long he has been drinking.

'The journalist who wrote the report, perhaps?' she says, peering down the road, willing the bus to arrive.

He shrugs. 'Who knows? I've never met this man Frank Parker, and I've got no idea how she would know him. She works at some government office or other, as a translator.'

Despite her anxiety, Miriam feels a momentary lift of pride. Her daughter, working in a government office, doing an important job, even without the university degree she longed to achieve, and having arrived in the UK as a refugee, with almost nothing.

At last, the red double-decker comes into view and pulls to a stop, and they climb to the top deck. It has always given Miriam a childish thrill, riding along on the level of the first storeys of the passing buildings, being able to see glimpses of people's lives through their windows, and into their gardens. But today all she can think of is Rosa.

'What about you, Daniel? Are you working?' she asks, to break the silence.

He hesitates. 'Yes, I'm the floor manager at an engineering company. It's not bad, though the pay is poor.' He pauses and turns to her, his eyes focusing and softening, as though recognising her properly for the first time. 'We never expected to see you again, you know. Rosa was told you'd been taken to the camps. She'll be so ...' He breaks off.

'We *were* taken to the camp.' Miriam lowers her voice. 'To Auschwitz. Hans and Willi were killed. I never saw them again.'

'*Scheisse,*' he hisses. 'I'm sorry. Those bastards.'

'Have you any news of your family?'

He sighs. 'Only that they too were transported to a camp. I was going to ask at the Jewish Relief place but they told Rosa the liberations were so chaotic, it may take months, even years ...'

'I'm so sorry, Daniel. Even though I was there and saw it for myself, it's hard to believe.'

'How did *you* survive, Miriam?'

'Luck,' she says simply. It is too shameful. She will never tell anyone about the warehouse where they sorted through the belongings of dead people. 'Just luck.'

'I hope my family had that kind of luck. But as time goes by, it seems less and less likely,' he whispers.

The enormity of their losses silences them both for a few moments. She watches the East End of London passing by,

Saturday markets taking place among the bomb-damaged streets, people greeting each other, laughing, children playing.

'They may never meet their grandson,' he says, out of the blue.

'Your sister has a son?'

'No, *we* have a son. Rosa and me.'

'You have a son?' She repeats it in her head, trying to focus. Can this really be true? 'I have a *grandson*?' she repeats, too loudly. *Mein enkel*. My grandson. I am a grandmother! She wants to embrace him, but holds back, placing a hand on his arm instead. There are other people on the bus, staring at them. 'What wonderful news. Congratulations. What's his name, Daniel? How old is he?'

'Hans. He's six.'

'Hans? After her father?'

'And my grandfather.' Another Hans. She rolls the name around on her tongue. Hans, my little Hans. *Hänschen klein. Hübscher Junge.* She smiles to herself, picturing the little boy already, dark hair, big brown eyes looking up at her, the heat of his small body on her lap. The next generation. How proud her dearest Hans would be to know that his grandchild had been named after him. She will tell little Hans all about his grandpa and his uncle Willi, how they would have been had they lived.

The image of Hans and Willi being led away at the camp invades her mind, Hans whispering in his son's ear. They both smiled bravely and gave tiny, discreet waves before a guard shouted and shoved them forwards, onwards with all the other men.

She returns to the present, to the bus, to Daniel. 'But where is he today?'

'With Mrs Tanner, our childminder. She collects him from school each day, but now she's offered to have him till Rosa is ...' He stutters to a halt. 'He's happy there. We can go and see him later, if you want. It's only down the road.'

'Tell me about him,' she says.

It is the first time she has seen Daniel smile. 'He's tall for his age, and handsome, of course. Everyone says how much he looks like me. He's bright, and funny, and clever, and he loves West Ham football club more than anything in the world.'

'The children here are crazy about football, aren't they? Does he play, too?'

For the first time, it feels as though she and Daniel are having a normal conversation, mother-in-law to son-in-law.

'Oh yes, every weekend, in Victoria Park. A proper English kid. I usually take him, but ...' He tails off as the bus draws up to their stop outside St Thomas's Hospital, and they glance at each other, reminded of why they are here.

32

Inside this building my daughter is fighting for her life, Miriam thinks as they climb down from the bus. It is just past six o'clock, according to the clock on the wall in the foyer of the hospital.

A starched-looking matron regards them fiercely: 'No visitors till seven.'

'It's my wife,' Daniel says. 'Rosa Cooper, the woman who was punched in Leicester Square last night. She is gravely ill. We don't mind waiting, but please can you tell us how she is?'

The woman huffs and disappears. Miriam's heart is pounding so hard she's afraid it might simply pack up. And what if the news is bad? What if Rosa has taken a turn overnight? What if the matron returns with a solemn expression and tells them that Rosa has passed away? She feels dizzy with dread.

The matron reappears with a clipboard. 'What name again?'

'Rosa Cooper,' Daniel says.

She traces her finger down a list, then turns the page and with slow, painful deliberation traces almost to the bottom of that, too. 'Ah yes, Bluebell Ward. You'll have to wait until seven, though, as I said. It is supper time for the patients, you understand.'

Miriam has been determined not to beg, but the tension is too great and the words now burst from her mouth. 'Please, I have travelled so far, waited so long. She is my only child – the rest of my family were killed in the camps, you understand. I haven't seen her for seven years. Seven years! And you tell me I have to wait another whole hour. Have you no pity?'

'Listen, madam, if we made an exception—'

She is interrupted by the appearance of a grey-haired, avuncular-looking man. Judging by his white coat and his air of authority, he is obviously a doctor. 'Is there something I can help with?' he asks mildly.

'These people ...' the matron begins, and at the same time Daniel says, 'We want to see Rosa Cooper. I am her husband, and this is her mother. They haven't seen each other for seven years.'

The man nods, with a kindly smile. 'Let me deal with this, Matron,' he murmurs, and she backs away, scowling.

'Now, what you need to know is that Mrs Cooper has a fractured skull and is still unconscious, but her condition is stable for the moment.' Miriam's racing heart eases just a fraction. 'There is still a long way to go, however. Head injuries are very hard to predict. You can see her, of course you can, but I ask you to respect the rules of the hospital.' He reaches for his pocket watch. 'The other patients are having their meals at the moment, so the staff are very busy but in just under an hour, you will be able to sit with her, for a short while only, please. Bluebell Ward, where we have our critical patients, is just up there, on the left-hand side. Meanwhile, please take a seat down here. It won't be long.'

Those fifty minutes feel like a lifetime. They make sporadic attempts at conversation, but their whispers echo discourag-

ingly around the cavernous entrance hall. At last the clock
chimes and the bossy matron shouts: 'Visiting time. Just one
hour. All out by eight.'

They climb the stairs and follow the green signs to Bluebell
Ward. A nurse in a crisply starched blue and white uniform
greets them.

'Who are you here to see, please?'

'Mrs Rosa Cooper,' Daniel says.

She checks her clipboard. 'Ah yes. Next of kin only. And
you are?'

'Daniel Cooper, her husband, and Mrs Miriam Kauffman,
her mother.'

'Follow me.'

They pass at least a dozen beds lining the sides of the long
room and reach an area partitioned off with wooden panels.
Miriam can see that there are four beds there, each containing a
long white motionless hump with a face at the pillow end. She
struggles to recognise her daughter, but fails.

The nurse is speaking again, in a low voice. 'You understand
that Mrs Cooper has not yet regained consciousness and is still
seriously ill. You can have just ten minutes.'

And now they are at the bedside. Rosa's face is disfigured by
a large reddish-purple swelling below her right eye and across
her cheek, but the rest of her is deathly pale, hands folded
neatly across her chest. She looks as though she is asleep and
could open her eyes at any moment. Her hair is darker and
longer than Miriam remembers, brushed out across the pillow –
she feels a swell of gratitude for the care she has been given
here.

'Can I kiss her?' she asks the nurse.

'Gently, mind. You can hold her hand and talk to her, too.
In fact we believe that talking to patients in this state may actually help them recover consciousness more quickly, especially if
it is familiar voices.'

She cradles Rosa's face in her hands, then kisses her on both cheeks. 'Rosa, my darling girl,' she whispers. 'I am here, your mama. I have come such a long way to see you.' The words choke in her throat. Her heart feels as though it might break, here and now. Aware of Daniel on the other side of the bed, she stands back to allow him to kiss his wife, but he doesn't seem interested.

She sits down and strokes Rosa's hand, willing her to respond. She squeezes it gently: the flesh is warm and a pulse moves beneath the pale skin, but it is otherwise terrifyingly lifeless. She takes a deep breath to calm her racing heart, reminding herself that she too was unconscious, for three whole weeks, in the convent hospital, and she recovered with no apparent ill effects. There is no reason why Rosa cannot do the same.

'My dearest girl,' she starts. 'You have to wake up now, because I have come so far to see you today, and we only have a short while. If you can hear me, please squeeze my hand, or move your head. Anything just to show that you know we are here.'

There is no reaction.

'Look, Daniel is here too. He told me about your lovely boy Hans, my darling. I am so, so proud of you, and cannot wait to meet my grandson. Perhaps we will bring him to see you when you are feeling better. Would you like that?'

She looks across the bed at Daniel. He shrugs and turns his face away, and she wonders what is going through his mind. Perhaps he is simply paralysed with fear that Rosa will never wake up, that little Hans may never see his mother again.

'It's been a long, long journey for me, my darling. I was in the camps but I managed to survive.' It is on the tip of her tongue to mention Hans and Willi, but she stops short. If Rosa can hear her, it will not help her recovery to learn that her beloved father and younger brother are dead. 'Anyway,' she carries on, 'I walked all the way to the border, and with the help of a charming young officer, I was given papers to come to England to find you. I have been living with a lovely family as their housekeeper in Knightsbridge, and searching everywhere I could think of to find you. In the end, it was Mrs Geller who told me. Remember that you wrote to her looking for me? Praise God that my letter reached her and she replied.'

Rosa's expression is as blank as ever, her hand just as limp and unresponsive. The nurse approaches and peers around the panels: 'Two minutes, please.'

Surely not already? 'Do you want to say anything, Daniel?'

He shakes his head. 'What's the point,' he says. 'She can't hear us anyway.'

Miriam shushes him with a finger to her lips. 'You don't know that. What if she *can* hear? Tell her about Hans, for heaven's sake.'

'What can I say?' He shuffles in his seat, looking embarrassed, and she understands now that the root of his coldness is actually self-consciousness. She needs to engage him in conversation. 'Where is Hans today, Daniel?' she says, rather too loudly.

'He's with Mrs Tanner, and I think they are going to the park,' he replies.

'What does he like doing in the park?'

'Playing football, of course, like I told you. Never goes anywhere without his ball.'

'Does Mrs Tanner play with him?'

Daniel scoffs. 'She's too old to run around after him, but he usually finds a friend of his own age to play with.'

Miriam squeezes Rosa's hand. 'You see, Rosa, your little boy is in good hands, so you mustn't worry about him. And I am sure you will wake up soon and then we can bring him in to see you. Isn't that worth opening your eyes for?'

She pauses, scanning her daughter's face, hoping for just the tiniest twitch of an eyelid, or movement of her lips, but there is nothing. The gentle breathing continues just as before, the hand lies motionless in her own.

The nurse returns and announces that time is up.

Miriam can hardly bear to leave. It seems too cruel to tear her away so soon. 'It's taken us such a long time to travel here,' she pleads, but the woman shakes her head.

'Doctor's orders,' she says. 'It is for the good of the patient. We don't want to tire her. She needs all her strength to recover. Perhaps tomorrow you will be able to stay a little longer. We'll see what the doctor says.'

As they leave, they see a scruffy-looking man at the entrance to the ward, carrying a large bunch of flowers, and hear the matron ask: 'Who are you here to see, sir?'

'Rosa Cooper.'

Miriam can sense Daniel tensing beside her as the matron explains that only next of kin are allowed to visit Mrs Cooper, but that she will take the flowers and show them to her when she regains consciousness.

'That's a shame, but thank you anyway, Matron.' The man hands over the flowers. 'There's a card attached.'

'Who's that? Someone you know?' Miriam whispers, but Daniel is already striding towards the man.

'Hello,' he booms. 'Let me introduce myself. Daniel Cooper, Rosa's husband.'

The man darts a glance at Miriam, as though trying to gauge the situation. 'And I am Rosa's mother,' she says. 'Miriam Kauffman.'

He seems momentarily taken off guard, but gathers himself and holds out a hand. 'Frank Parker, *The Times* newspaper. Pleased to meet you.'

Daniel recoils. 'What? You ...' Words fail him for a second, and then he begins to shout. 'Matron? Get this man out of here.

At once! He's that low-life journalist who wrote the story about my wife.' His hands bunch into fists.

Mr Parker is trying to explain. 'All I want is to see how Mrs Cooper is getting on, and bring her some flowers. I was at the premiere with her when that brute punched her. I stayed with her till the ambulance came.'

'You were ... What on earth ...?'

'I think you'd better explain,' Miriam says. She turns to the matron. 'Don't worry, I think we can sort this out.' She draws the two men away from the entrance to the ward and into the corridor. Daniel is still bristling, but she senses that Mr Parker, despite his untidy appearance, is actually a reasonable sort of man. She likes his face. His curly hair and gentle expression remind her a little of Jack Preston.

'Let's have a sensible conversation,' she says. 'First of all, Mr Parker, you need to know that my daughter is still unconscious and the doctors cannot predict when she will wake up, but they say her condition is stable, whatever that means.'

'Thank goodness. It was such a shock to all of us. I was really worried about her.'

'But what we want to know is why she was at this premiere in the first place. I understand that she went there to meet Erich Steiner?'

'That's right.' He rubs his chin, clearly considering how much to tell them. A considerate man, Miriam senses, not the hard-bitten type of journalist the movies like to portray.

'I am a friend of a friend,' he starts. 'My school friend married a German girl called Marta Muller, and it turns out that Marta and Mrs Cooper know each other from Hamburg.'

'Marta Muller? Good heavens. The Mullers were neighbours of ours. Rosa and Marta were good friends. And you say she is in England?'

'Yes, married with a son the same age as Hans. She's Marta Wilson now.'

'How extraordinary.'

'It seems that when Mrs Cooper discovered that Erich Steiner had escaped from Germany after the war, she wanted to find out more about him, and Marta suggested she contact me. I was able to discover that his new wife, who is a film star, was coming to London, and we took a chance that he might come with her, travelling incognito. And that is exactly what happened.'

Daniel cuts in, his voice low and threatening. 'Did you not consider that might have been a dangerous thing to do, encouraging my wife to confront a former Nazi and threaten to expose his identity?'

'Of course we knew he would be surprised and probably angry, but we had absolutely no reason to think that he might actually attack her in public, with the police watching.'

'He's been arrested now, though, hasn't he?'

Mr Parker nods. 'We had alerted the police in advance. It was all carefully planned. And that is exactly what Mrs Cooper wanted: to see him brought to justice for his ...' he pauses, weighing his words, 'his activities in the Nazi party. He's also been charged with assault.'

'And my wife is lying unconscious in a hospital bed, and her son is motherless,' Daniel says.

'Not motherless,' Miriam chides. 'She'll recover soon, I'm sure of it. Thank you for your explanation, Mr Parker.' There are so many more questions she wants to ask, but they can wait for another day.

As they are preparing to leave, Frank Parker says: 'Forgive me, Mrs Kauffman, but does your daughter know you are here? In England, I mean? She told me all her family had been killed in the camps.'

'I was lucky,' Miriam says. 'The rest of our family were not so fortunate. But I survived, and have been looking for Rosa for nearly a year. And now I am here, and we are just praying that she will wake up so that we can be reunited.'

He starts for the stairs, but turns back. 'I don't suppose we could keep in touch?'

'I'm not sure what purpose that would serve, Mr Parker,' Daniel interrupts. 'Haven't you caused enough harm already? I think it is best if you leave our family alone now.'

Mr Parker takes out a reporter's notebook from an inside pocket. He hastily scribbles something, then tears off the page and hands it to Miriam. 'This is Marta Wilson's address and phone number. She would be so pleased to hear from you. She's been going spare, thinking that she's somehow responsible for what happened. I am sure that speaking to you would help.'

'Just so long as we get Rosa home, all will be well. But I will get in touch with Marta, I promise. She was a dear friend to my daughter, and her own family suffered too. I would like to hear what happened to them. And she can keep you posted about Rosa's progress, perhaps?'

'Thank you, Mrs Kauffman.' He doffs his hat. 'It was a pleasure to meet you both.'

As they leave, Daniel is distracted, folded in upon himself – shocked at seeing Rosa in such a perilous state, Miriam assumes. She asks whether he will visit again tomorrow, and he seems uncertain. 'I have to work tomorrow. Someone has to pay the bills,' he mutters. 'But I'll do my best.'

'Perhaps you could bring Hans with you,' she says, 'It might help Rosa wake up.' But he shrugs and she decides not to press him. She will meet her grandson soon enough, she reminds herself. It's already been a long, bewildering day. But she has found her daughter, and even though she failed to respond, Miriam feels certain that she will come back to life, given time.

33

It is a short bus ride from St Thomas's Hospital to the Greenes' house, and as she enters, she discovers that Jack is already there.

'You didn't waste any time,' she says, delighted. Seeing him always makes her feel better.

'I got on the train just as soon as I received your telegram.'

'Thank heavens you're home,' Sam says. 'We were starting to wonder what had happened to you.'

'Indeed. It's been quite a day.'

'Did you find her?' Jack asks.

'Give the poor woman a chance to take her coat off,' Sarah says, shooing the men away. 'We've kept a plate for you in the warming oven.'

Miriam hastily washes her hands and collects her dinner – beef stew, one of her favourites, and so similar to the goulashes she used to cook in Hamburg back when they could afford to buy beef. She realises that she hasn't eaten since breakfast. A glass of red wine is waiting for her at the table, and she sits down, taking a couple of sips, feeling grateful for this life of order and plenty. What a contrast to Rosa's meagre little house.

'In answer to your question, yes, I have found her,' she says.

Jack leaps to his feet, throwing his arms in the air. 'Oh my goodness,' he shouts. 'At last. Where is she? How is she?'

She takes a breath. 'I went to their house in Bethnal Green.' She pauses, wondering how to describe the sparsely furnished rooms. It feels an age ago. 'Daniel was there. But ...' she struggles for the words to describe what she now knows, 'I'm afraid Rosa is in hospital. She's gravely ill, and unconscious. The doctors can't tell us whether she will wake up.'

'What? How?' Jack's voice is high and tight with shock.

'She was punched,' Miriam says. 'It's a long story.'

'Who by, for heaven's sake?' Sam gasps.

She takes another sip of wine, and Sarah leans forward to replenish her glass. Miriam sips again, and then starts speaking.

By the time she's finished the story, Sam has already taken out a notebook and is waiting, pen poised. 'What name does your daughter go by these days?'

'Rosa Cooper.'

'And that journalist. What was his name again?'

'Frank Parker. *The Times*.'

'What day was it in the paper, do you remember?'

'Today, I think.'

He goes to the living room and they hear him searching, but he returns empty-handed. 'Dammit. I must have left my copy at the office. I'll check tomorrow. Now, I'm going to telephone the hospital.'

He goes into the hallway and they hear him dialling. 'Directory enquiries? Give me the number of St Thomas's Hospital, please.' He puts down the phone, and as he dials again, they all leave the table and gather at the doorway to listen.

'St Thomas's Hospital? Right. You have a patient by the name of Mrs Rosa Cooper?' A pause. 'Now listen. I am calling from the Home Office. Perhaps you are not aware, but Mrs

Cooper's assailant is a Nazi criminal, now being held on behalf of the international courts. She has helped us to apprehend him. So I am sure you would not want to impede the progress of justice by refusing ... Ah, yes, I can wait while you put me through.'

He winks, as Miriam shares an admiring glance with Jack.

'Hello? Ah, yes. Thank you, Dr Berryman. Yes, it is the progress of Mrs Rosa Cooper we want to find out about. As you probably know, we are most anxious to question her as a witness to the international crimes her assailant is alleged to have committed. How is she this evening?'

A longer pause as Sam listens, his face sombre.

'Well, thank you, Doctor. That is most helpful. Perhaps I could give you my number, in case of any change in her condition. Yes, twenty-four hours a day. This is most important, you understand? A matter of national security.'

'Well?' Jack says as Sam replaces the heavy receiver on its cradle, and Miriam finds that she has been holding her breath. She is speechless with admiration.

'No change as yet. They don't know how much, or how little, her brain has been affected by the skull fracture. He'll let us know if there is any change.'

'Let's all have a cup of tea,' Sarah says, ever practical, and Miriam remembers her role in this household. She is not a friend, not a guest, but the housekeeper.

'I'll make it,' she says, ignoring Sarah's protests. 'I'd be glad of something to keep me busy.'

As she is waiting for the kettle to boil, Sarah joins her in the kitchen.

'I'm so sorry, Miriam. This must all have been the most awful shock.'

Miriam turns to the kettle. She cannot look at Sarah or she will crumple and cry.

'Yes, it is,' she allows herself to admit. 'A terrible shock. But my daughter is strong, always has been. Something in my heart tells me that she will pull through.' And then she remembers: 'Oh, I forgot to say. She has a child. A son called Hans, after his grandfather, my husband.'

'Oh, my dearest Miriam. What a miracle. Such a wonderful tribute.'

And now she is in Sarah's arms, and they are both crying.

After a few moments, they gather themselves, wipe their faces, make the tea and carry the tray through to the living room. They have to move a decanter off the table to find a place for it. Sam and Jack are already clasping glasses of whisky.

'You'd better pour another couple,' Sarah says. 'We can have the tea in a minute. But right now we need to make a toast.'

When they are all holding a glass, Sarah nudges Miriam. 'Go on, then.'

'I learned today that I have a grandson,' she says. 'They have named him Hans, after his grandfather, my husband.'

They cheer, and congratulate her, and raise their glasses to Grandma Miriam.

'You make me feel like an old woman with a shawl, knitting in hand.' As she joins in the laughter, she notices that Jack seems distracted.

'How old is he, this boy?' he asks with an air of studied casualness.

'Six.' As she says it, his cheeks drain of colour and, with a bolt of sudden clarity, Miriam understands. She tries to remember what he said about Daniel and Rosa moving to London, and cannot place the date. Before the start of the war, she thinks, which would make it ... just possible. But now is not the time.

· · ·

Next morning, Sarah insists that Miriam return to the hospital. 'It's not every day you find a daughter you haven't seen for seven years,' she says.

'Will Daniel be going with you?' Jack asks.

'He wasn't sure. He had to go to work today, he said.'

'Then can I come instead?'

'They won't let you in,' she says. 'Yesterday it was next of kin only. And they're terribly strict. That journalist who was with her at the premiere turned up and they refused to let him in.'

'Perhaps I could be a long-lost cousin?'

'I don't think that will ... what is it you say? That's it: cut the mustard.'

'I'll never get over your extraordinary mastery of the English language,' he says, laughing. 'It was one of the things that persuaded me to give you a second chance when we met at that godforsaken border post. I thought that if you'd taken the trouble to learn our language, you must really want to go there.'

'And here I am, thanks to you,' she says.

'Here we both are, and off to see Rosa together this afternoon,' he says, almost happily. 'I never dreamed that this day would arrive.'

'Don't get your hopes up,' Miriam warns. 'She is probably still unconscious.'

'We can talk to her, though? Isn't that what you said yesterday?'

'Yes, the nurse said it was good to talk. She might hear us, and it could stimulate her brain, she said.'

'So you don't mind if I come with you?'

'Of course not. It would be wonderful to have your company. Afternoon visiting hours are three till four. But this morning I thought I might make a little visit.' She takes from her pocket the slip of paper on which Frank Parker wrote Marta's address, and peers at it. 'I don't think this is very far away from here.'

She goes to the living room and returns with the A to Z map book of London that has been her bible since arriving here. How else would anyone ever find their way around?

'Now, let me see.' She checks the index for St George's Terrace, Regent's Park. 'Aha, here it is.' She points to the spot on the map, checking. 'I wonder if I could walk there.'

'Who lives there?' Jack asks.

'An old friend of Rosa's from Hamburg days,' Miriam explains. 'It's a long story, but it seems they met by chance and have become firm friends in London. It was Marta who put Rosa in touch with the journalist she went with to the premiere. We met him at the hospital and he gave me her address. So, how far away do you think this is?'

Jack peers at the map. 'A nice walk through Hyde Park, then another twenty minutes to Regent's Park. I'd allow forty-five minutes.'

Miriam is all for setting off right away, but a sudden thought stops her: 'What if she's not in?'

'Have you got a telephone number?'

She has never used the heavy Bakelite machine that squats like an ugly toad on the Greenes' hall table, so it simply hasn't occurred to her that the words and numbers Frank Parker scrawled at the end of the address could be a telephone number. 'Regent's Park 5620,' she reads. 'Could that be it?'

'Let's give it a try.'

'Shouldn't we ask first? How much does it cost?'

'They won't mind. I'll pay if necessary.' Jack goes to the phone and dials, speaks into it: 'Regent's Park 5620, please.' He passes the receiver to Miriam. 'Here, you answer it.'

It feels awkward in her hand, this strangely shaped piece of equipment. In her ear, she hears a disembodied telephone ringing in some distant place. She nearly drops the receiver when a light female voice answers: 'Hello? Regent's Park 5620. Marta Wilson speaking.'

Miriam is unprepared, and the words freeze in her mouth.

'Hello?' the voice says again.

'Say something,' Jack prompts.

'Hello,' Miriam says.

'Who is this?'

'Frau Kauffman, Miriam Kauffman. Is that Marta Muller?'

There is a gasp at the other end of the line. 'Heavens! Did you say Miriam Kauffman?'

'Yes, from Hamburg, Rosa's mother. Do you remember me?' Miriam says in German.

'Oh my goodness. We thought you were dead. Where are you calling from, Mrs Kauffman? Have you heard about Rosa?'

'I am in London. Knightsbridge. Listen, I went with Daniel to the hospital yesterday. That's where we met Frank Parker and he gave me your address. But Rosa is still unconscious.' She is getting the hang of this telephone thing now: she can hear little squeaks of surprise from the other end, and she can almost picture Marta – older now, of course – as she speaks.

'I can't believe it. Rosa has been searching everywhere for you, and now you are here. I feel so guilty about putting her in touch with Frank, but she was completely obsessed with Erich Steiner. She was ready to fly to Argentina to confront him, would you believe?'

'Please don't feel guilty, Marta. Mr Parker explained that no one could have predicted that Steiner would actually attack her.'

'Are you going to see her again?'

'Yes, this afternoon.'

'I would love to come too, but when I rang the hospital, they said close family only. Will you give her my love?'

'If she is awake, of course.'

There is a momentary pause. Then, 'Listen, when are you going?'

'Visiting hours are three o'clock till four.'

'Can I meet you beforehand? There's a Lyons on the corner, not far from the hospital, near the Tube station. Could you get there by two-ish? There's something I would like you to take to her for me. And it would be so lovely to see you – I really want to learn more about how you come to be in London.'

34

Marta is so altered that Miriam scarcely recognises her. She remembers a gawky kid with blonde curls, always dressed in hand-me-downs and usually wearing slacks. Her pallid, spotty complexion seemed never to have seen a decent diet, or the light of day.

Today, she is beautiful and sophisticated, like a model. Her hair is pinned up in a victory roll, her make-up is flawless and she is wearing a smart wool jacket in a delicate lilac, picking out colours from the flowery dress beneath. On her feet are elegant heels of a similar tone. As they approach the window table where she is already seated, it is all Miriam can do to stop herself gasping in amazement. Beside her Jack emits a hushed 'Wow.'

Marta leaps to her feet as they draw near. 'Mrs Kauffman! It is so wonderful to see you. However long has it been? But I would recognise you anywhere. And this is ...?'

'Apologies,' Miriam says, recovering from the surprise. 'This is Jack Preston. His family sponsored Daniel and Rosa when they came to England before the war.'

'Such a pleasure to meet you, Jack. Rosa has told me a little

about the time she had with your family – in Suffolk, wasn't it?'
Marta's face seems to light up as they shake hands, and Miriam
sees through this young woman's eyes what a handsome man
Jack is.

'You have a good memory,' he says, as they take their seats
and the waitress arrives at the table. They order tea all round.
'So terribly English,' Marta jokes, clicking open a sleek silver
cigarette case and offering it around. Miriam declines, but Jack
takes one.

'This is so extraordinary, seeing you again,' Miriam starts.
'Now, tell me again how you met Rosa here in London,'

'We bumped into each other completely by chance in
Trafalgar Square before Christmas last year. Freddie, that's my
son, is the same age as Hans, and they're best buddies now too.'

A memory flashes into Miriam's brain. The carols, the
lights, and that face that reminded her of … Marta Muller, the
young woman now sitting across the table from her.

'In Trafalgar Square? The night they sang the carols and lit
the lights on the Norwegian tree?'

'Exactly.'

The coincidence, the might-have-been, is dizzying. She was
in the same square as her daughter that night, but they
never met.

'Are you okay?' Jack whispers

Miriam pulls herself back to the present. 'Yes, it's fine.
Except that I was there too. But then there were thousands of
people. It's not so surprising …'

'What a terrible shame,' Marta says.

No good dwelling on the past. The present is much more
important. 'You said she'd talked about Steiner?' Miriam asks.
'Why did she want to meet him so much?'

'It was something in a letter from our old neighbour, Mrs
Geller, that convinced her he had betrayed you to the SS. You
remember Mrs Geller?'

'Of course I do,' Miriam says. 'It was through her that I finally got Rosa's address in London yesterday. A day too late,' she tails off, sadly.

'Not too late,' Jack says quietly. 'Remember what you told me last night: you were convinced that she will wake up and be well again.'

'I believe that too,' Marta says. 'We have to hold on to that hope.'

The tea arrives and Marta pours, milk first. These charming English rituals make Miriam feel safe in her adopted country.

'What was it Mrs Geller told Rosa?' she prompts.

'I never saw the letter, but I gather she said she feared that Erich Steiner was determined to find you, and she was very afraid that her mail had been tampered with, so he could have discovered your address that way. Then a bit later, Rosa heard from the daughter of the farmer you stayed with after leaving Hamburg. Before he died he told her about how you and your husband and son were arrested, and he assumed you'd been betrayed by someone, though he never knew who.'

'Poor Mr Schmidt. Such a kind man. He gave us shelter when we most needed it. I wonder what happened to him after we left. I hope they didn't punish him for harbouring us.'

'Apparently he was also imprisoned but released after a couple of months as they couldn't prove his involvement, so he was always grateful that you had never given him away,' Marta says. 'But tell me, what happened after that? And how do you come to be in London?'

Miriam takes a breath, and swallows. 'We were captured and put on a transport train to Auschwitz. My husband and my son died there and I only survived through luck – I was put on a work detail that saved my life, although it was touch and go at the end when we were all starving.'

Marta gasps. 'I am so sorry.' She opens her handbag, takes out a handkerchief and dabs her eyes.

Miriam places a hand over hers. 'Your parents too?'

Marta nods, sniffing. 'As you know, my father was a commu-nist. After you left, the police raided our apartment and arrested him for the second time. They also found incriminating evidence against my mother, so they took her, too. That was when my English auntie wrote and said I was to go to the British embassy. She had pulled some strings there, and I got one of the last trains out of Hamburg before war started.'

'I take it you've had no word from them since?'

Marta shakes her head. 'It is all about luck, good and bad, isn't it?' She looks up and smiles at Jack, who has been listening quietly. 'The Preston family were Rosa's good luck, she told me.'

'It was my father,' he demurs, but Miriam notices his neck beginning to colour. 'Nothing to do with me really.'

'And it was Jack who helped me get to London,' she says. 'Without him, neither Rosa nor I would be here. We all owe him a great debt.'

The deep pink blush now floods his cheeks. 'I'll go and pay,' he says.

Miriam shares an amused glance with Marta. 'Men are so bad at accepting compliments.'

Marta hands her a small gift bag. 'This is for Rosa,' she says. 'There's a card from me and another one Freddie has made for his little friend Hans, as well as something for when she is feeling better. Please give her all our love. And I would really appreciate it if you could telephone me when there are any developments, good or bad.' She kisses Miriam on both cheeks, the continental way that Miriam has almost forgotten.

'I promise,' Miriam says, gathering her coat and bag. 'It has been so lovely to meet you again. But now I am afraid we must leave you.'

. . .

Jack and Miriam arrive just before three o'clock and enter the now familiar hallway along with crowds of other visitors waiting to be allowed in.

When the dragon matron with the clipboard asks Jack for his relationship to Mrs Cooper, he replies without hesitation: 'Brother.' She frowns, looking up at him with a sceptical expression and then down again at the clipboard. For a fleeting moment Miriam fears she might question him further – Jack could not look more different from her if he tried – but she grunts and ticks something off on her list.

'Bluebell Ward – you'll remember the way from yesterday,' she says.

Miriam grabs Jack's arm before the matron can change her mind. 'Come along, son,' she says.

'"Come along son",' he mimics as soon as they are safely out of earshot. 'How you said that with a straight face, I'll never know.'

'There's truth in it, you know,' Miriam giggles. 'You do feel a bit like a son to me.'

'So come on then, Mum,' Jack says. 'Let's go and see my sister.'

'I need to warn you that her face has taken quite a battering.'

'I am sure she is still beautiful, all the same,' he says, and from the tenderness in his voice, it is now even more obvious to Miriam that Jack Preston loves her daughter.

She has dared to hope that Rosa may have opened her eyes, but when they reach the ward, the nurse says, 'No change, I'm afraid. She still seems to be deeply unconscious, not reacting to any stimuli. But the doctor will be along shortly, so you can ask him about her prognosis.'

'What's a prognosis?' Miriam whispers.

'It's what they think about her recovery and ...' Jack's voice tails off as he sees the still, silent form of Rosa, pale as a corpse.

Miriam tries to judge whether there has been any change in her condition, for better or worse, but decides there is nothing to see. She kisses the cool cheeks and forehead, smoothing Rosa's hair before taking a seat beside the bed and gesturing to Jack that he should pull up the chair on the other side.

'Hello, my darling,' she says, taking a limp hand in hers. 'How are you doing today?' She studies Rosa's face, desperate to detect the slightest sign of movement, but there is none.

'Rosa, my darling, open your eyes. I hope you have been having some sweet dreams in this long sleep of yours. Anyway, I'm back again, your mother, come all the way from Germany to find you after these seven long years. It has been such a journey trying to find you, my love. If you can't open your eyes, that doesn't matter in the slightest. But I would dearly love some kind of sign to show that you know I am here.'

She pauses, squeezing Rosa's hand gently, holding her breath. Nothing. She squeezes again, and is about to give up when ... Is she imagining it? No, something is happening, a small pressure, the slightest twitch of a forefinger. It happens again, and she knows it is not just wishful thinking. There is a tiny but unmistakable movement.

She lets out a small squeal of delight. 'She squeezed my hand, Jack. A definite squeeze! Take her other hand – she might do the same for you. Don't be afraid.'

He reaches forward and gingerly lifts Rosa's other hand into his own.

'Oh my darling,' Miriam says. 'You can hear us, and you know we are here, don't you? I am sure this is the start of your recovery. And today I've brought a special surprise for you. We both owe him so much, sweetheart. The person holding your other hand is Jack Preston. Remember him? The one who made it possible for you and Daniel to come to England, and then helped me come here too, to find you.'

She looks across the bed at Jack, who seems to be gripping

Rosa's hand almost too tightly, his gaze fiercely focused on her face.

'Say something,' she urges.

He tries, but it comes out as a croak. He tries again. 'Rosa, it's me, Jack. Do you remember? From Suffolk? Those wonderful summer days on the hill, the canoe trip along the river? I know it was such a long time ago, and the world has been turned upside down by war since then, but I'm still the same old Jack, and it would be …'

He stops suddenly, as though he has had an electric shock. 'Oh. She squeezed my hand too, Miriam. You were right. Oh, my darling Rosa.' He glances up at Miriam and corrects himself. 'Rosa, you dear thing. Thank you for letting me know that you can hear my voice.'

Miriam goes into the main part of the ward and hails a nurse. 'Come and see. She's responding. Squeezing our hands. What do you think?'

The nurse lifts Rosa's wrist and takes a pulse, shines a bright torch into each eye by lifting each lid in turn. She sticks a thermometer into her mouth and clamps the lifeless lips around it, while cuffing Rosa's arm and taking a recording of her blood pressure.

'Her vital signs are unchanged, I'm afraid,' she says at last. 'But if you think you have experienced a response, I suggest you continue what you are doing: talking to her, holding her hand. I will send the doctor in as soon as he arrives.'

35

Rosa is swimming in the freshwater lake near their home in Hamburg. It is a favourite spot for city-dwellers in the heat of the summer, and the beaches are always crowded. But when you swim down below the surface, into the dim green depths sliced through with shafts of sunlight, everything is silent and still.

She loves the weightlessness of being underwater. It is how she learned to swim, aged about five, rising to the surface to gasp a breath before paddling downwards once more. She keeps her eyes closed because the water makes them sting. If only she still had the mask that came as a present for her tenth birthday. After that, she would spend hours floating on the surface, head down, watching the fish flitting away with a flash of silvery scales, swarms of freshwater shrimps darting hither and thither like flies, clams closing their shells tight as fists as she approached.

Now she is rising to the surface, feeling the sunlight through her eyelids. She hears voices, still muffled by the water. There must be other swimmers nearby, or perhaps people on the shore. She tries to open her eyes, but they feel glued together and won't move. She listens, concentrating hard. It is her mother's voice, much closer than she expected. Perhaps Mama is underwater too.

'Hello, my darling.'

She attempts to move her lips, but they too seem to be stuck together. 'Hello, Mama,' she wants to say. 'What are you doing here under the lake with me?'

But she is sliding back through the water, down, down into the depths, the shafts of sunlight dimming, the voices fading. And then, nothing.

She has no idea how long she has been in the lake. Surely it is time to get out now? Her skin will be wrinkly, the picnic will be drying out in the sun, Mama will be worried. She must swim to the surface again. She must take a breath. It is becoming urgent now.

Something touches her hand. Is it someone helping her out of the water? Why would they bother? She is perfectly capable of getting out herself. She feels with her toes to see if she can touch the bottom, where the lake becomes shallower closer to the shore.

There is that voice again. 'Rosa, my darling, open your eyes.'

She tries to obey, but they are heavy, so heavy. She can feel the touch on her hand, and tries to respond, tries again. Then she hears Mama shriek: 'She squeezed my hand, Jack.'

Jack? She doesn't know anyone called Jack in Hamburg. She must have misheard. And then she hears a deeper voice, a quiet voice that seems to enfold her with happiness. It is a man's voice, familiar but for the moment unrecognisable. Not Papa, not Willi, not Daniel.

'She squeezed my hand too, Miriam. You were right,' the voice says. 'Oh, my darling Rosa.'

She tries to move her hand again. It is exhausting, this struggle to move, and she wonders whether she will ever be able to do those things again, those everyday actions that once seemed so easy, so natural. Perhaps it is because she is no longer floating weightlessly in the water. Her body still feels heavy, but she is content to be lying here on the soft sandy beach in the warm sunlight, with those familiar, beloved voices around her. She feels so sleepy, though, exhausted from all the swimming. Perhaps she will just have a little ...

Later, although she cannot tell how much later, when someone is washing her face with a warm flannel, Rosa opens her eyes.

'Hello, Mrs Cooper,' a woman says. 'You're back with us again, are you?'

The world is blurred, out of focus, but she can just about make out colours: the dark blue dress of the person wiping her face, the glint of something pinned to her chest, the white of the walls, the pink of the curtains around the bed.

Then there is a man's voice she doesn't recognise, who booms: 'Excellent, excellent. She is definitely coming round. Hello, Mrs Cooper, can you hear me?' She wants to tell him not to shout because she can hear him perfectly well, thank you, but although she feels her throat vibrating, no sound comes out.

Someone opens her lips, placing a straw between them. 'Can you try to suck, Mrs Cooper? It's only orange squash, but it will taste delicious, I promise, after all this time.'

She sucks as best she can, but none of the promised deliciousness arrives in her mouth. So the woman tips her head back, opens her mouth and pours in a few drops. The taste and smell of orange is almost overwhelming, the sweetness irresistible. She swallows and opens her mouth for more.

By the following day, Rosa can open and close her eyes at will. They have propped her up on the pillows and she can see the largely still, silent mounds of the other patients in their beds, hear the busy scuffle of nurses' feet and witness the approach of white-coated doctors.

She can suck from a straw and has even been able to swallow small amounts of a soft, tasteless paste that reminds her of the baby food she used to feed to Hans when he was being weaned. She can wriggle her fingers and her toes, but when she smiles or tries to talk, her cheekbone is painful. Her head aches horribly too, but the nurse is kind. 'You'll feel better soon, don't you worry,' she says. 'Can I get you any more pain relief?'

The nurse explains that she was punched by a man called Eric Stewart, although a bit later, thinking it over, she remembers that it was Erich Steiner.

The memories return slowly, like a bus emerging from London fog: headlights first, the reassuring rumble of the engine and then the bulk of the vehicle in full view. The headlights are the most recent events: the red carpet, the floodlights, Frank Parker, the heavy camera around her neck, recognising Steiner despite his disguise, the pain in her cheekbone when he hit her and the audible crack in her head when she fell.

The background memories return soon enough: the wedding ring reminds her that she is married to Daniel, and then she remembers with a frisson of joy that she has a son, little Hans. She cannot wait to hold him in her arms once again. Perhaps Daniel will bring him to visit her in this hospital. Then she recalls Mrs Tanner, Paula and Marta; the solid friendship of women that makes her feel safe. She hopes they aren't too worried about her. She will write to them when she's a bit stronger.

Finally, the bigger picture emerges from the fog, along with a deep, overwhelming sense of sorrow: the letters from Mrs Geller and the farmer's daughter, the news that her family were lost …

But hold on! One of those voices she heard was Mama. Was that all a dream?

'Nurse, Nurse?' she calls. 'Come, please.'

'Mrs Cooper, are you all right?'

'Yes, but tell ... tell me. Dream?'

'Did you dream what, dearie?'

'Mama? My mother?'

'Ah yes, Mrs Kauffman. She was here yesterday, dearie. And she will come again today, she said.' The nurse says this in a completely matter-of-fact way, as though mothers visit daughters in hospitals every day of the week. Which of course they do, but not mothers who were supposed to have been killed in a concentration camp.

'Mother? Alive?'

'Very much so, I'd say. Oh now look, there's nothing to cry about. The doctor says you will make a full recovery. Quite a little miracle, he's calling it. Here, let me wipe your tears. Your visitors will be here soon enough. Why don't you have a sleep, conserve your strength for visiting time?'

It seems so improbable. Mama, here in London, coming to visit her in hospital? As she drifts off to sleep, Rosa refuses to allow herself to believe it.

She wakes to the voice of little Hans.

'Mummy!' He is running down the ward towards her, ducking and diving like an expert footballer to avoid the outstretched hands of nurses.

'Oi, no running, young man!'

He launches himself onto her bed.

'Off the bed, mister,' the nurse says, catching up.

And then another woman arrives and says, 'For goodness' sake, he's her son. Let them have a cuddle for a minute or two, at least.'

Rosa holds Hans close and peers up at the two other people by her bedside. One of them is Daniel. He looks terrible, with the dark bruises of sleeplessness around his eyes, his skin grey, his face strained. But who is this woman who has just spoken with her mother's voice? She looks so small, so withered.

'Mama?' It is when the woman smiles that Rosa knows.

'Yes, it is me, my darling,' she says. 'Can I hug your mummy too, Hans?'

He shuffles over, and Mama moves close. Soon they are both laughing and crying, all at once.

'Why are you crying, Mummy?' Hans asks.

'Because ...' The words won't come.

'It is because she is happy, my darling,' Mama explains. 'That you are here, that Daddy is here, and that her own mummy is here. We are all so happy to be together again.'

Mama settles by the bedside with Hans on her knee. 'This is like a dream come true,' she says. 'I've come so far, looked high and low, and when I finally found you, it seemed possible that you might actually die. And now,' she strokes Hans's hair, 'look what I've found. Not only my daughter, alive and well, but a beautiful grandson, too.' She beams again, wiping her eyes with the back of her sleeve.

'I not believe,' Rosa says. 'I look ...' She gestures with her hands, frustrated, as she struggles for the words.

'Don't worry, the doctor told us that your speech will be back to normal soon,' Mama says. 'For the moment you must just concentrate on getting well. We can leave those conversations till later.'

So she doesn't ask about Papa and Willi, she doesn't ask how her mother came to be here, how she found her. That can all come in good time. For the moment, she feels blessed. What she most wants now is to go home to her family, to her little house, with Hans, and Daniel and now Mama.

. . .

That evening, she has another visitor. A man, dressed casually, with light curly hair and a slightly crooked grin that is powerfully familiar, except that she cannot put a name to him. She tries desperately to remember, and then, in a thrilling flash of recollection, it comes to her: Jack Preston.

He clears his throat. 'Hello, Rosa,' he says, looking strangely awkward. 'Long time no see.'

She manages only to nod. It is her beautiful boy, the one who showed her what love could be like but then disappeared from her life for ever. Whatever is he doing here?

'Sorry to appear unannounced like this. It must be a bit of a shock after all this time.'

'Jack?' she whispers.

'Yes, it's me,' Jack Preston says, eyes crinkling at the corners in that adorable way.

'How?'

'How did I get here? That's a long story, for another day.'

She reaches up to touch the dimples in his cheeks. They always did melt her heart.

'Jack, darling Jack,' she whispers. 'I never forgot.'

The last time she saw him, he was just a boy on the brink of manhood. Now he has grown into a man: physically taller and broader, and quietly confident. She looks into his concerned eyes, feels the heat of his hand on hers and feels herself falling in love with him all over again. 'I cannot believe.'

'Me neither,' he says. 'I had lost hope of ever seeing you ever again.'

'You find me?'

'So thoughtless of you to get punched, and damned inconvenient,' he says, and his laughter seems to peel away the years.

'How you are, Jack?'

He briefly summarises his war, how he met Miriam, how she nearly died of pneumonia and he found her a place to stay with an old school friend. How tirelessly she searched for Rosa.

'She is a remarkable woman, your mother.'

'Mama, and now you.'

'Miriam tells me you have a son,' he says.

'Hans.' She smiles fondly. 'My boy. Loves football and crisps.'

He falls silent, and then, 'Can I ask ...?'

She takes a breath. She has never wanted to contemplate the idea, but now that she sees Jack again, with those hazel eyes flecked with green, and the way his cheeks dimple when he smiles, she realises there is an outside chance Hans might be his.

'I don't know, Jack.'

A bell rings somewhere, and a nurse calls out: 'Five minutes to end of visiting time.'

Jack seems to hesitate. 'I had to come and see you. But now you have your boy, and your husband, and your mama, is it best if I just disappear again?'

'Daniel. I never love him. But you? It never stop.'

He whispers, simply: 'I won't interfere, but I will always be there, Rosa. You know where to find me.'

He reaches out his arms, gently enfolding her, and she feels his warmth and strength radiating through her as though they have never been apart. The touch of his skin is the same, and as she breathes in his familiar scent of fresh air and sandalwood, her heart fills with gratitude that she is alive, and he is here.

EPILOGUE
GERMANY, DECEMBER 1947

Mother and daughter cling to each other as they stumble through the rubble-strewn streets of central Hamburg on a dreary winter's day. Their own street is almost unrecognisable, their apartment building long gone, flattened by Allied bombs along with most of the area around the docklands.

Some rebuilding of the city centre has already started, but even now, more than two years after the end of the war, progress seems painfully slow. They wrap scarves around their faces against the dust that swirls relentlessly in a freezing breeze.

The notion of making this trip began during an evening of nostalgia a few months ago. Rosa recovered well from her injuries and has been back at work for over a year now. Miriam is still living with the Greenes, but spends every weekend in Bethnal Green. On Saturday mornings she takes Hans, now a leggy seven-year-old, to the flicks, as he calls them, and in the afternoon stands on the touchline watching him play his beloved football. She enjoys shopping and cooking for the family, usually staying for supper and overnight. She loves the boy like a son, and the more she gets to know him, the more she sees in him his grandfather and his uncle Willi. He helps her towards accepting life without them.

That evening, she bought a bottle of German wine – Liebfraumilch, as she recalls – to accompany the schnitzel she was preparing. As Daniel prefers beer, she and Rosa drank most of it. After supper, they stoked up the coal fire and, feeling slightly tipsy, began to reminisce about life in Germany.

'Remember the penguins in the zoo?'

'I so loved them. With their little surprised faces.'

'And the parks. Such wonderful parks.'

'We taught you to swim in the Stadtparksee. Remember that?'

'How could I forget? It was so cold.' Rosa gave a melodramatic shiver.

'Afterwards we always went to the café for hot chocolate and strudel.'

'Yum. Shall we make some tomorrow, Mama?'

'We can, but they are never the same here somehow. Something to do with the ingredients. We'll just have to go back to Hamburg one day.'

'Are you serious?'

'About going back?' Miriam paused, sighed and took a sip of her wine. 'Sometimes I wonder. What is it like these days? Germany was my home, you know. Yours too.'

'I can't believe you would go back to that country after everything that happened.'

'Out of curiosity,' Miriam said. 'Aren't you curious, too?'

It might at least lay some ghosts, Rosa thought to herself.

And now they are here, having crossed a very choppy North Sea on a cargo ship from Harwich, organised with the help of Sam Greene, and endured an uncomfortable night trying to sleep on the benches in the seamen's mess. For their stay in Hamburg, the captain has recommended a *Gasthof* that turns out to be very comfortable. It is in an area that largely escaped the bombing, not far from the Steiners' building, which makes Rosa feel panicky at first, until she gives herself a little talking-to. Those days are in the past. Steiner is in jail and his family will be long gone.

Today, feeling refreshed after a good sleep and a wash, they are heading out to explore the ruins of their city. They pass the synagogue, which is still boarded up, and negotiate the piles of rubble that are all that is left of the neighbourhood in which they lived. The zoo is an area of devastation, and they wonder whether the animals were rehoused before the bombing, or whether they escaped and are still roaming the streets, searching for food. The park has become a village of temporary housing, shed-like buildings with lines of washing strung between them and children playing in the mud outside. It is a desolate scene, and after the initial excitement of being back in their home city, they walk together in silence, saddened to see what has become of it.

At last they find a café, and the hot chocolate and pastries are just as they remember.

'What do you think, Mama?' Rosa asks, biting into a delicious layer of crisp flaky pastry enclosing sweet apple. 'Would you come back to live here?'

Miriam shakes her head. 'The Hamburg I knew has gone, my darling. Best to look forward now.' It's a relief to hear this. Rosa knows without any doubt that England is her home. She enjoys her job and her son is happy at school, growing up like a little Englishman. There is nothing left for her in Germany.

Daniel still talks about making a new start in America, and sometimes she wishes he would just up sticks and go without her. But she knows he will never leave his son, and in any case, she would not want Hans to grow up without his father. Their marriage is over, but they tolerate each other for the sake of the boy.

Her mother still sees Jack Preston from time to time at the

Greenes' house, and Rosa sometimes dreams about him, wondering what might happen should she find herself free.

Miriam finishes her pastry and heads off to the *Damentoilette*. While she waits, Rosa reaches for one of the newspapers folded into a rack beside their table. She scans the headlines and sees: *LAWYERS' TRIAL DRAWS TO A CLOSE IN NUREMBERG*.

Lawyers? Her eyes flick quickly to the text, and the list of names. She was only vaguely aware of the additional military tribunals being organised by the United States; somehow the English newspapers seem to have lost interest since the International War Crimes Tribunal held two years before.

Steiner was a lawyer. With a dry mouth and thudding heart she reads on and, sure enough, there is his name among those of fifteen other senior lawyers and judges indicted for 'furthering the Nazi plan for racial purity by implementing the eugenics laws of the Third Reich'. The trial has been going for some weeks and is already approaching its conclusion. The judges will retire to consider the sentences in the next day or so.

As she sees her mother returning, she hastily refolds the newspaper and places it back in the rack, wishing she'd never picked it up in the first place.

'Are you okay?' Miriam asks. 'You look a bit pale, sweetheart. Too much pastry, perhaps. Come on, let's get some fresh air.'

Later, as they are waiting at the station for the train that will carry them back to the Hook of Holland to catch the ferry, Rosa glances up at the departures board and sees that another train is departing for the city of Nuremberg in just twenty minutes. All at once, she is struck by an overwhelming, irresistible notion. If she can see Steiner in the dock, if only for a few moments, she will live the rest of her life in peace. She must witness justice being served; there is something strangely biblical about it.

Miriam thinks she is crazy, but Rosa is determined. 'If you don't want to come, Mama, that's fine. But it's just something I need to do.' In the end, Miriam agrees to go with her. They change their tickets and settle down for the six-hour journey south.

Even though Nuremberg is where Hitler held his rallies, the Allied bombers seem to have let the city off lightly. Many of the buildings, including the imposing Palace of Justice made famous by the first Nuremberg trials, are untouched by war. It is mid-afternoon by the time they arrive, only to be told that proceedings have finished for the day. 'Come early enough tomorrow and you might just get a seat in the public gallery,' the clerk says. 'It'll be busy, though, let me warn you. It's judgement day.'

Rosa and Miriam are sitting high up in the public gallery of Courtroom 600, crammed in with around fifty other men and women of all ages with one thing in common: they are keen enough to arrive before breakfast to ensure they witness this momentous day.

Rosa hasn't slept a wink and has no appetite for the cheese roll her mother takes from a paper bag and offers her while they wait. The room is stuffy and overheated, harshly lit with strip lights in the ceiling. It was here, in this very place, that twenty-four leaders of the Third Reich, including Goering, Hess, Speer and von Ribbentrop, declared in turn that the deaths of millions had been caused because they were only following orders. She read the reports in the English newspapers, fascinated and appalled by the way the men had tried to evade responsibility.

At last there is a disturbance in the courtroom below. The

door opens, and as the sixteen defendants are led to their seats in the dock, she feels her mother's hand taking hers.

She assumed Steiner would be instantly recognisable, but as the men shuffle forward, she can barely distinguish between them. How could such ordinary men, looking for all the world like used-car salesmen in their ill-fitting second-hand suits, have committed such terrible crimes?

Only when they are seated do some of them raise their faces, and now, at last, she sees him, third from the end. It is less than two years since that fateful day in Leicester Square, but he seems to have aged a decade: his skin is grey, his cheeks hollow and his eyes sunk in deep shadows. His hair is thinning and he looks like an old man. Gone is the arrogant jut of the chin, the fierce, piercing gaze. Even his commanding height seems to have been diminished; he appears no taller than his neighbour.

Does he know that he is defeated, Rosa wonders, or does he hold out hope of being exonerated and freed? Her empty stomach clenches painfully at the possibility.

Everyone is asked to stand when the three judges arrive and, once they are settled, those in the body of the court put on headsets for the simultaneous translation. There are none for the public gallery, and Rosa and Miriam are grateful that they can follow the proceedings with ease in both of the main languages.

After this, the trial moves at quite a pace; it feels as though everyone is keen to get today over with. The chief judge describes what will happen and outlines the four main categories of crime of which the defendants are accused. The legal wording is dry, describing nothing of the horror these men have caused: 'conspiracy to commit war crimes and crimes against humanity', 'abuse of the judicial and penal process', 'membership of a criminal organisation'.

At last the judgement begins. In a sonorous voice, the judge calls each defendant to stand. He tells each of them on which counts they are guilty, and what their sentence will be: death by hanging, life imprisonment, or a shorter term. On hearing their verdicts, the defendants react in different ways. Some throw up their hands in despair, others start to weep, one shouts, 'No, it's wrong, all of it', while a few stand impassively, facing their fate with dignity.

When it is Steiner's turn, he rises purposefully, regaining his proud demeanour for a few moments. But as the verdict is read out – guilty on three counts, sentenced to life imprisonment – he crumples, slumping to the bench with his head in his hands, a broken man.

Rosa doesn't hear much of the other remaining verdicts. She exhales deeply, her shoulders relaxing as though a great weight has been lifted from them, feeling lighter, freer. Even the dismal courtroom seems sunnier. She can see a future. Steiner no longer wields any power over her.

Only as the judge dismisses the court and the men are led away from the dock does she start to weep.

'Take me home now please, Mama,' she whispers. 'It's over.'

A LETTER FROM LIZ

Dear Reader,

Thank you so much for choosing to read *Searching for My Daughter*. The story feels very personal to me, so I really hope you enjoyed it and that it gave you food for thought. If you would like to be the first to hear about my new releases please sign up using the link below. Your email address will never be shared and you can unsubscribe at any time.

www.bookouture.com/liz-trenow

Like many of my novels, *Searching for My Daughter* was inspired by stories that I heard from older family members. My uncle John was a remarkably modest character who died aged one hundred after an extraordinary life that included enlisting as a bomber pilot in World War II. He was shot down, then rescued after forty-eight desperate hours floating in a tiny life raft on the North Sea, and put back together by German doctors before being sent to a prisoner-of-war camp. There, he was invited to take part in the 'Wooden Horse' escape, but opted to stay in the camp because his fluent German made him invaluable as an interpreter. When the war ended, he signed up to work as an intelligence officer for the Control Commission (see 'A Note on the History That Inspired *Searching for My Daughter*'), helping displaced people return to their own countries.

His memories helped me appreciate, for the first time, the immensity of the refugee crisis caused by the Nazis and the heartbreaking echoes with the plight of today's refugees fleeing regime-sponsored wars and ethnic cleansing around the world. How sad that it is a problem we still don't seem able to solve.

I knew it was a story that had to be told, and chose to tell it through the experiences of a mother and daughter. I am the mother of two daughters, and can hardly bear to imagine what it would be like not knowing whether they were still alive.

If you loved the book, I would be really grateful if you could write a review. It makes such a difference helping new readers to discover my books for the first time.

Do get in touch via my Facebook page, through Twitter or my website.

Thanks,

Liz Trenow

www.liztrenow.com

 facebook.com/liztrenow

 twitter.com/liztrenow

 instagram.com/liztrenow

A NOTE ON THE HISTORY

Following their victory over Nazi Germany in May 1945, the Allies were faced with occupying and administering a country in ruins. It had been agreed at the Yalta Conference in February that Germany would be divided into sectors overseen by each of the key Allied countries, Russia, America, Britain and France. As well as managing local services, these Control Commissions would be responsible for monitoring the movement of displaced people seeking to return to their homelands as well as intercepting Nazi criminals trying to evade justice.

Nazi persecution in the 1930s and 1940s followed by a worldwide war had created a refugee crisis on a scale never seen before, with an estimated five million people displaced from their homes across the world. Multiple organisations in many countries worked tirelessly to help them relocate and be reunited with their families, but sadly many never saw their relatives again. There are no records of how many were successfully reunited.

Before the war, Nazi persecution prompted hundreds of thousands of Jewish people to try to get out of Germany and Austria. Sadly, just as today, many countries were frightened of allowing in too many refugees. By the start of the war, only a few hundred thousand visas had been issued, of which Great Britain granted only forty thousand. The Kindertransport programme enabled a further ten thousand unaccompanied Jewish children to escape to the UK.

Those left behind, unable to get visas or afford the fares, found themselves trapped, and were subsequently rounded up and sent to their deaths in Nazi concentration camps. We now know that around six million European Jews died, along with at least five million prisoners of war, Roma, Jehovah's Witnesses, gay and disabled people and others. Few inmates survived long enough to be liberated.

The Kanada warehouses were facilities in the Auschwitz concentration camp used to store and sort the stolen belongings of prisoners who had been murdered in the gas chambers. They were dubbed Kanada because they were seen as a land of plenty. Prisoners working there could – at great risk – procure goods such as food and medicines for themselves and other inmates, meaning that their chances of survival were greatly increased.

Between November 1945 and October 1946, the famous Nuremberg International Military Tribunal tried twenty-four leading Nazis and charged them with crimes against peace, war crimes and crimes against humanity. Eleven were executed and the others sentenced to varying terms of imprisonment.

Nuremberg was chosen because the Palace of Justice was spacious and largely undamaged (one of the few buildings that had escaped Allied bombing), and had a large prison as part of the complex. It was also the ceremonial birthplace of the Nazi party and had hosted its annual propaganda rallies, which made it a fitting place to mark the party's symbolic demise.

Between December 1946 and April 1949, the Americans conducted twelve further military tribunals at Nuremberg for groups of 'lesser' war criminals, which included doctors, judges and lawyers as well as those responsible for running the concentration camps at Auschwitz, Belsen, Dachau and others.

The Nuremberg tribunals established landmark principles for dealing with international crimes against humanity and resulted in the establishment of the Universal Declaration of Human Rights, as well as the first definition of genocide as a crime.

ACKNOWLEDGEMENTS

Thank you to my lovely editor, Laura Deacon, Caroline Hogg and the team at Bookouture, as well as my brilliant agent, Caroline Hardman of Hardman & Swainson, for their clear-eyed advice and support in helping *Searching for My Daughter* make its way into the world. Thank you too to my good friend Anne Sherer Broom for her expert advice on all things Jewish, to Sharon Mire, who told me about the Kanada warehouses at Auschwitz, and to Jonathan Seath for his eagle eye on my use of German.

As ever, my family, David, Becky and Polly Trenow, have been amazingly supportive, as have other relatives and wonderful friends, without whom life would be infinitely less fun.

77984069R00177